DATE DUE

MAY 2 3 2007	
JUN 1 5 2007	

ZORRO®

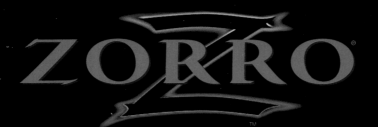

PAPERCUTZ™

ZORRO®

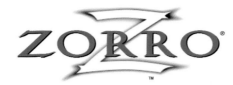

Graphic Novels
Available from Papercutz

1 Scars!
2 Drownings! (Coming December 2005)
3 Vultures! (Coming March 2006)

$7.95 each in paperback
$12.95 each in hardcover

ALL-NEW, FULL-COLOR GRAPHIC NOVEL
ZORRO
#1 SCARS!
DON McGREGOR • SIDNEY LIMA
PAPERCUTZ

ALL-NEW, FULL-COLOR GRAPHIC NOVEL
ZORRO
#2
PAPERCUTZ

ALL-NEW, FULL-COLOR GRAPHIC NOVEL
ZORRO
#3
VULTURES!
PAPERCUTZ

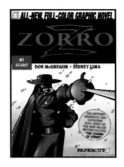

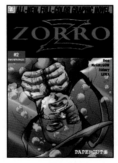

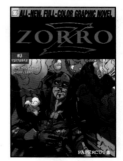

Please add $3.00 for postage and handling for the first book, add $1.00 for each additional book.
Send for our catalog:
Papercutz
555 Eighth Avenue, Suite 1202
New York, NY 10018
www.papercutz.com

DON McGREGOR • Writer
SIDNEY LIMA • Artist
Based on the character created by
JOHNSTON McCULLEY

New York

This is for my wife, MARSHA CHILDERS McGREGOR – 27
years from our first night and the image of her moving
with grace and beauty is a flesh and blood song in the
heart and mind and soul, making fantasy and love real.
– D.M.

Scars!
DON McGREGOR — Writer
SIDNEY LIMA — Artist
MARK LERER — Letterer
MARCOS de MIRANDA — Colorist
JIM SALICRUP — Editor-In-Chief

Special thanks to John Gertz and Sandra Curtis

ISBN 10: 1-59707-016-5 paperback edition
ISBN 13: 978-1-59707-016-4 paperback edition
ISBN 10: 1-59707-017-3 hardcover edition
ISBN 13: 978-1-59707-017-1 hardcover edition

10 9 8 7 6 5 4 3 2 1

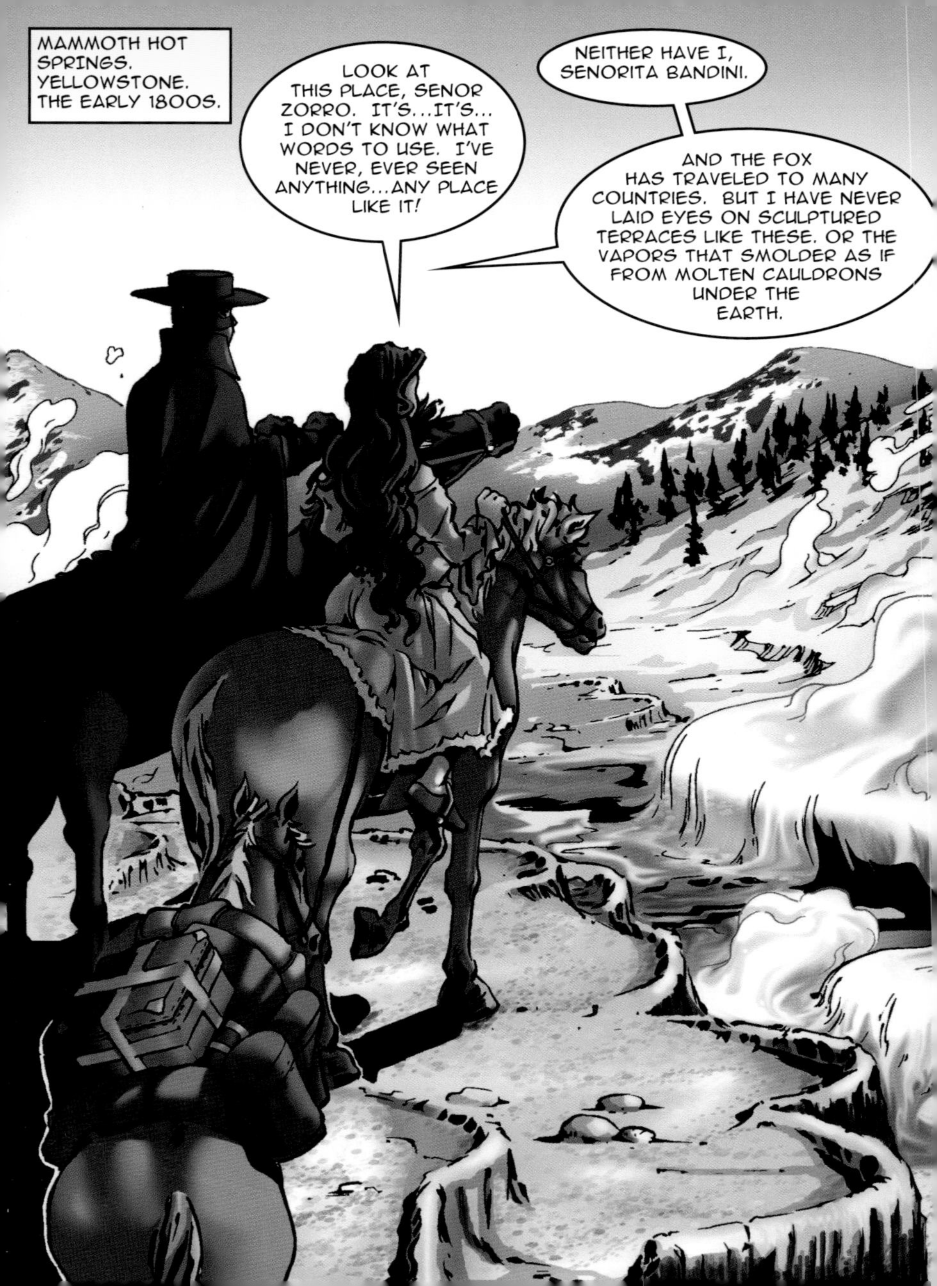
MAMMOTH HOT SPRINGS. YELLOWSTONE. THE EARLY 1800S.
LOOK AT THIS PLACE, SENOR ZORRO. IT'S...IT'S... I DON'T KNOW WHAT WORDS TO USE. I'VE NEVER, EVER SEEN ANYTHING...ANY PLACE LIKE IT!
NEITHER HAVE I, SENORITA BANDINI.
AND THE FOX HAS TRAVELED TO MANY COUNTRIES. BUT I HAVE NEVER LAID EYES ON SCULPTURED TERRACES LIKE THESE. OR THE VAPORS THAT SMOLDER AS IF FROM MOLTEN CAULDRONS UNDER THE EARTH.

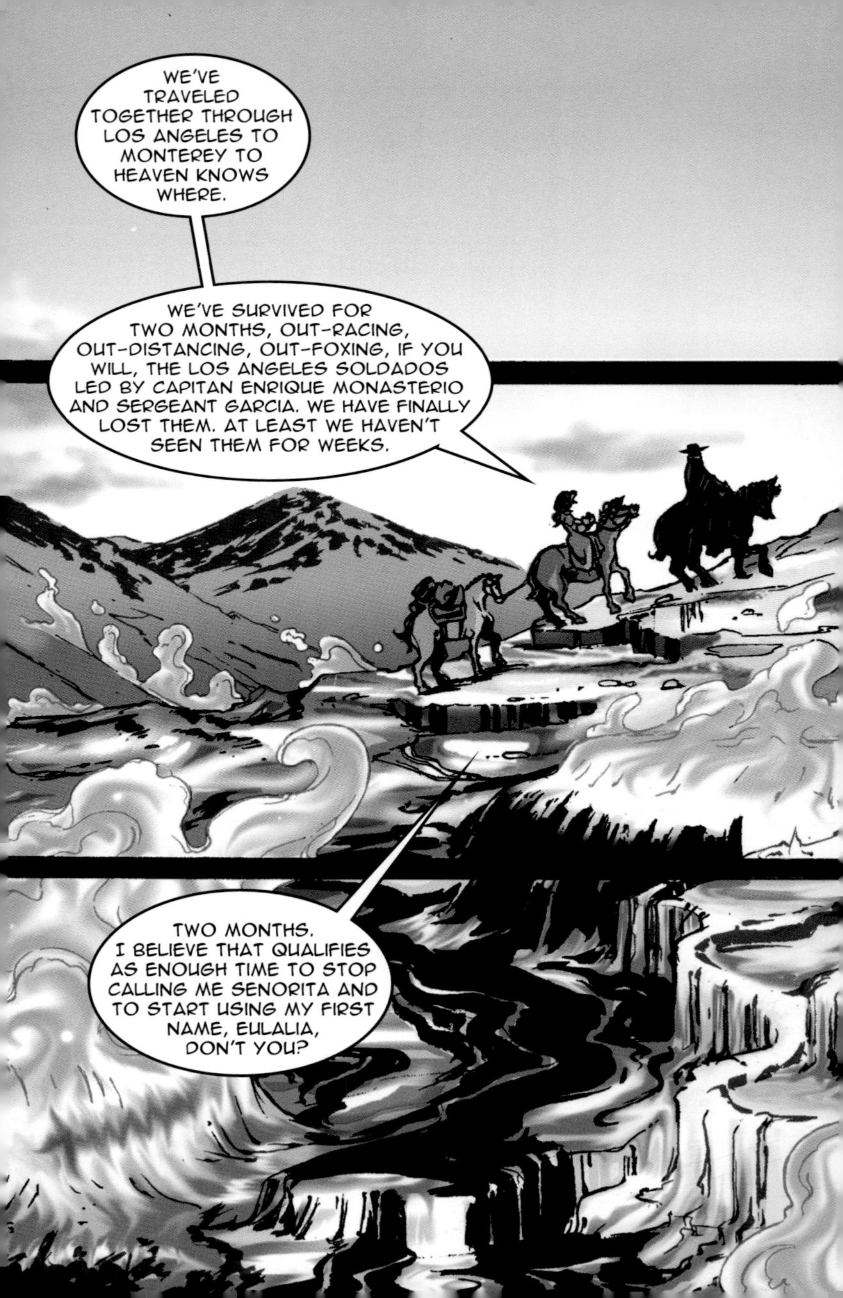
WE'VE TRAVELED TOGETHER THROUGH LOS ANGELES TO MONTEREY TO HEAVEN KNOWS WHERE.
WE'VE SURVIVED FOR TWO MONTHS, OUT-RACING, OUT-DISTANCING, OUT-FOXING, IF YOU WILL, THE LOS ANGELES SOLDADOS LED BY CAPITAN ENRIQUE MONASTERIO AND SERGEANT GARCIA. WE HAVE FINALLY LOST THEM. AT LEAST WE HAVEN'T SEEN THEM FOR WEEKS.
TWO MONTHS. I BELIEVE THAT QUALIFIES AS ENOUGH TIME TO STOP CALLING ME SENORITA AND TO START USING MY FIRST NAME, EULALIA, DON'T YOU?

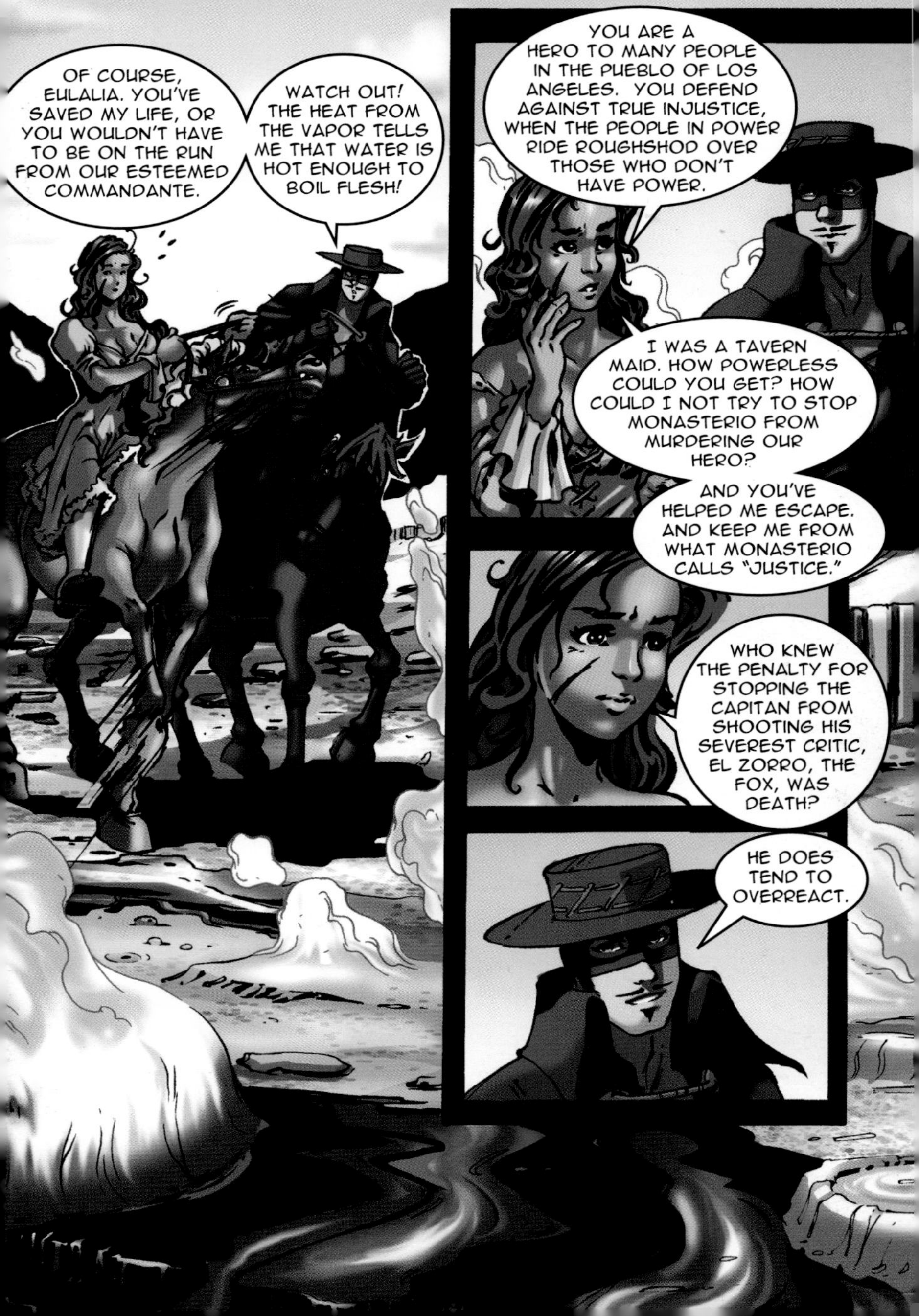
OF COURSE, EULALIA. YOU'VE SAVED MY LIFE, OR YOU WOULDN'T HAVE TO BE ON THE RUN FROM OUR ESTEEMED COMMANDANTE.
WATCH OUT! THE HEAT FROM THE VAPOR TELLS ME THAT WATER IS HOT ENOUGH TO BOIL FLESH!
YOU ARE A HERO TO MANY PEOPLE IN THE PUEBLO OF LOS ANGELES. YOU DEFEND AGAINST TRUE INJUSTICE, WHEN THE PEOPLE IN POWER RIDE ROUGHSHOD OVER THOSE WHO DON'T HAVE POWER.
I WAS A TAVERN MAID. HOW POWERLESS COULD YOU GET? HOW COULD I NOT TRY TO STOP MONASTERIO FROM MURDERING OUR HERO?
AND YOU'VE HELPED ME ESCAPE. AND KEEP ME FROM WHAT MONASTERIO CALLS "JUSTICE."
WHO KNEW THE PENALTY FOR STOPPING THE CAPITAN FROM SHOOTING HIS SEVEREST CRITIC, EL ZORRO, THE FOX, WAS DEATH?
HE DOES TEND TO OVERREACT.

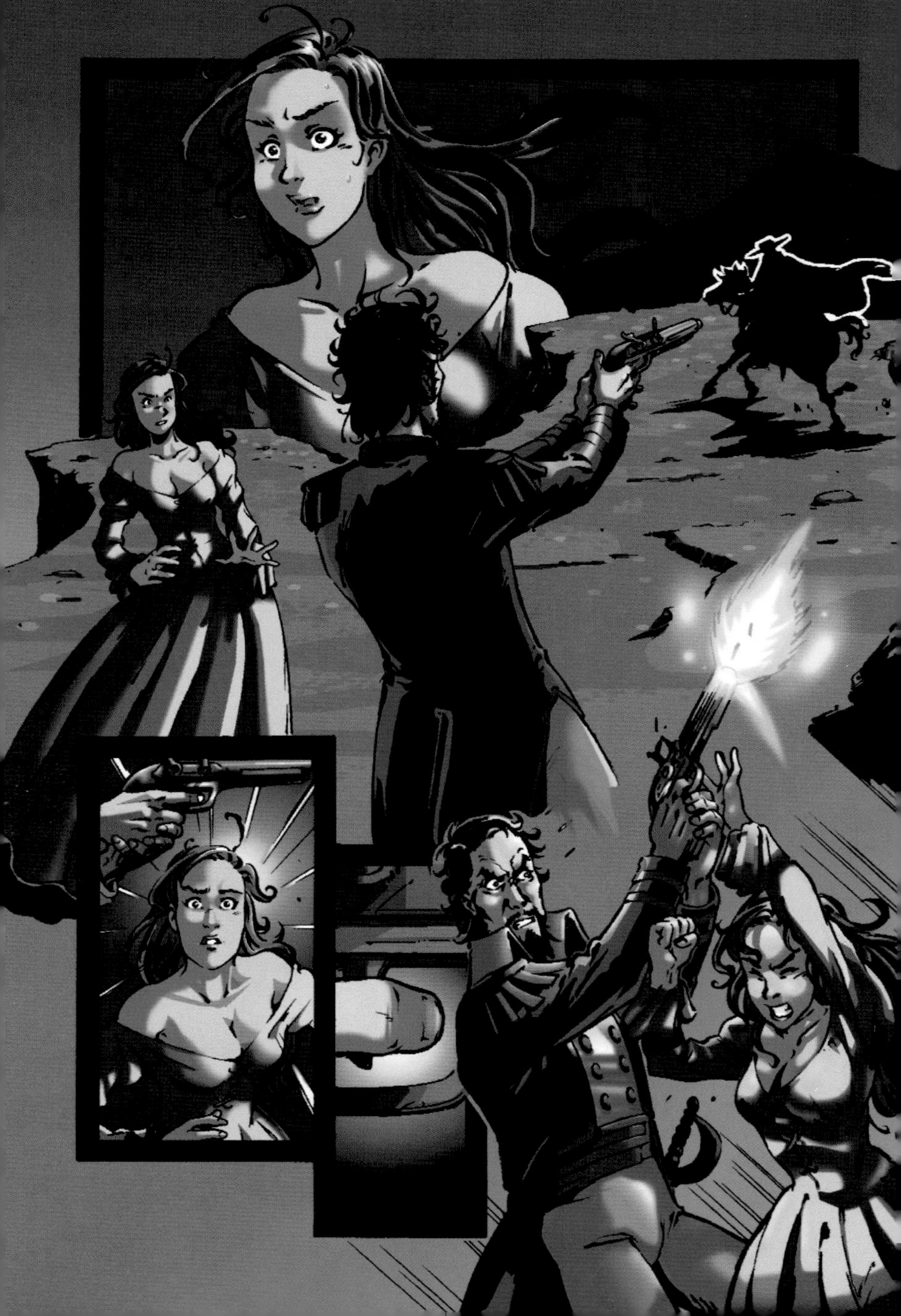

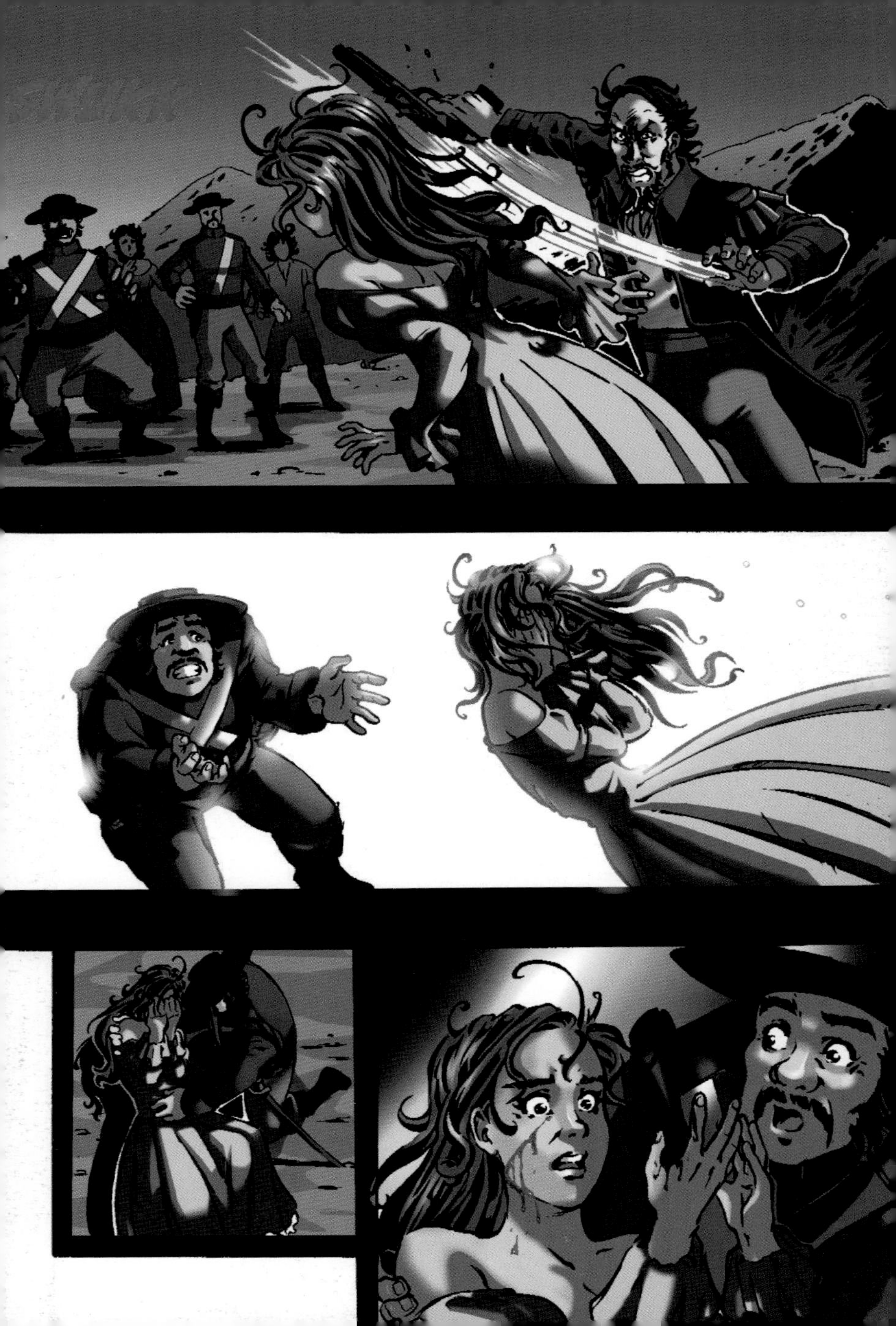

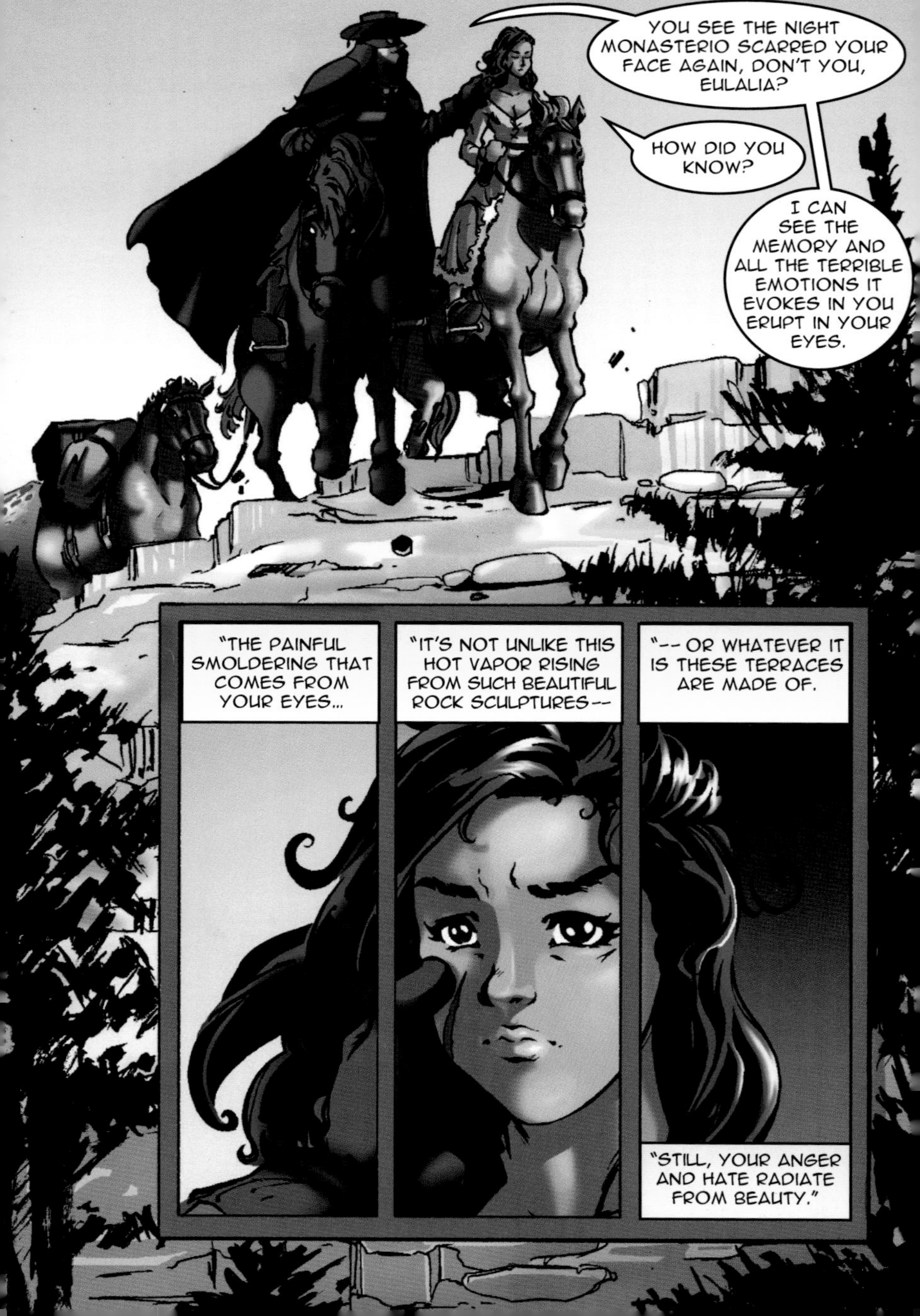
YOU SEE THE NIGHT MONASTERIO SCARRED YOUR FACE AGAIN, DON'T YOU, EULALIA?
HOW DID YOU KNOW?
I CAN SEE THE MEMORY AND ALL THE TERRIBLE EMOTIONS IT EVOKES IN YOU ERUPT IN YOUR EYES.
"THE PAINFUL SMOLDERING THAT COMES FROM YOUR EYES...
"IT'S NOT UNLIKE THIS HOT VAPOR RISING FROM SUCH BEAUTIFUL ROCK SCULPTURES--
"-- OR WHATEVER IT IS THESE TERRACES ARE MADE OF.
"STILL, YOUR ANGER AND HATE RADIATE FROM BEAUTY."

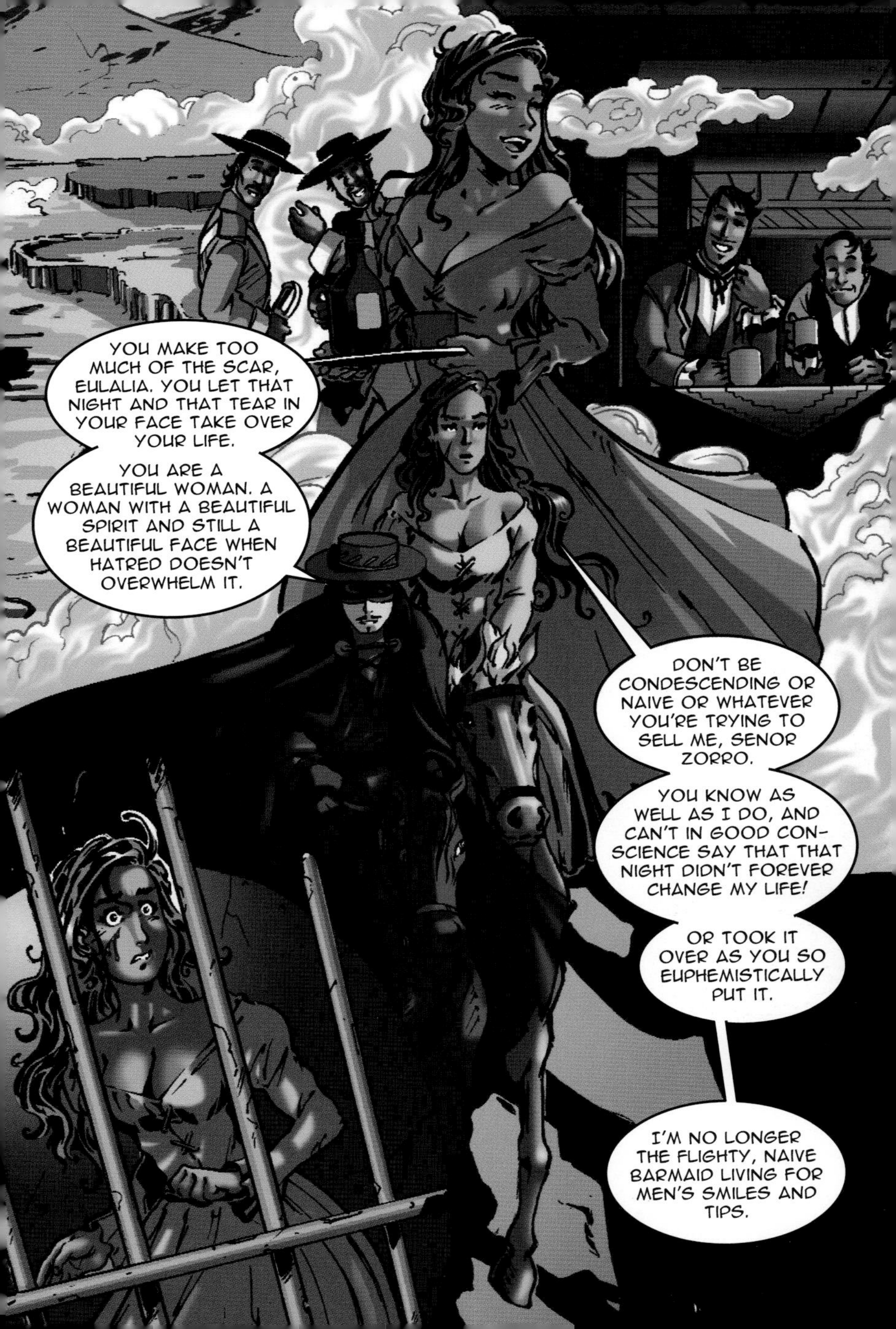
YOU MAKE TOO MUCH OF THE SCAR, EULALIA. YOU LET THAT NIGHT AND THAT TEAR IN YOUR FACE TAKE OVER YOUR LIFE.
YOU ARE A BEAUTIFUL WOMAN. A WOMAN WITH A BEAUTIFUL SPIRIT AND STILL A BEAUTIFUL FACE WHEN HATRED DOESN'T OVERWHELM IT.
DON'T BE CONDESCENDING OR NAIVE OR WHATEVER YOU'RE TRYING TO SELL ME, SENOR ZORRO.
YOU KNOW AS WELL AS I DO, AND CAN'T IN GOOD CONSCIENCE SAY THAT THAT NIGHT DIDN'T FOREVER CHANGE MY LIFE!
OR TOOK IT OVER AS YOU SO EUPHEMISTICALLY PUT IT.
I'M NO LONGER THE FLIGHTY, NAIVE BARMAID LIVING FOR MEN'S SMILES AND TIPS.

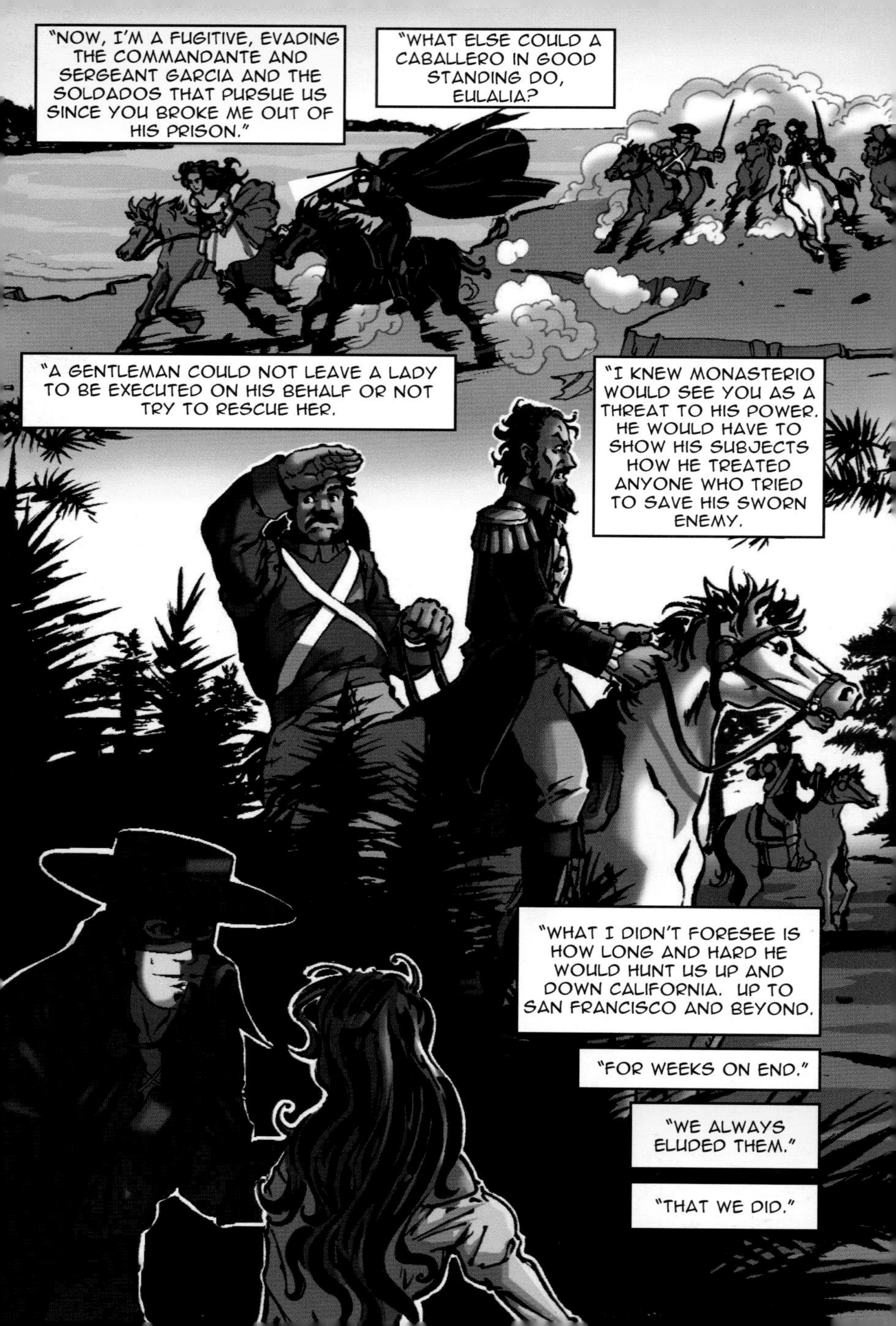
"NOW, I'M A FUGITIVE, EVADING THE COMMANDANTE AND SERGEANT GARCIA AND THE SOLDADOS THAT PURSUE US SINCE YOU BROKE ME OUT OF HIS PRISON."
"WHAT ELSE COULD A CABALLERO IN GOOD STANDING DO, EULALIA?
"A GENTLEMAN COULD NOT LEAVE A LADY TO BE EXECUTED ON HIS BEHALF OR NOT TRY TO RESCUE HER.
"I KNEW MONASTERIO WOULD SEE YOU AS A THREAT TO HIS POWER. HE WOULD HAVE TO SHOW HIS SUBJECTS HOW HE TREATED ANYONE WHO TRIED TO SAVE HIS SWORN ENEMY.
"WHAT I DIDN'T FORESEE IS HOW LONG AND HARD HE WOULD HUNT US UP AND DOWN CALIFORNIA. UP TO SAN FRANCISCO AND BEYOND.
"FOR WEEKS ON END."
"WE ALWAYS ELUDED THEM."
"THAT WE DID."

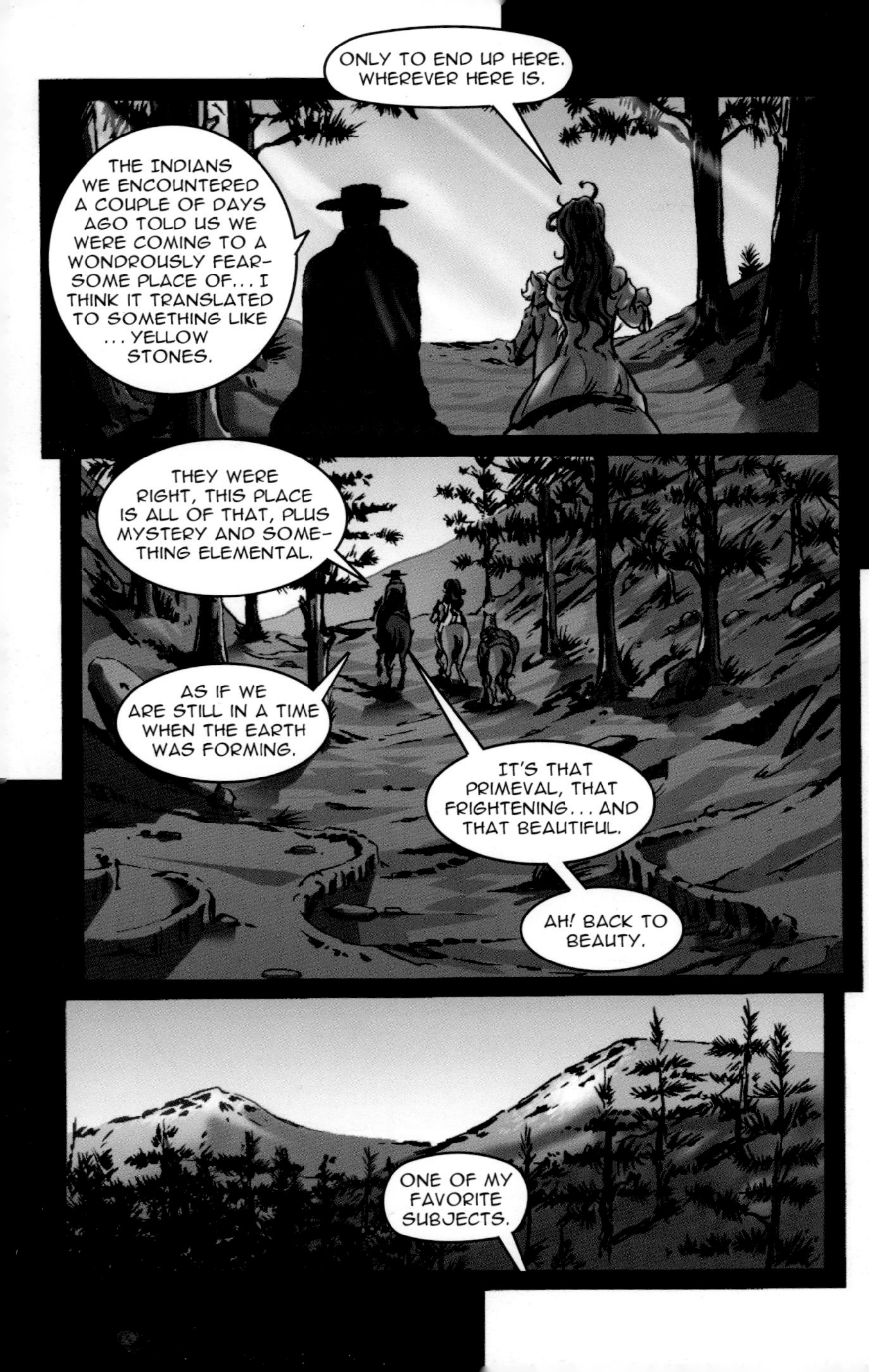
ONLY TO END UP HERE. WHEREVER HERE IS.
THE INDIANS WE ENCOUNTERED A COUPLE OF DAYS AGO TOLD US WE WERE COMING TO A WONDROUSLY FEAR-SOME PLACE OF... I THINK IT TRANSLATED TO SOMETHING LIKE ...YELLOW STONES.
THEY WERE RIGHT, THIS PLACE IS ALL OF THAT, PLUS MYSTERY AND SOME-THING ELEMENTAL.
AS IF WE ARE STILL IN A TIME WHEN THE EARTH WAS FORMING.
IT'S THAT PRIMEVAL, THAT FRIGHTENING... AND THAT BEAUTIFUL.
AH! BACK TO BEAUTY.
ONE OF MY FAVORITE SUBJECTS.

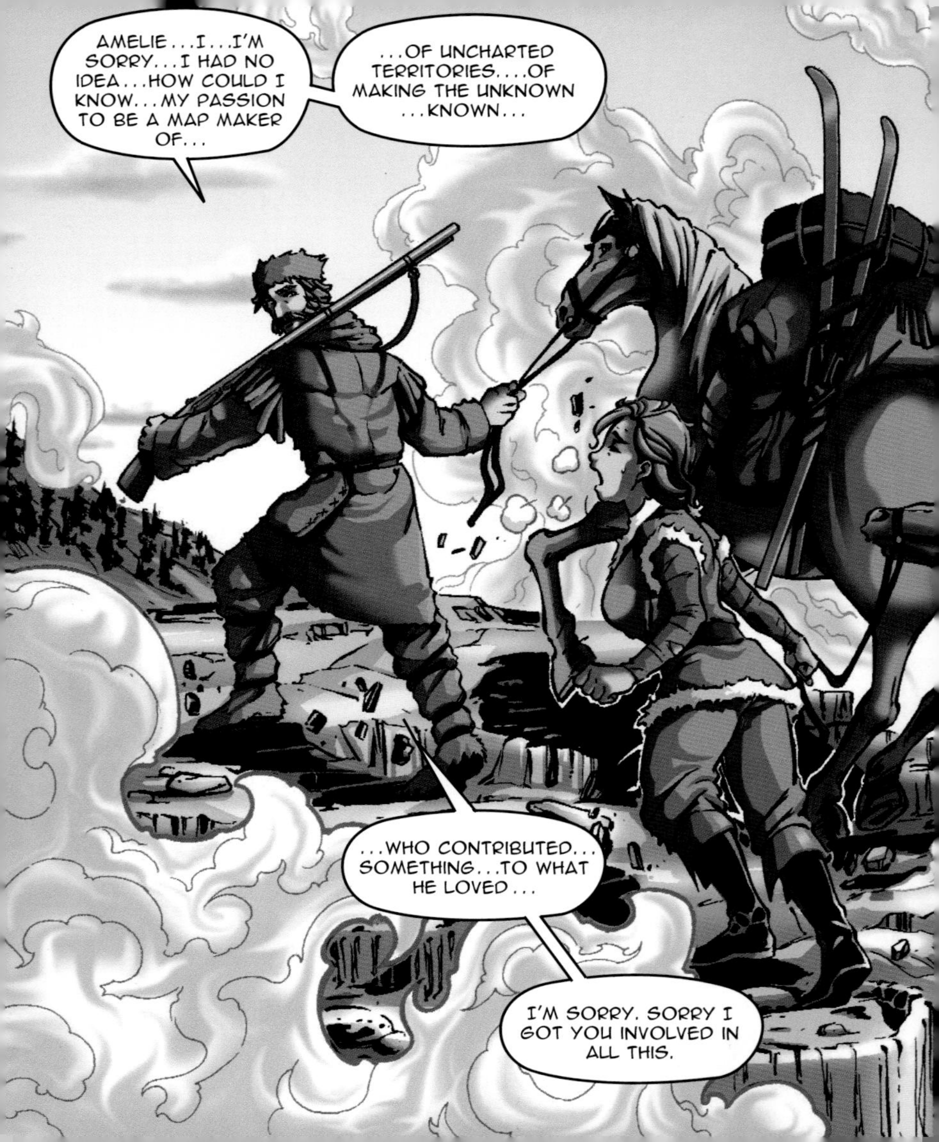
AMELIE...I...I'M SORRY...I HAD NO IDEA...HOW COULD I KNOW...MY PASSION TO BE A MAP MAKER OF...
...OF UNCHARTED TERRITORIES....OF MAKING THE UNKNOWN ...KNOWN...
...WHO CONTRIBUTED... SOMETHING...TO WHAT HE LOVED...
I'M SORRY. SORRY I GOT YOU INVOLVED IN ALL THIS.

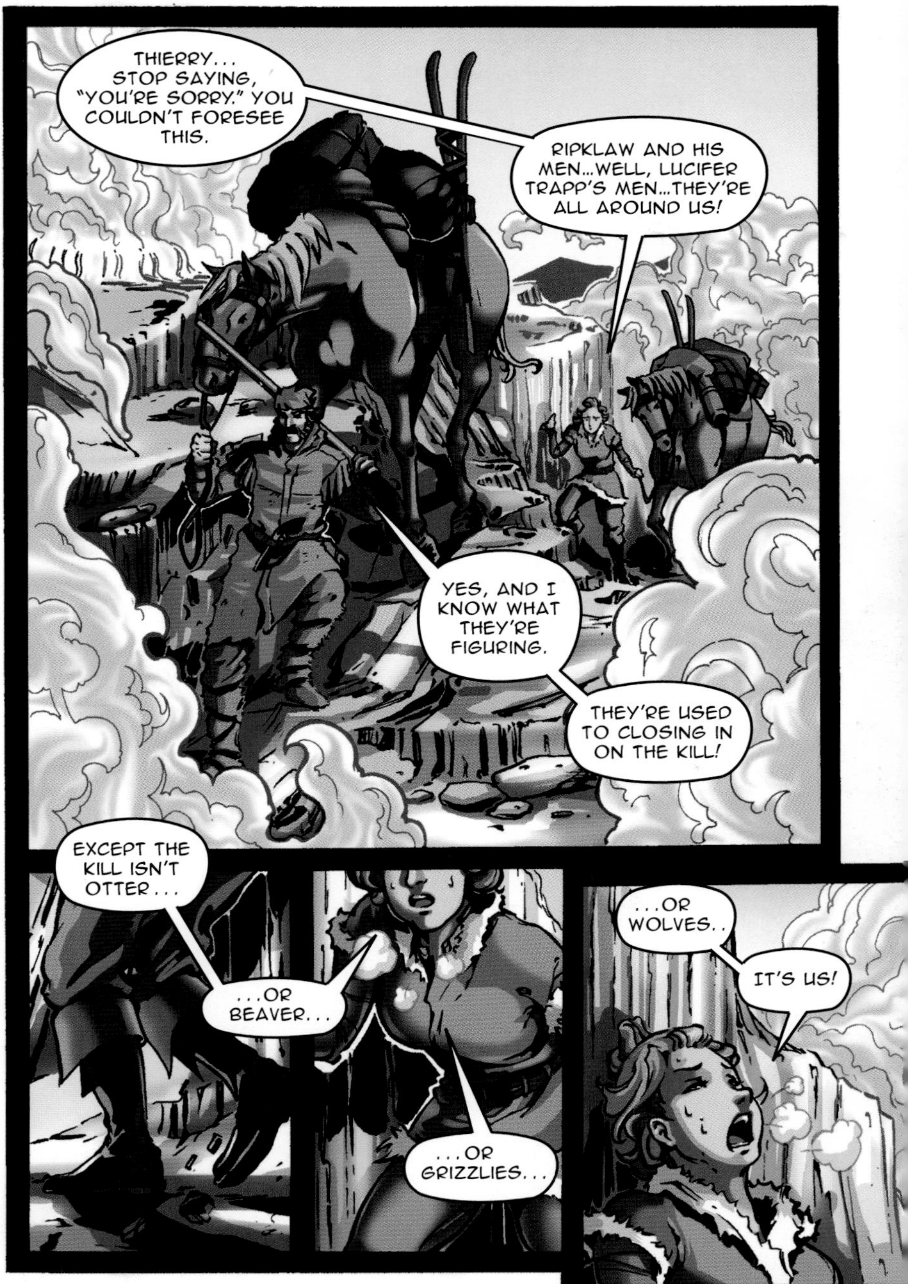
THIERRY... STOP SAYING, "YOU'RE SORRY." YOU COULDN'T FORESEE THIS.
RIPKLAW AND HIS MEN...WELL, LUCIFER TRAPP'S MEN...THEY'RE ALL AROUND US!
YES, AND I KNOW WHAT THEY'RE FIGURING.
THEY'RE USED TO CLOSING IN ON THE KILL!
EXCEPT THE KILL ISN'T OTTER...
...OR BEAVER...
...OR GRIZZLIES...
...OR WOLVES..
IT'S US!

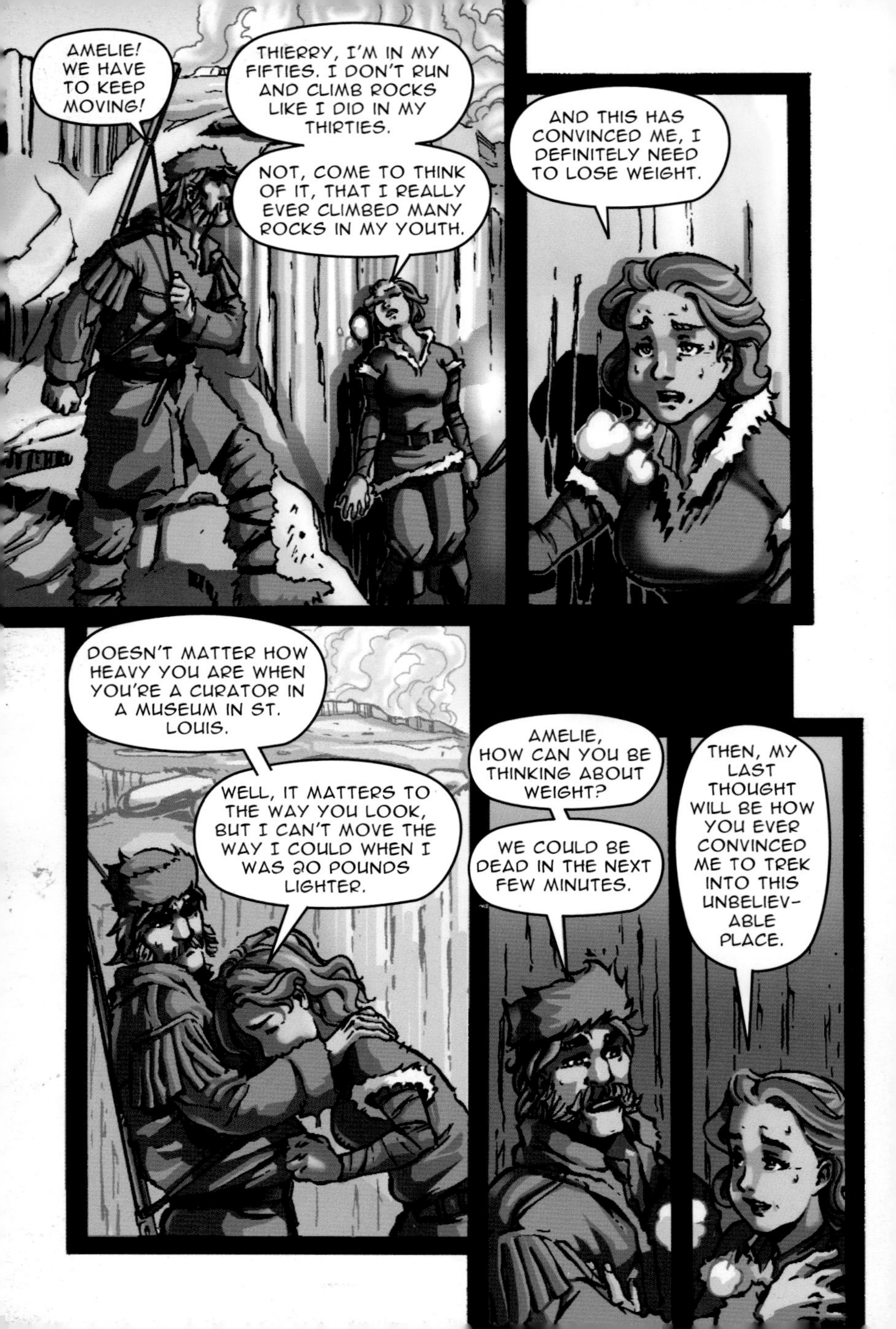
AMELIE! WE HAVE TO KEEP MOVING!
THIERRY, I'M IN MY FIFTIES. I DON'T RUN AND CLIMB ROCKS LIKE I DID IN MY THIRTIES.
NOT, COME TO THINK OF IT, THAT I REALLY EVER CLIMBED MANY ROCKS IN MY YOUTH.
AND THIS HAS CONVINCED ME, I DEFINITELY NEED TO LOSE WEIGHT.
DOESN'T MATTER HOW HEAVY YOU ARE WHEN YOU'RE A CURATOR IN A MUSEUM IN ST. LOUIS.
WELL, IT MATTERS TO THE WAY YOU LOOK, BUT I CAN'T MOVE THE WAY I COULD WHEN I WAS 20 POUNDS LIGHTER.
AMELIE, HOW CAN YOU BE THINKING ABOUT WEIGHT?
WE COULD BE DEAD IN THE NEXT FEW MINUTES.
THEN, MY LAST THOUGHT WILL BE HOW YOU EVER CONVINCED ME TO TREK INTO THIS UNBELIEV-ABLE PLACE.

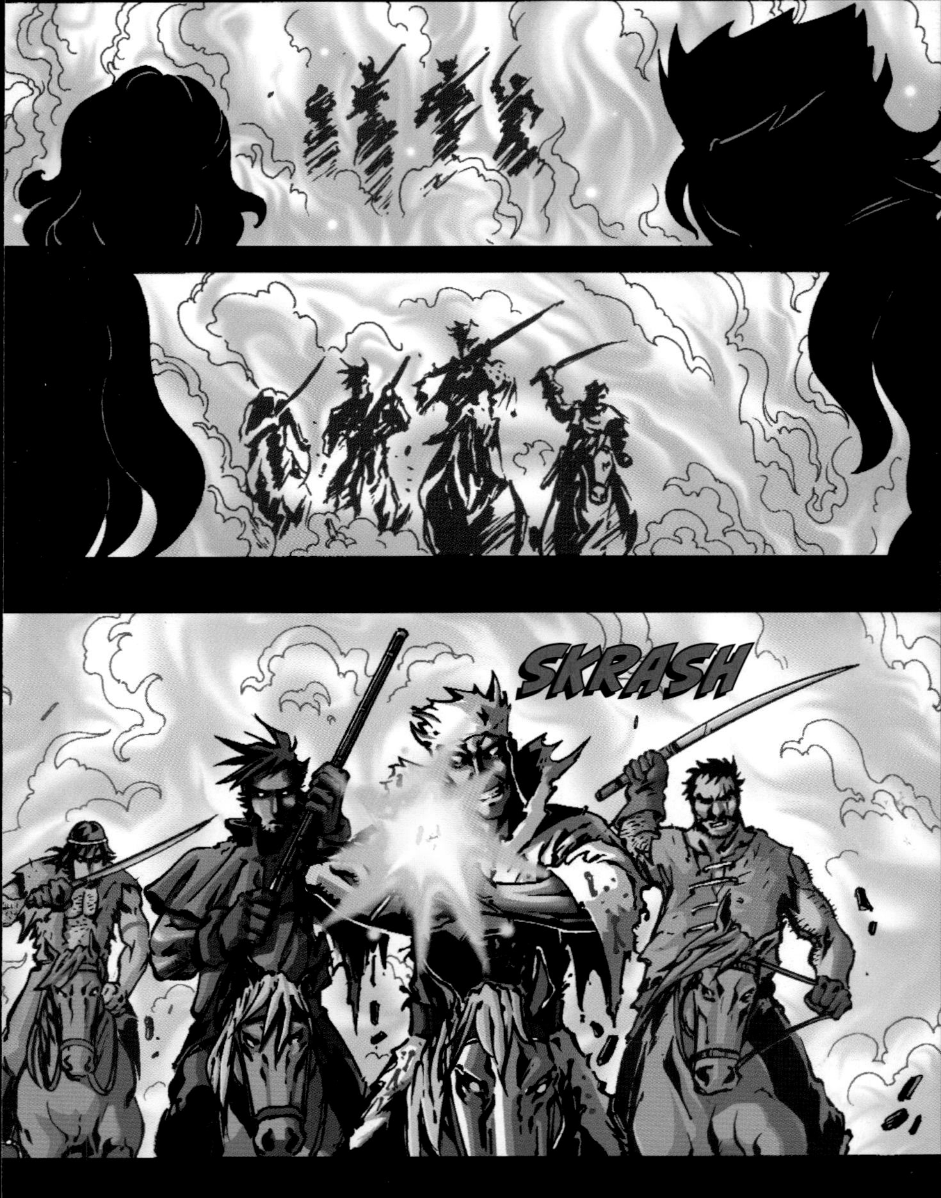
SKRASH

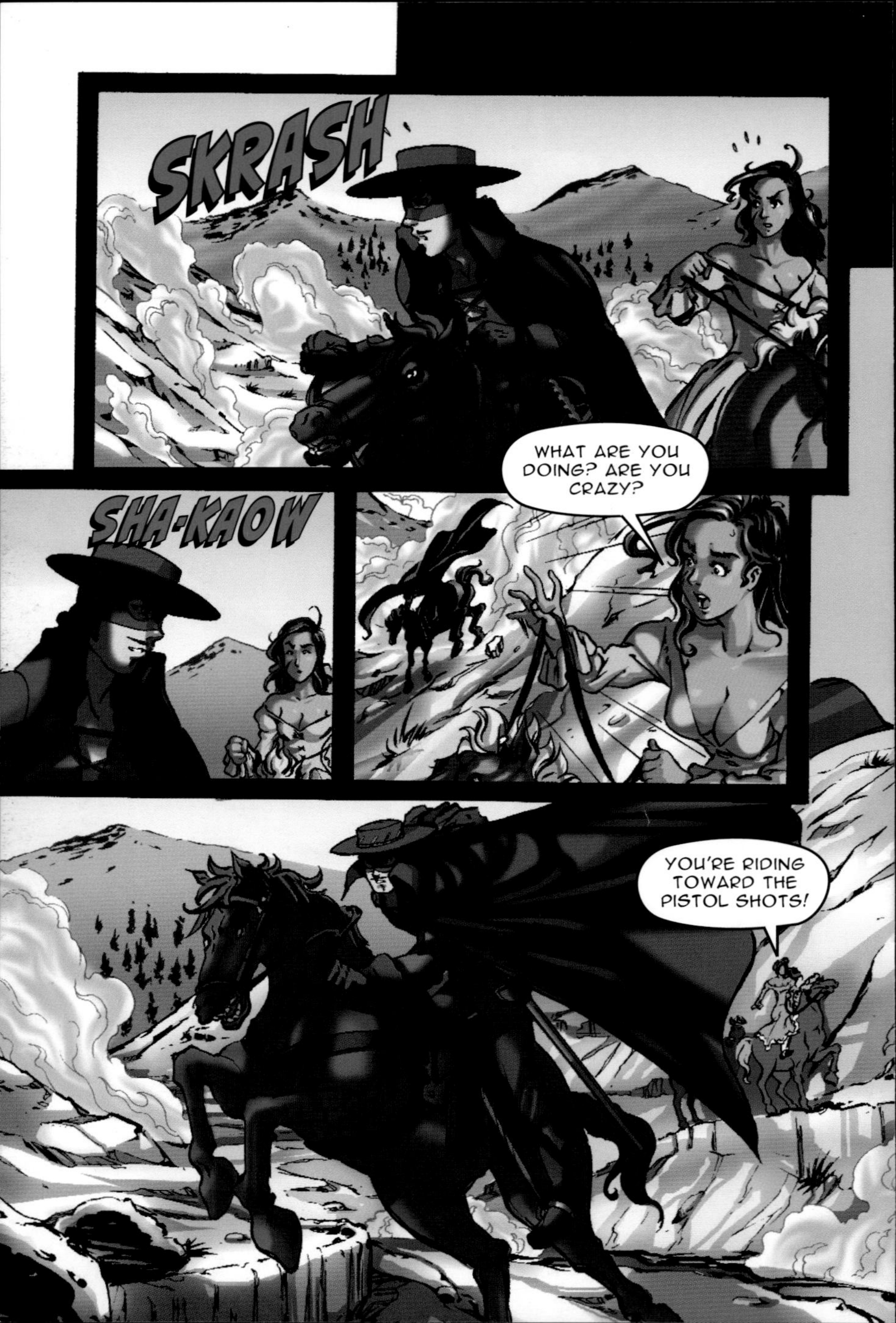
SKRASH
SHA-KAOW
WHAT ARE YOU DOING? ARE YOU CRAZY?
YOU'RE RIDING TOWARD THE PISTOL SHOTS!

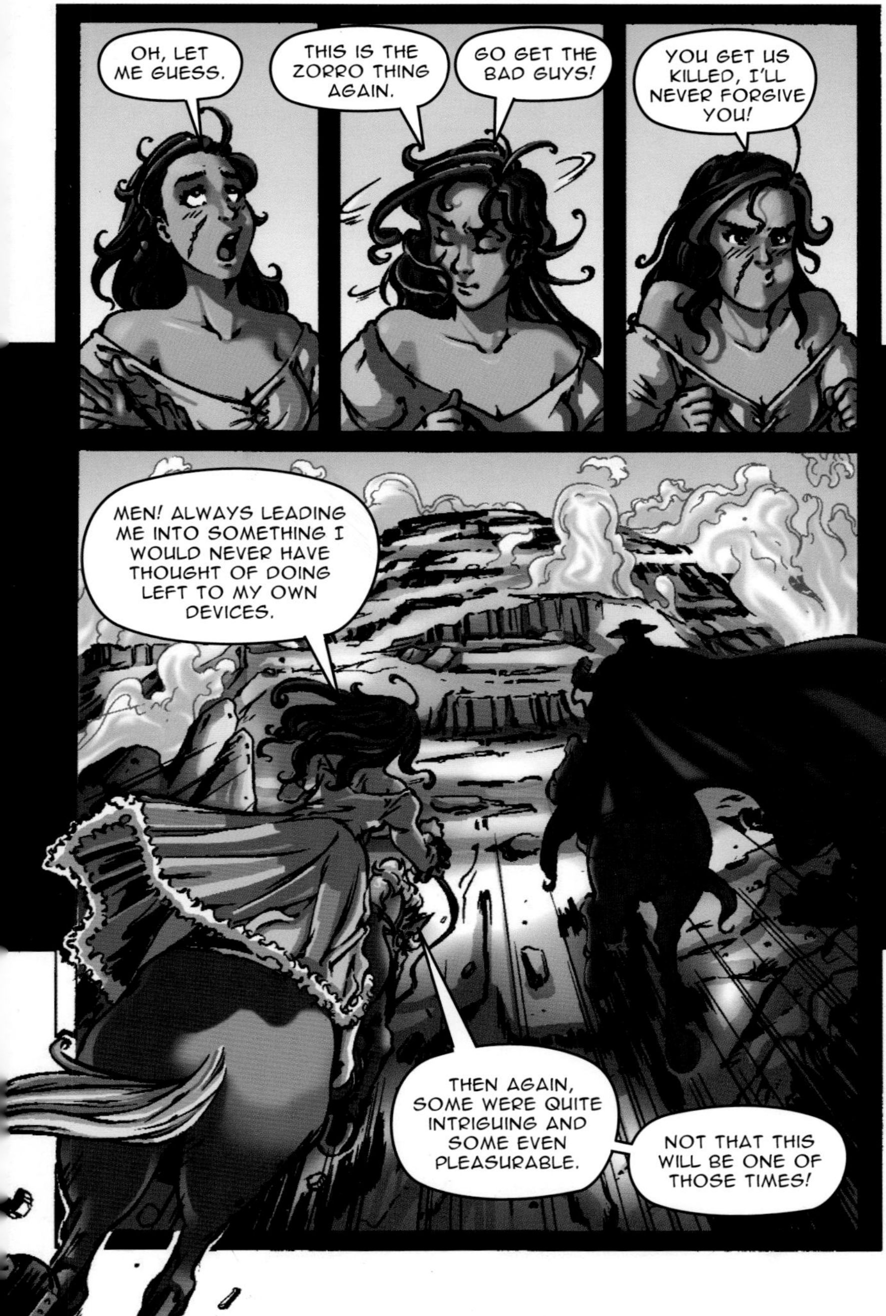
OH, LET ME GUESS.
THIS IS THE ZORRO THING AGAIN.
GO GET THE BAD GUYS!
YOU GET US KILLED, I'LL NEVER FORGIVE YOU!
MEN! ALWAYS LEADING ME INTO SOMETHING I WOULD NEVER HAVE THOUGHT OF DOING LEFT TO MY OWN DEVICES.
THEN AGAIN, SOME WERE QUITE INTRIGUING AND SOME EVEN PLEASURABLE.
NOT THAT THIS WILL BE ONE OF THOSE TIMES!

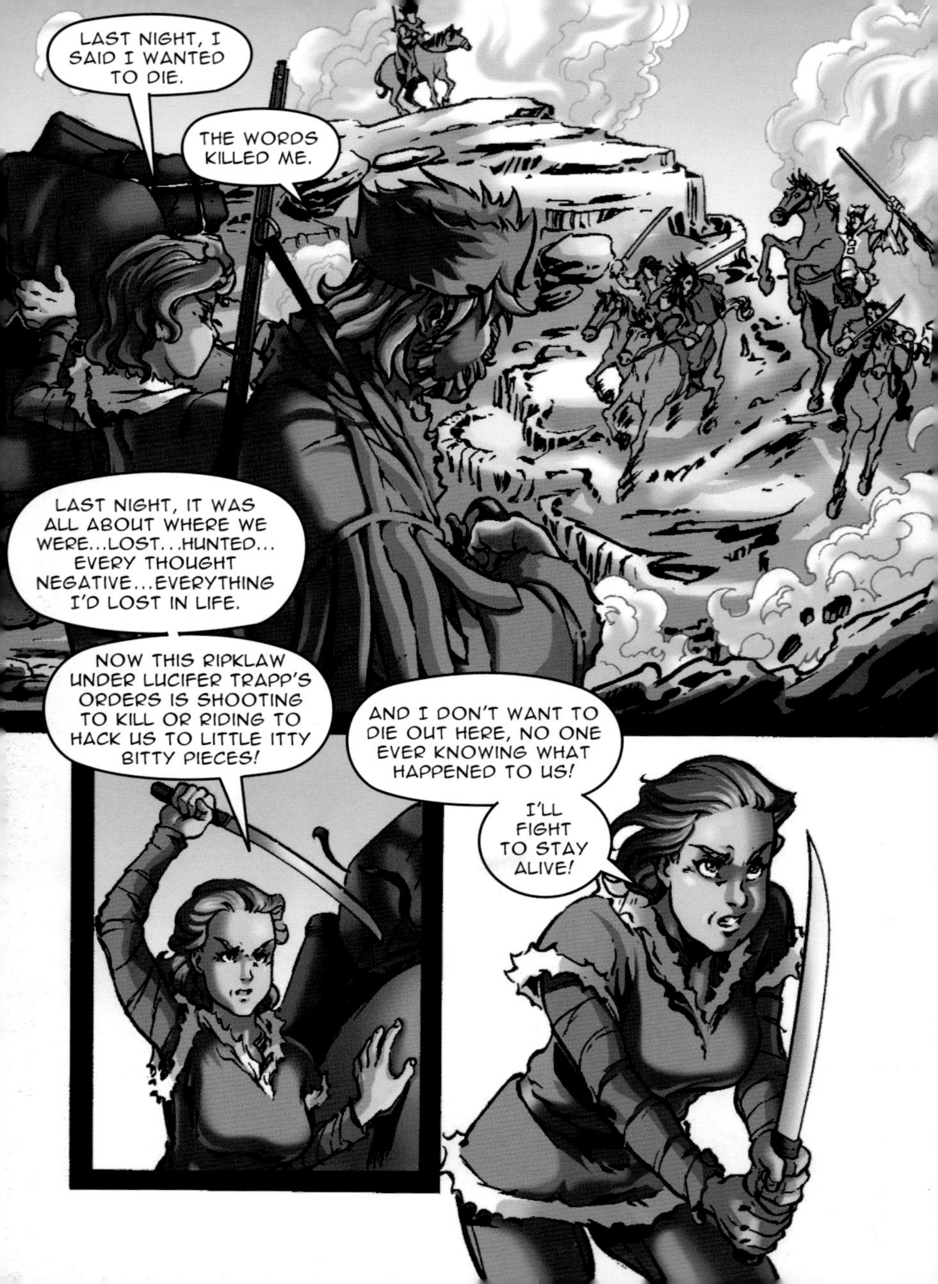
LAST NIGHT, I SAID I WANTED TO DIE.
THE WORDS KILLED ME.
LAST NIGHT, IT WAS ALL ABOUT WHERE WE WERE...LOST...HUNTED... EVERY THOUGHT NEGATIVE...EVERYTHING I'D LOST IN LIFE.
NOW THIS RIPKLAW UNDER LUCIFER TRAPP'S ORDERS IS SHOOTING TO KILL OR RIDING TO HACK US TO LITTLE ITTY BITTY PIECES!
AND I DON'T WANT TO DIE OUT HERE, NO ONE EVER KNOWING WHAT HAPPENED TO US!
I'LL FIGHT TO STAY ALIVE!

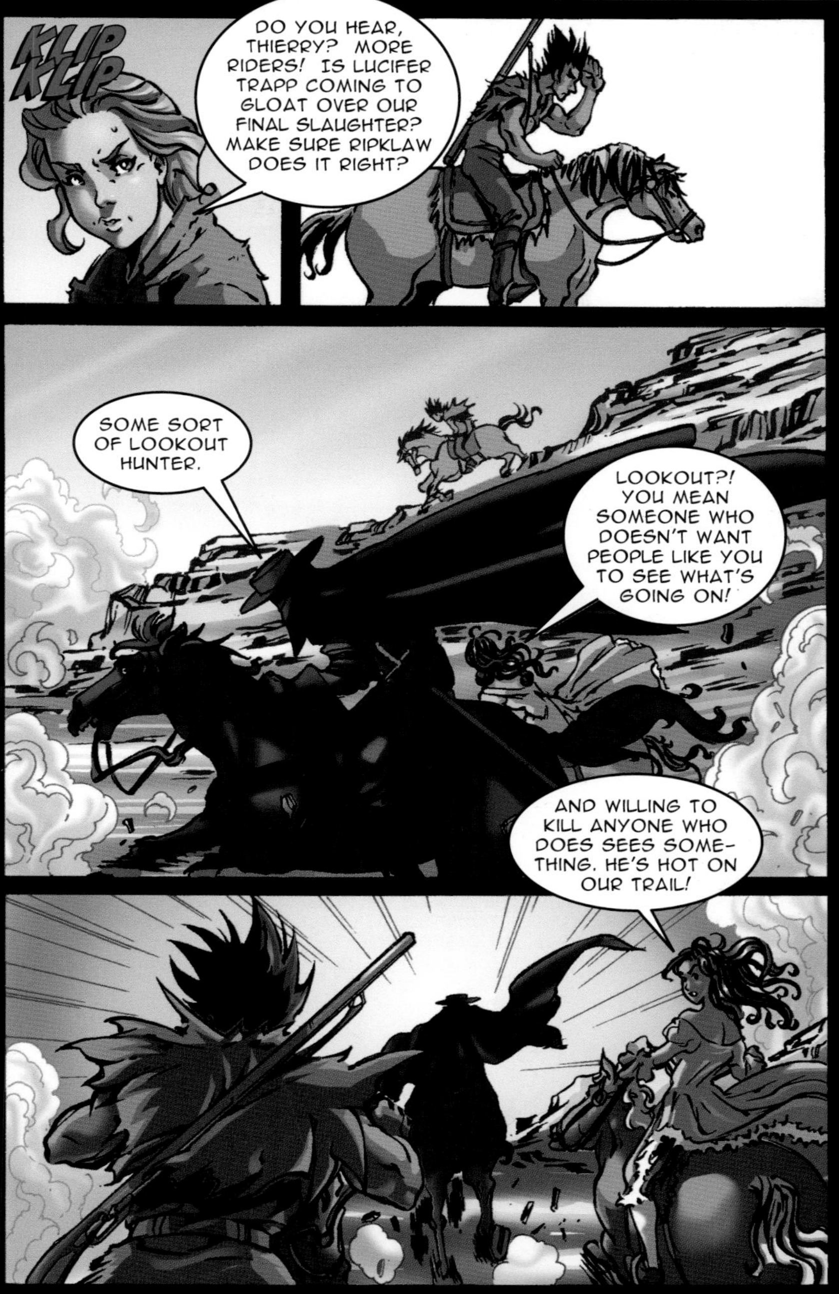
KLIP KLIP
DO YOU HEAR, THIERRY? MORE RIDERS! IS LUCIFER TRAPP COMING TO GLOAT OVER OUR FINAL SLAUGHTER? MAKE SURE RIPKLAW DOES IT RIGHT?
SOME SORT OF LOOKOUT HUNTER.
LOOKOUT?! YOU MEAN SOMEONE WHO DOESN'T WANT PEOPLE LIKE YOU TO SEE WHAT'S GOING ON!
AND WILLING TO KILL ANYONE WHO DOES SEES SOME-THING. HE'S HOT ON OUR TRAIL!

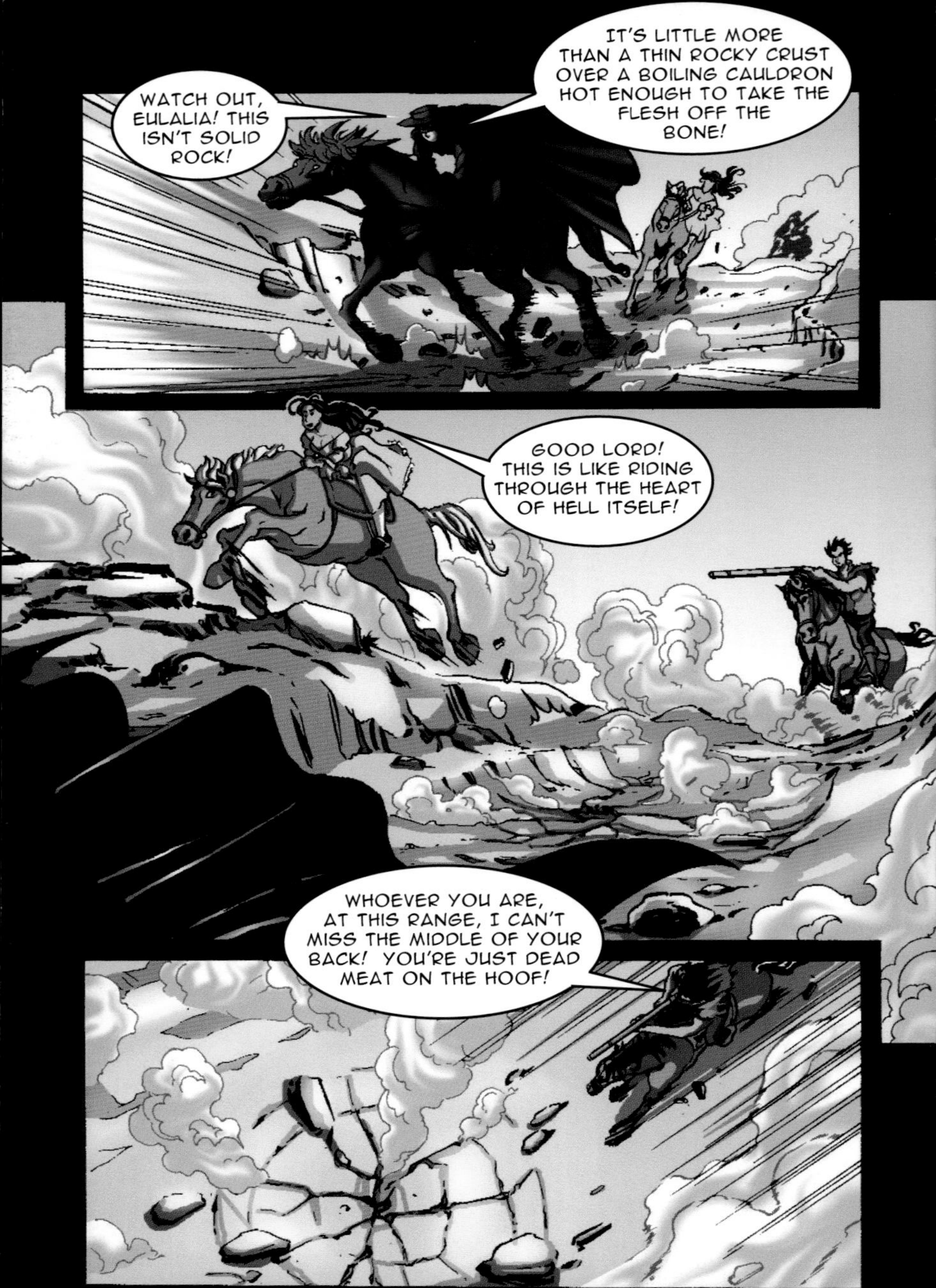
WATCH OUT, EULALIA! THIS ISN'T SOLID ROCK!
IT'S LITTLE MORE THAN A THIN ROCKY CRUST OVER A BOILING CAULDRON HOT ENOUGH TO TAKE THE FLESH OFF THE BONE!
GOOD LORD! THIS IS LIKE RIDING THROUGH THE HEART OF HELL ITSELF!
WHOEVER YOU ARE, AT THIS RANGE, I CAN'T MISS THE MIDDLE OF YOUR BACK! YOU'RE JUST DEAD MEAT ON THE HOOF!

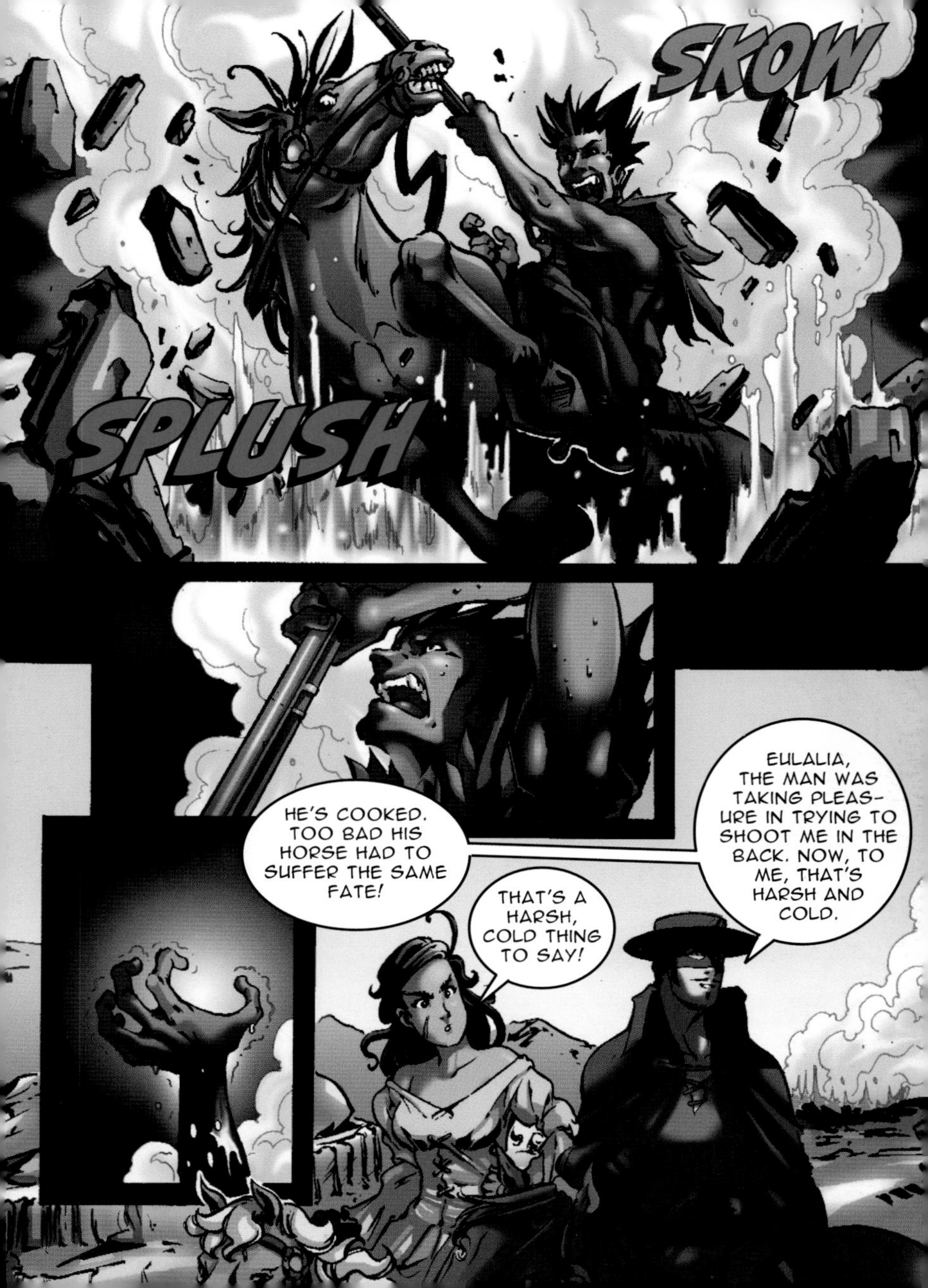
SKOW
SPLUSH
HE'S COOKED. TOO BAD HIS HORSE HAD TO SUFFER THE SAME FATE!
EULALIA, THE MAN WAS TAKING PLEAS-URE IN TRYING TO SHOOT ME IN THE BACK. NOW, TO ME, THAT'S HARSH AND COLD.
THAT'S A HARSH, COLD THING TO SAY!

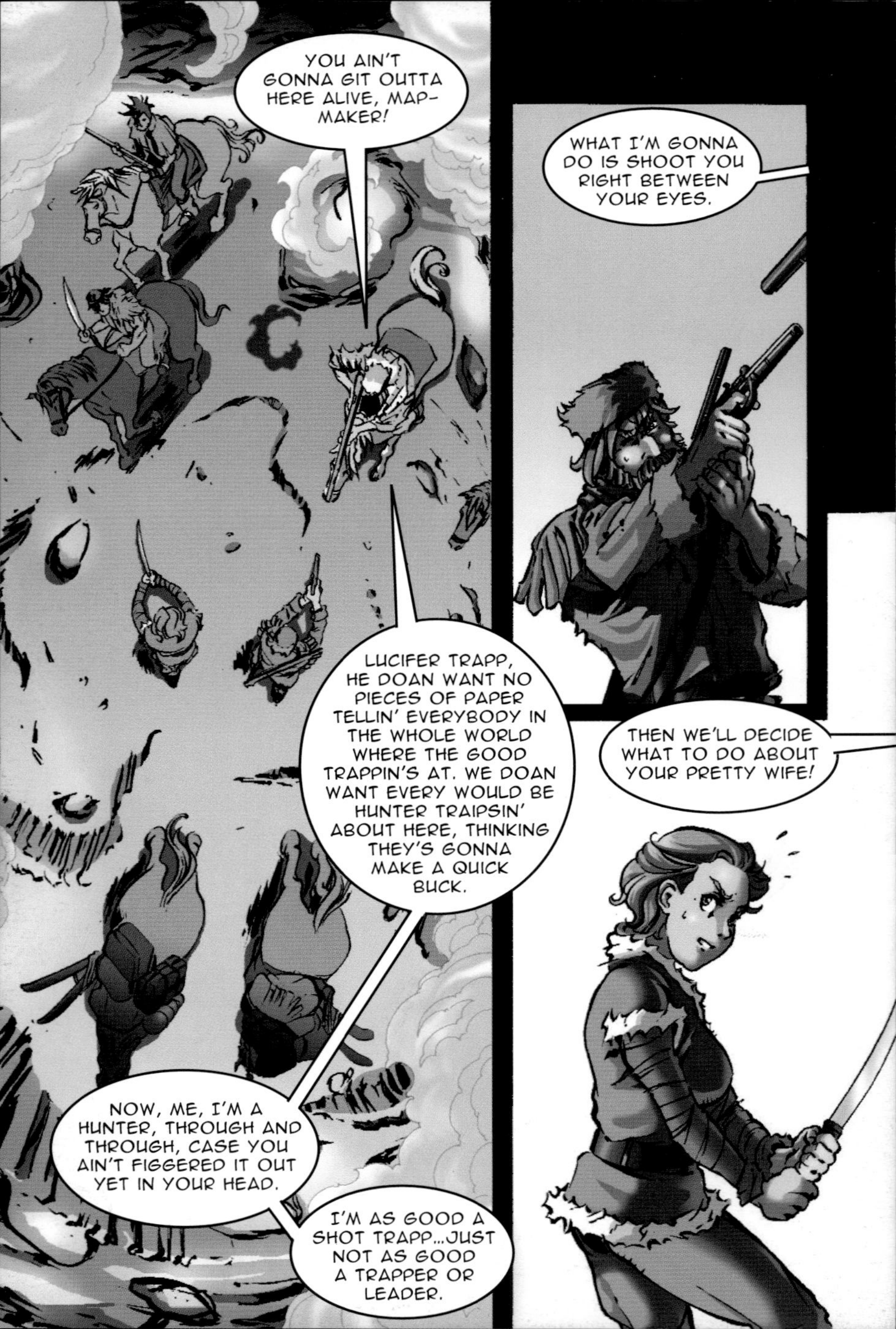
YOU AIN'T GONNA GIT OUTTA HERE ALIVE, MAP-MAKER!
LUCIFER TRAPP, HE DOAN WANT NO PIECES OF PAPER TELLIN' EVERYBODY IN THE WHOLE WORLD WHERE THE GOOD TRAPPIN'S AT. WE DOAN WANT EVERY WOULD BE HUNTER TRAIPSIN' ABOUT HERE, THINKING THEY'S GONNA MAKE A QUICK BUCK.
NOW, ME, I'M A HUNTER, THROUGH AND THROUGH, CASE YOU AIN'T FIGGERED IT OUT YET IN YOUR HEAD.
I'M AS GOOD A SHOT TRAPP...JUST NOT AS GOOD A TRAPPER OR LEADER.
WHAT I'M GONNA DO IS SHOOT YOU RIGHT BETWEEN YOUR EYES.
THEN WE'LL DECIDE WHAT TO DO ABOUT YOUR PRETTY WIFE!

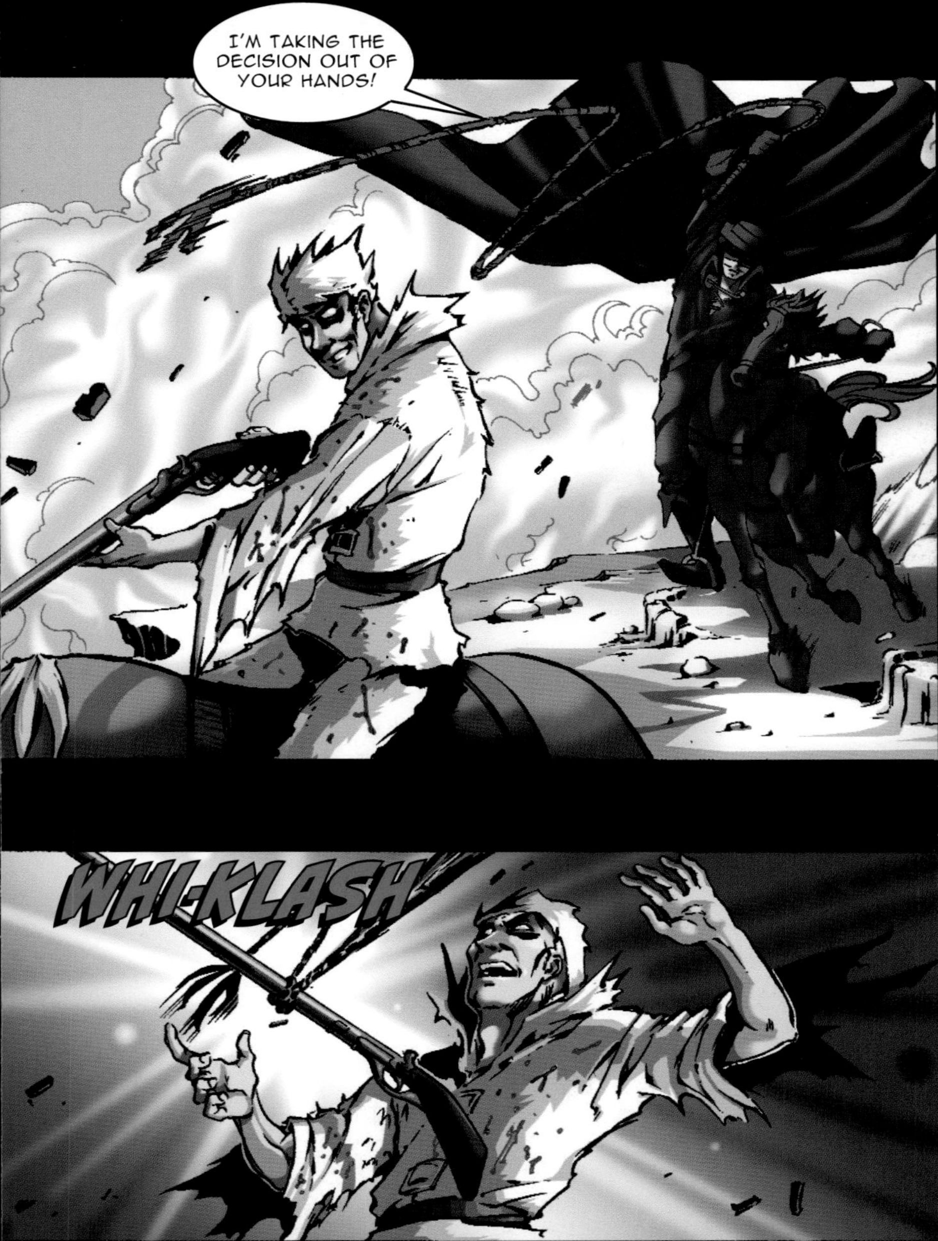
I'M TAKING THE DECISION OUT OF YOUR HANDS!
WHI-KLASH

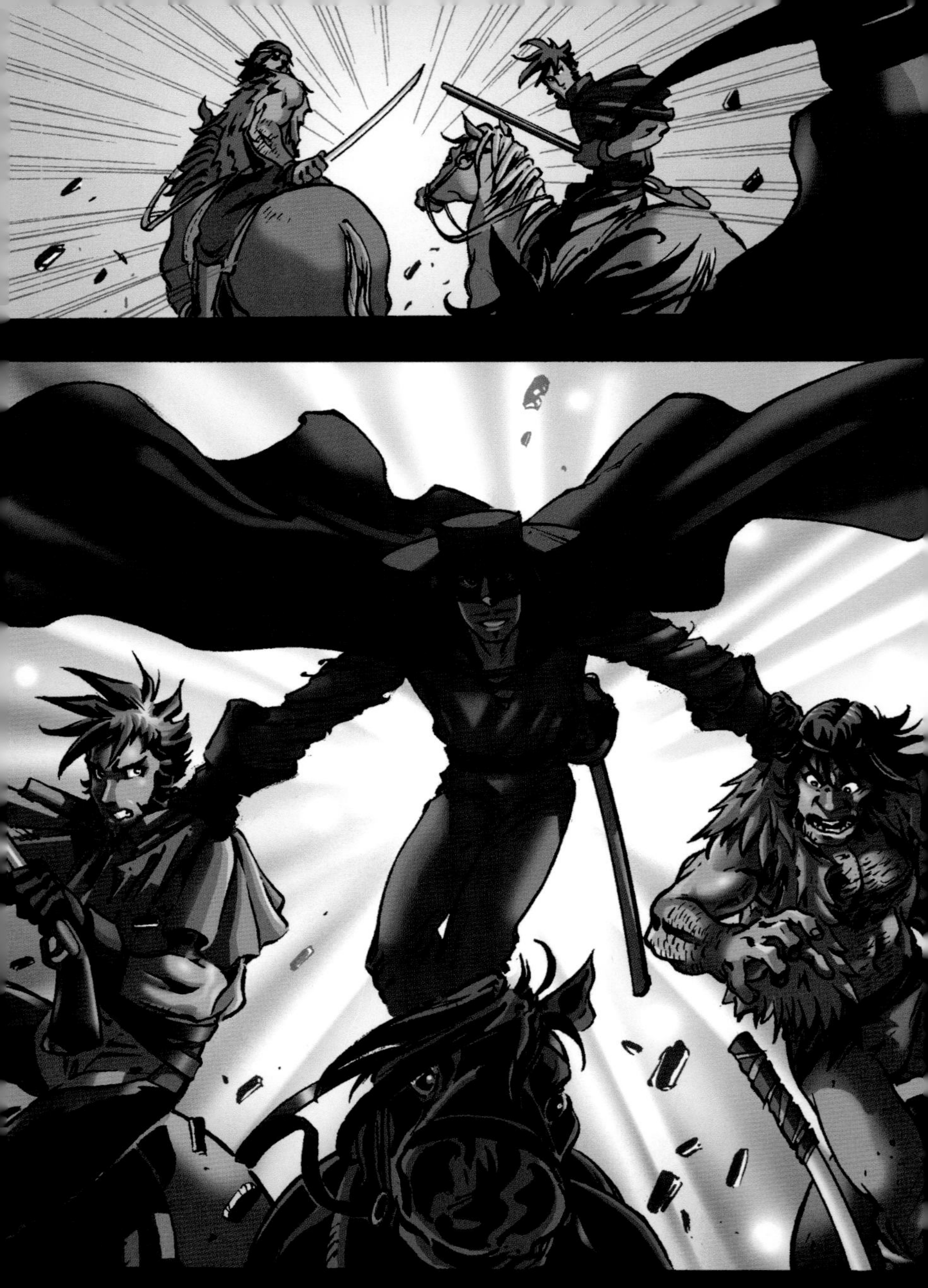

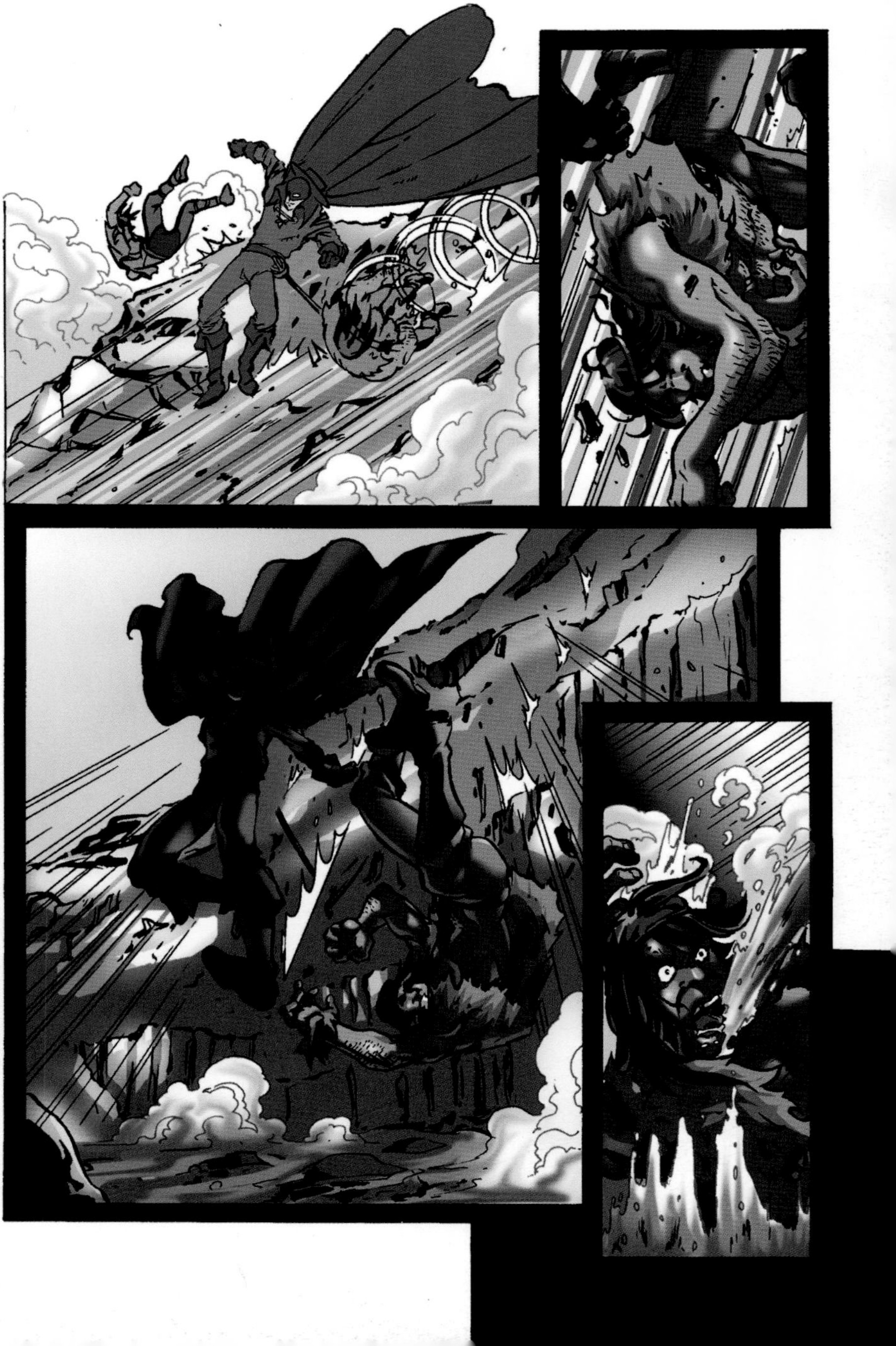

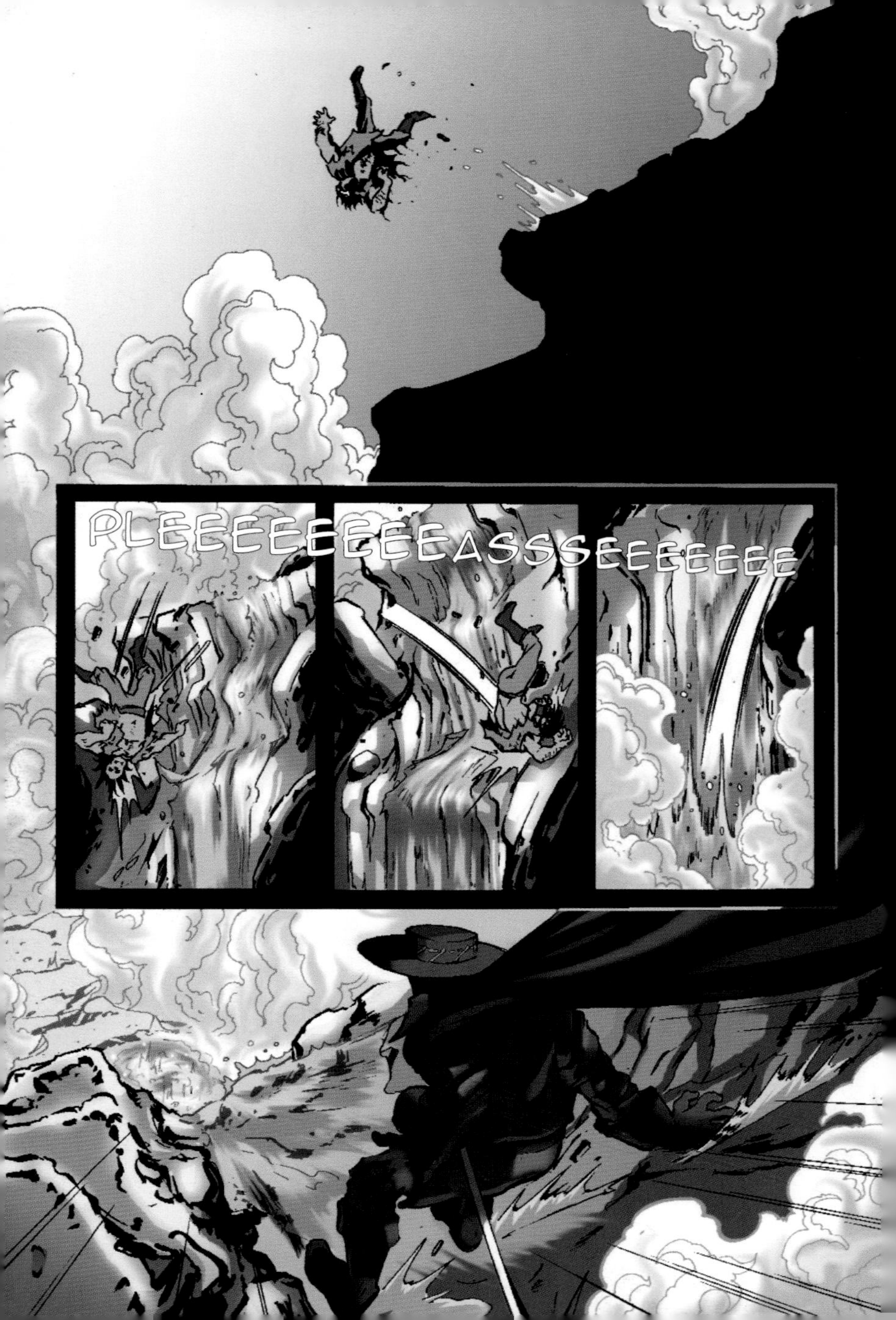
PLEEEEEEEEEASSSEEEEEEE

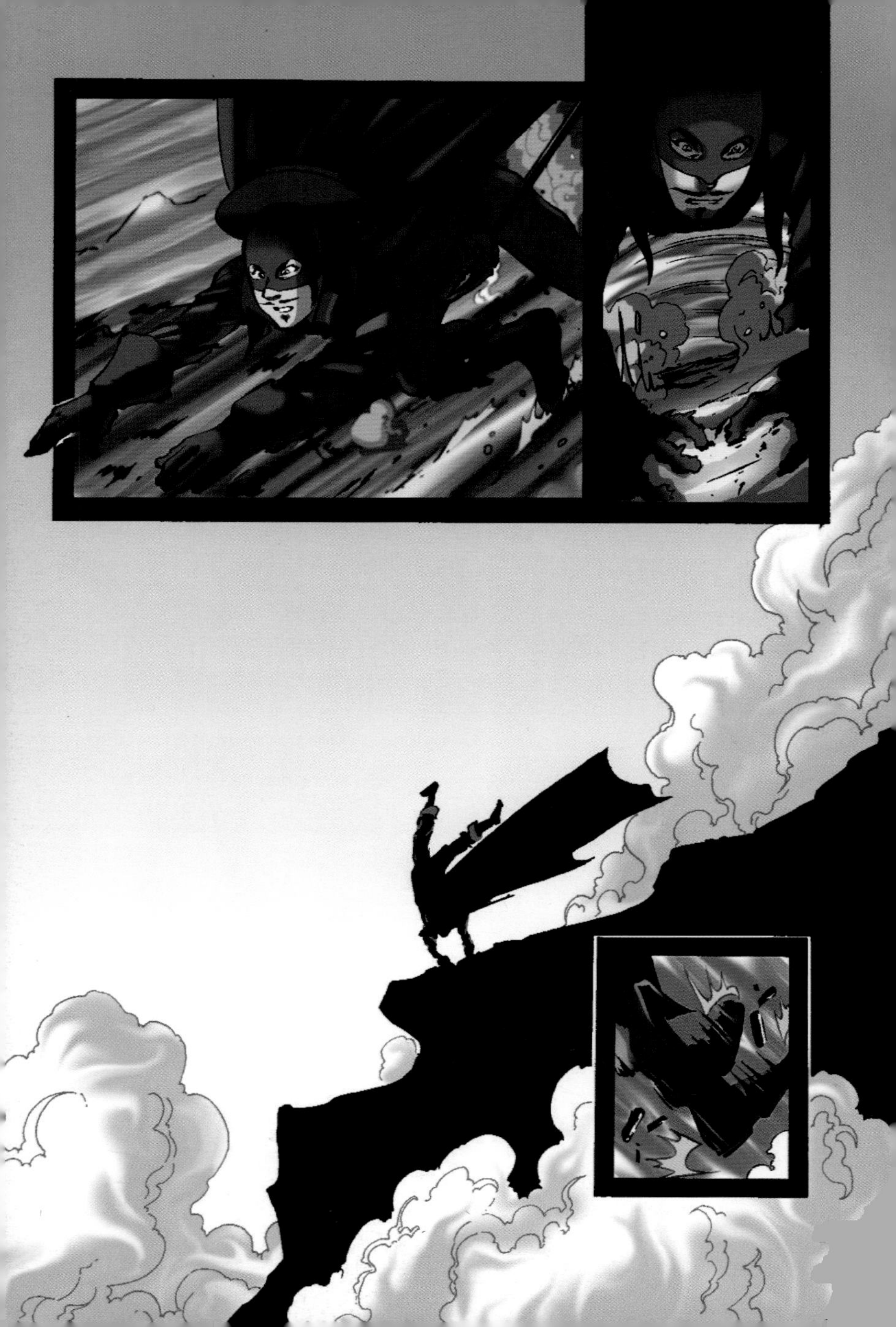

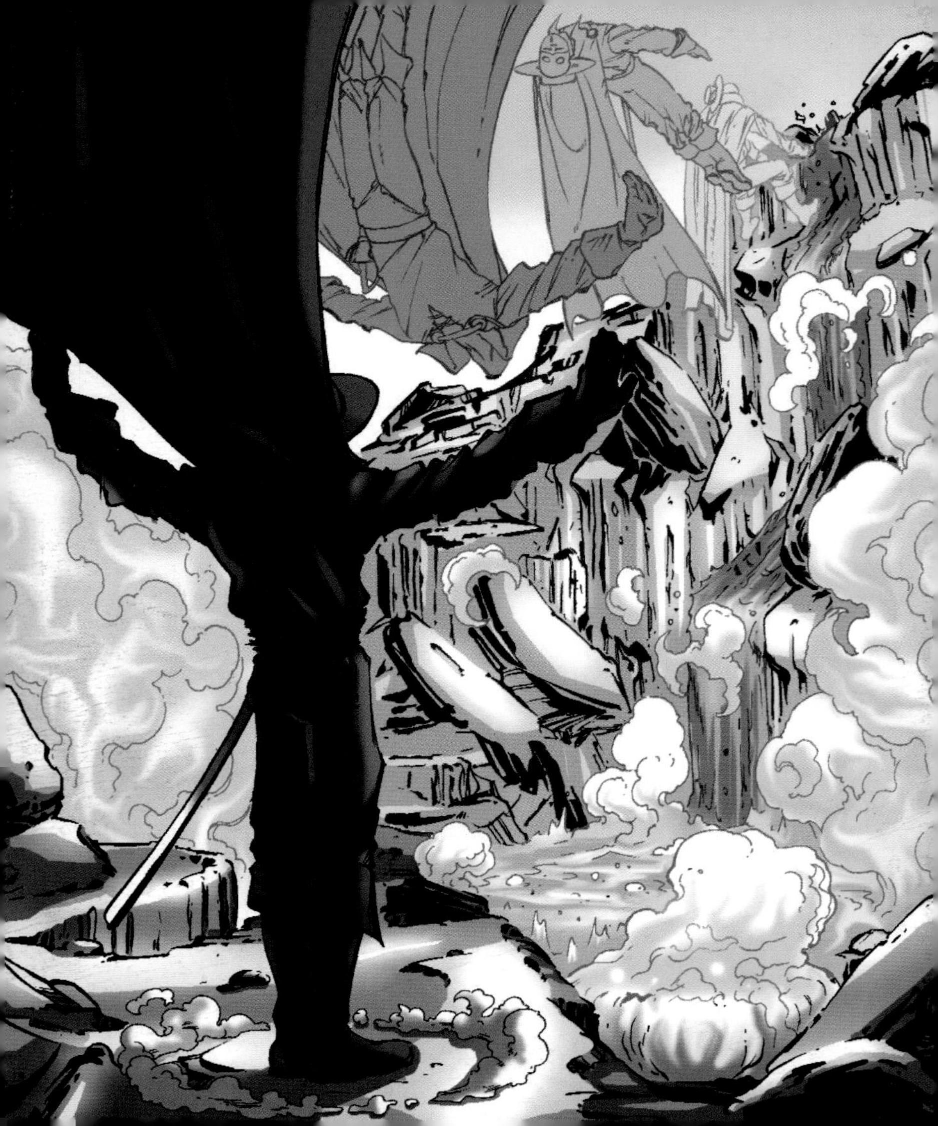

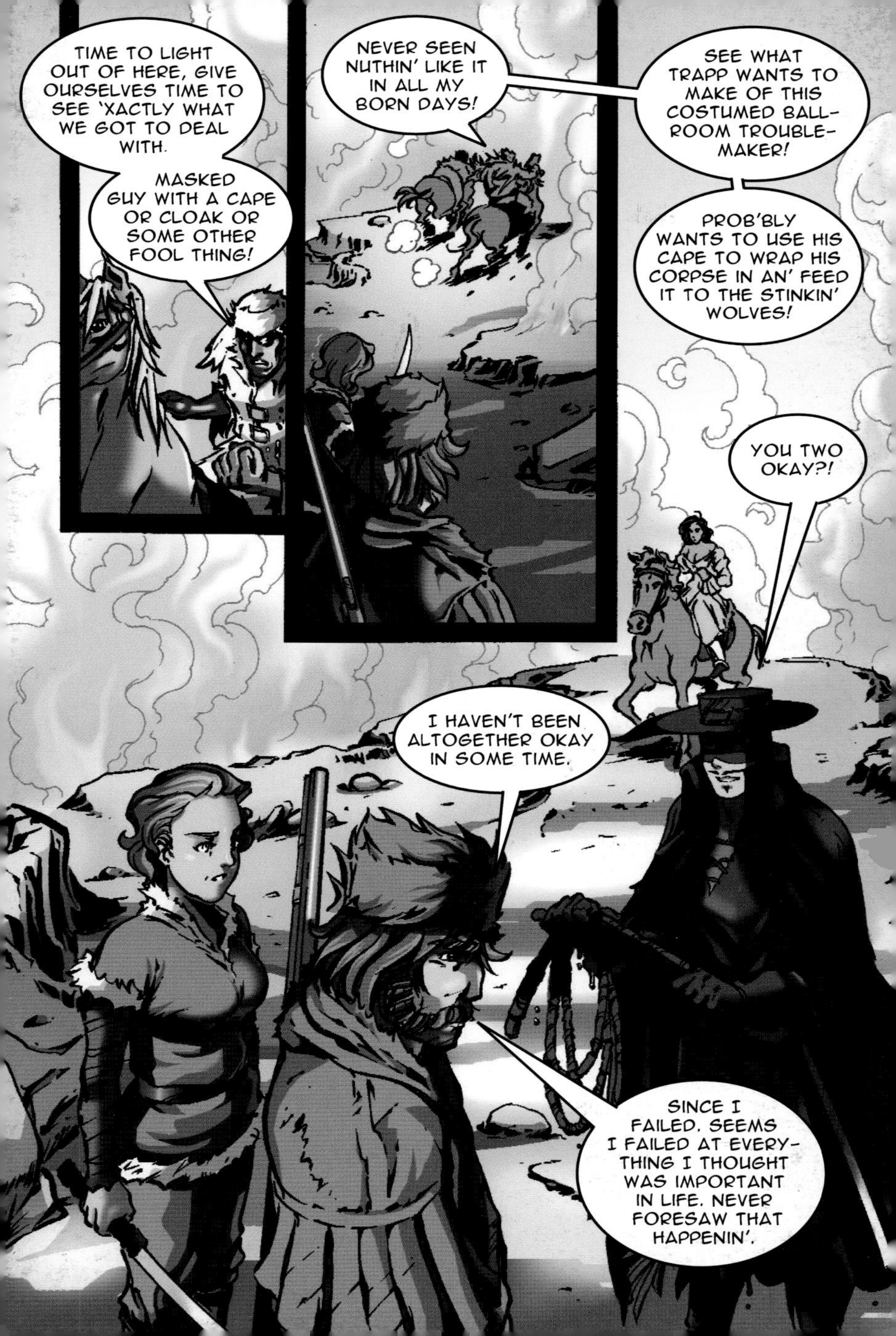
TIME TO LIGHT OUT OF HERE, GIVE OURSELVES TIME TO SEE 'XACTLY WHAT WE GOT TO DEAL WITH.
MASKED GUY WITH A CAPE OR CLOAK OR SOME OTHER FOOL THING!
NEVER SEEN NUTHIN' LIKE IT IN ALL MY BORN DAYS!
SEE WHAT TRAPP WANTS TO MAKE OF THIS COSTUMED BALL-ROOM TROUBLE-MAKER!
PROB'BLY WANTS TO USE HIS CAPE TO WRAP HIS CORPSE IN AN' FEED IT TO THE STINKIN' WOLVES!
YOU TWO OKAY?!
I HAVEN'T BEEN ALTOGETHER OKAY IN SOME TIME.
SINCE I FAILED. SEEMS I FAILED AT EVERY-THING I THOUGHT WAS IMPORTANT IN LIFE. NEVER FORESAW THAT HAPPENIN'.

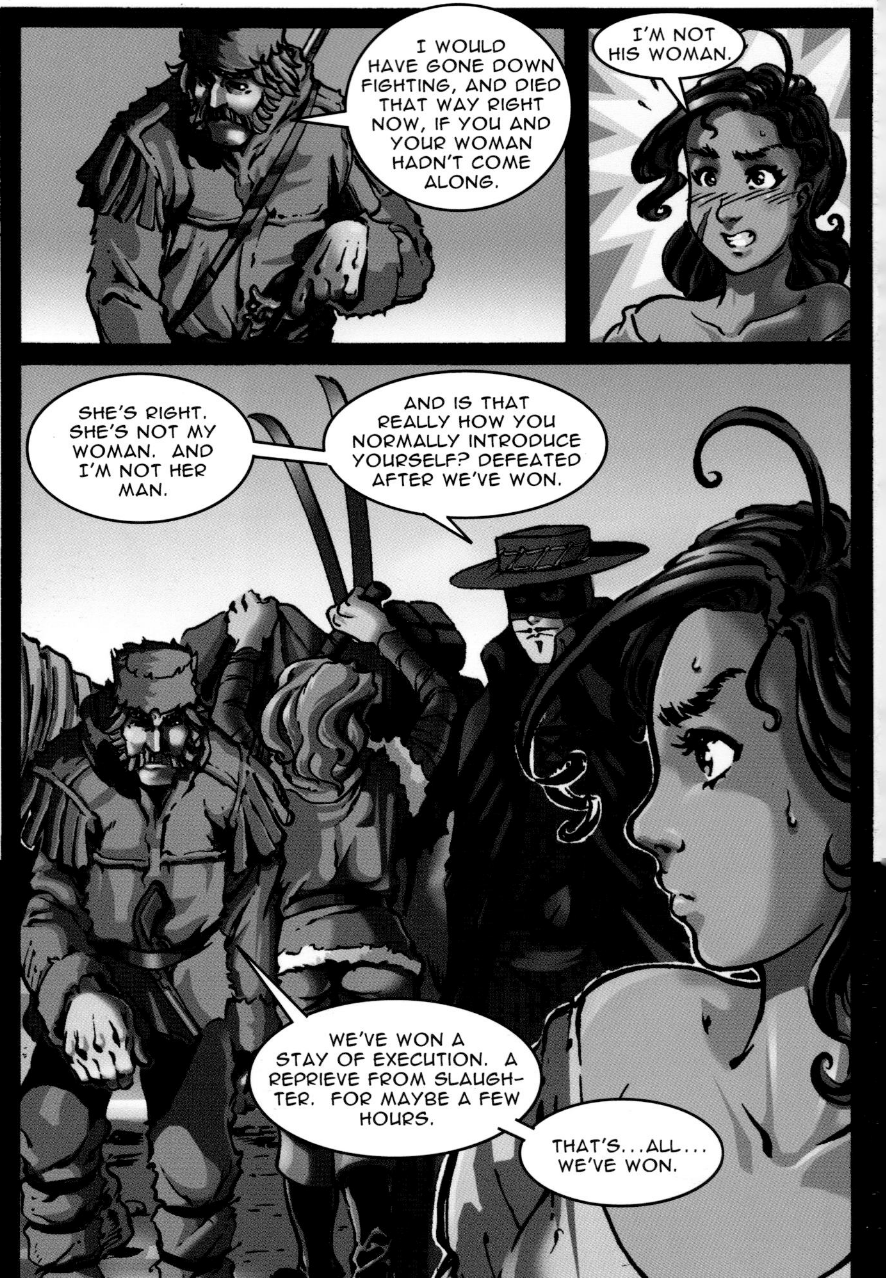
I WOULD HAVE GONE DOWN FIGHTING, AND DIED THAT WAY RIGHT NOW, IF YOU AND YOUR WOMAN HADN'T COME ALONG.
I'M NOT HIS WOMAN.
SHE'S RIGHT. SHE'S NOT MY WOMAN. AND I'M NOT HER MAN.
AND IS THAT REALLY HOW YOU NORMALLY INTRODUCE YOURSELF? DEFEATED AFTER WE'VE WON.
WE'VE WON A STAY OF EXECUTION. A REPRIEVE FROM SLAUGH-TER. FOR MAYBE A FEW HOURS.
THAT'S...ALL... WE'VE WON.

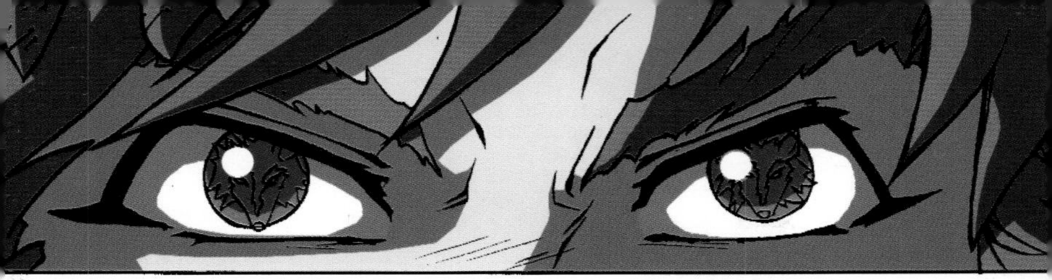

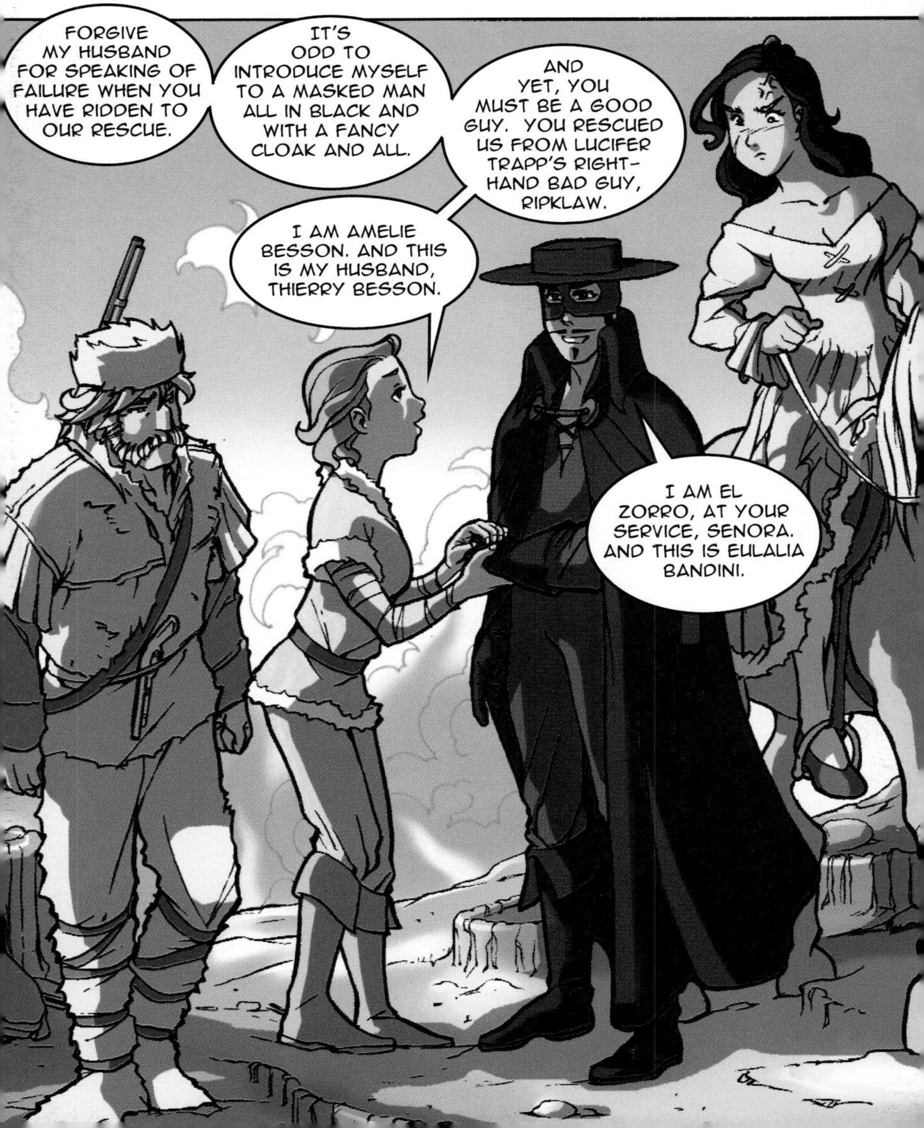
FORGIVE MY HUSBAND FOR SPEAKING OF FAILURE WHEN YOU HAVE RIDDEN TO OUR RESCUE.
IT'S ODD TO INTRODUCE MYSELF TO A MASKED MAN ALL IN BLACK AND WITH A FANCY CLOAK AND ALL.
AND YET, YOU MUST BE A GOOD GUY. YOU RESCUED US FROM LUCIFER TRAPP'S RIGHT-HAND BAD GUY, RIPKLAW.
I AM AMELIE BESSON. AND THIS IS MY HUSBAND, THIERRY BESSON.
I AM EL ZORRO, AT YOUR SERVICE, SENORA. AND THIS IS EULALIA BANDINI.

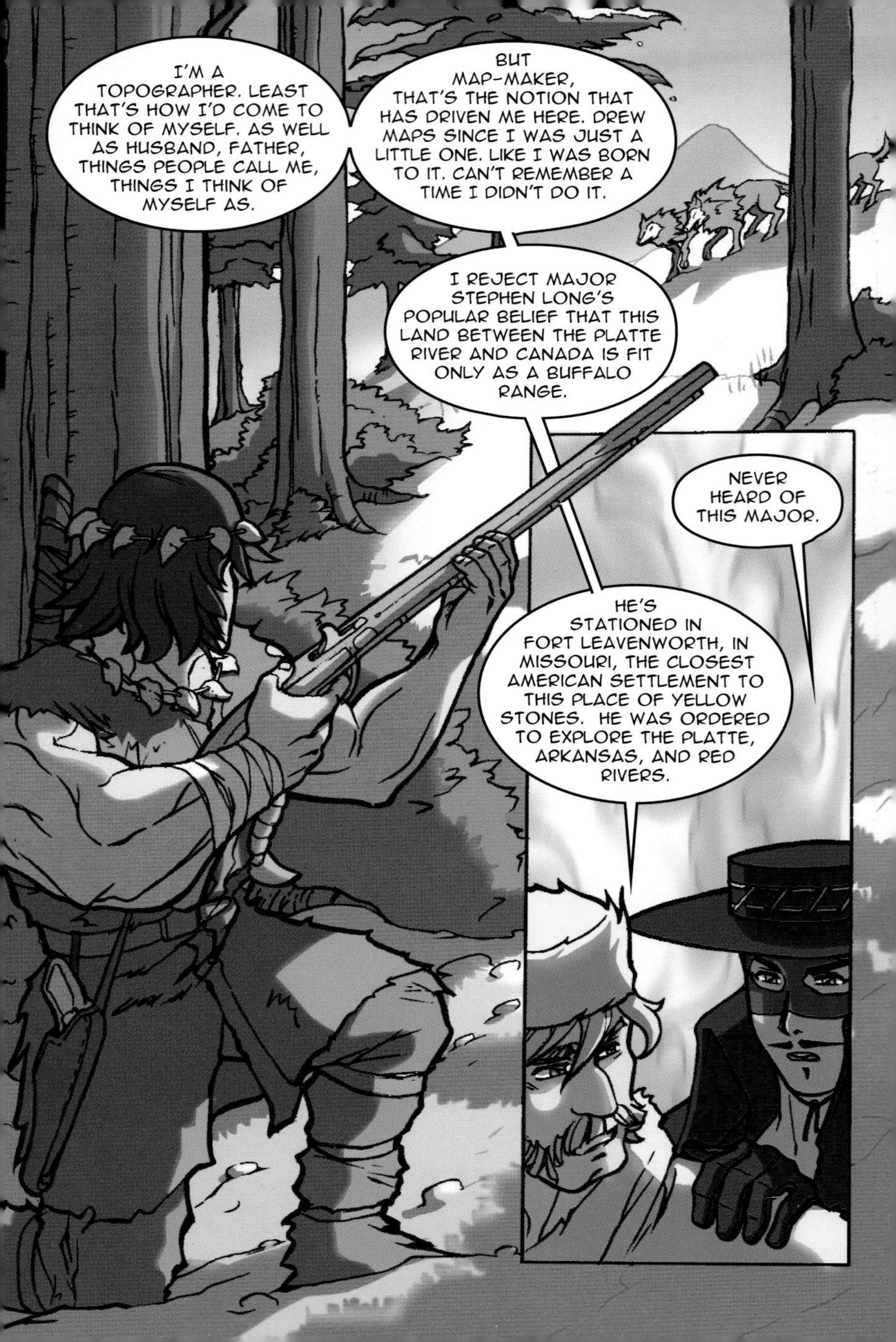
I'M A TOPOGRAPHER. LEAST THAT'S HOW I'D COME TO THINK OF MYSELF. AS WELL AS HUSBAND, FATHER, THINGS PEOPLE CALL ME, THINGS I THINK OF MYSELF AS.
BUT MAP-MAKER, THAT'S THE NOTION THAT HAS DRIVEN ME HERE. DREW MAPS SINCE I WAS JUST A LITTLE ONE. LIKE I WAS BORN TO IT. CAN'T REMEMBER A TIME I DIDN'T DO IT.
I REJECT MAJOR STEPHEN LONG'S POPULAR BELIEF THAT THIS LAND BETWEEN THE PLATTE RIVER AND CANADA IS FIT ONLY AS A BUFFALO RANGE.
NEVER HEARD OF THIS MAJOR.
HE'S STATIONED IN FORT LEAVENWORTH, IN MISSOURI, THE CLOSEST AMERICAN SETTLEMENT TO THIS PLACE OF YELLOW STONES. HE WAS ORDERED TO EXPLORE THE PLATTE, ARKANSAS, AND RED RIVERS.

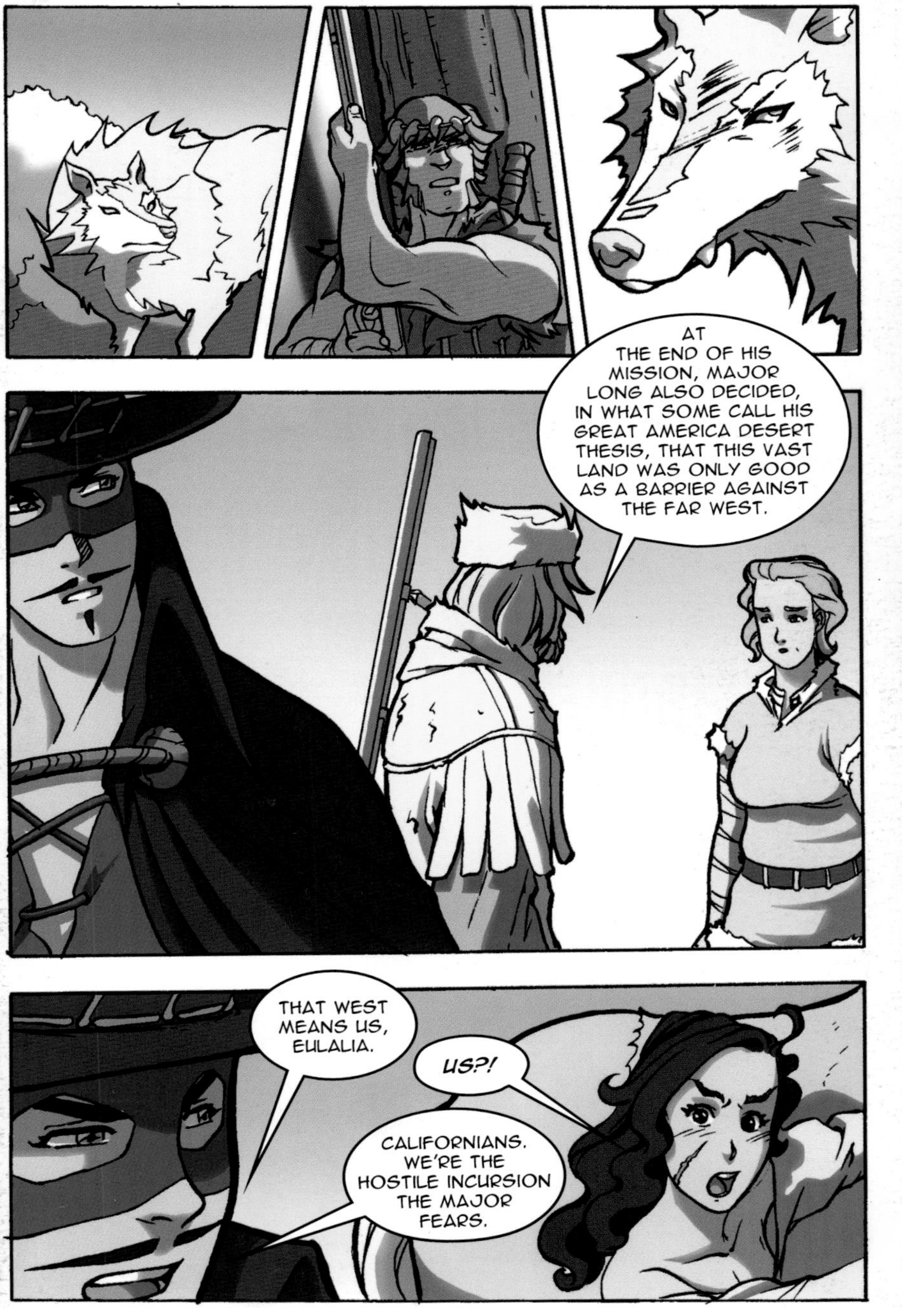
AT THE END OF HIS MISSION, MAJOR LONG ALSO DECIDED, IN WHAT SOME CALL HIS GREAT AMERICA DESERT THESIS, THAT THIS VAST LAND WAS ONLY GOOD AS A BARRIER AGAINST THE FAR WEST.
THAT WEST MEANS US, EULALIA.
US?!
CALIFORNIANS. WE'RE THE HOSTILE INCURSION THE MAJOR FEARS.

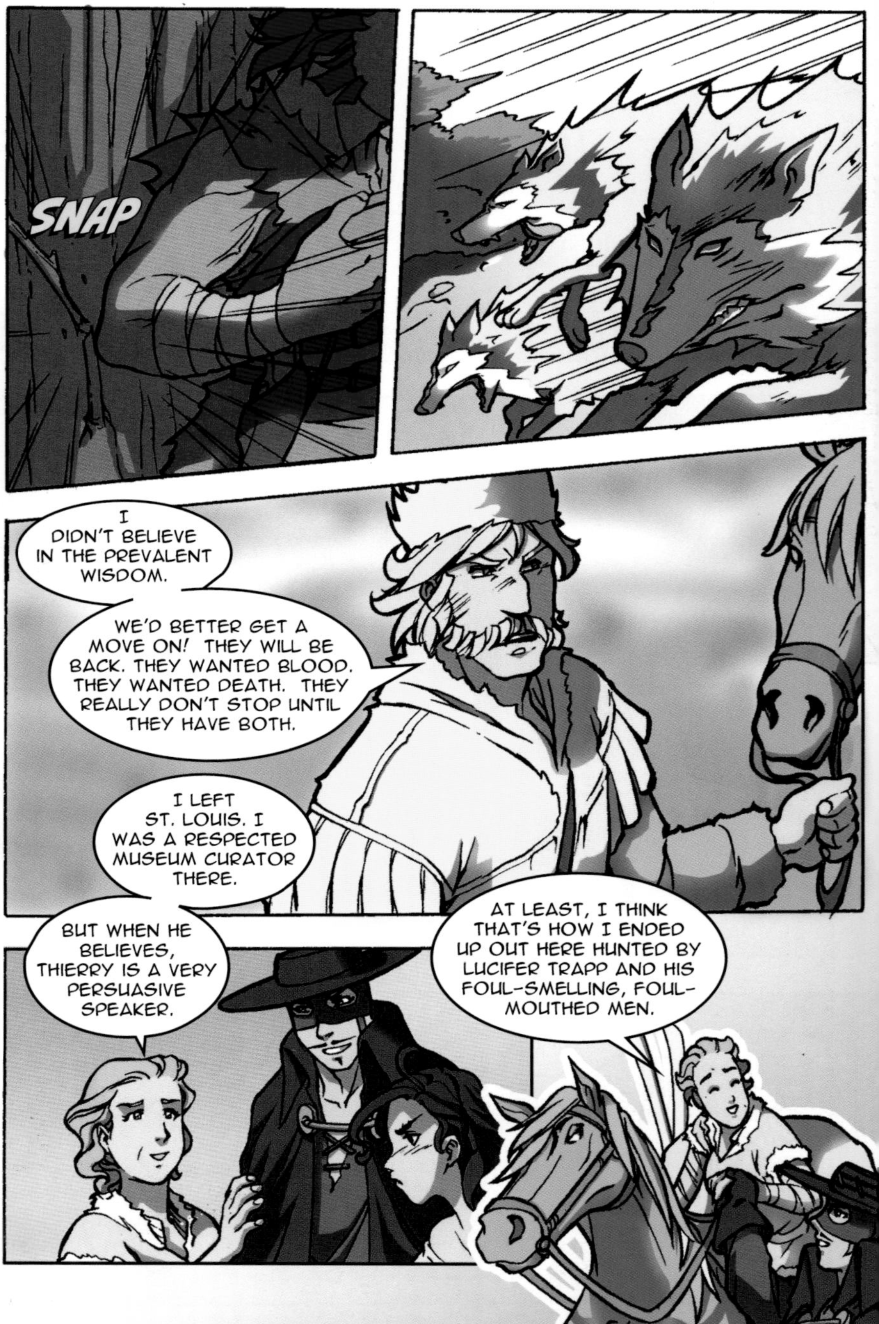
SNAP
I DIDN'T BELIEVE IN THE PREVALENT WISDOM.
WE'D BETTER GET A MOVE ON! THEY WILL BE BACK. THEY WANTED BLOOD. THEY WANTED DEATH. THEY REALLY DON'T STOP UNTIL THEY HAVE BOTH.
I LEFT ST. LOUIS. I WAS A RESPECTED MUSEUM CURATOR THERE.
BUT WHEN HE BELIEVES, THIERRY IS A VERY PERSUASIVE SPEAKER.
AT LEAST, I THINK THAT'S HOW I ENDED UP OUT HERE HUNTED BY LUCIFER TRAPP AND HIS FOUL-SMELLING, FOUL-MOUTHED MEN.

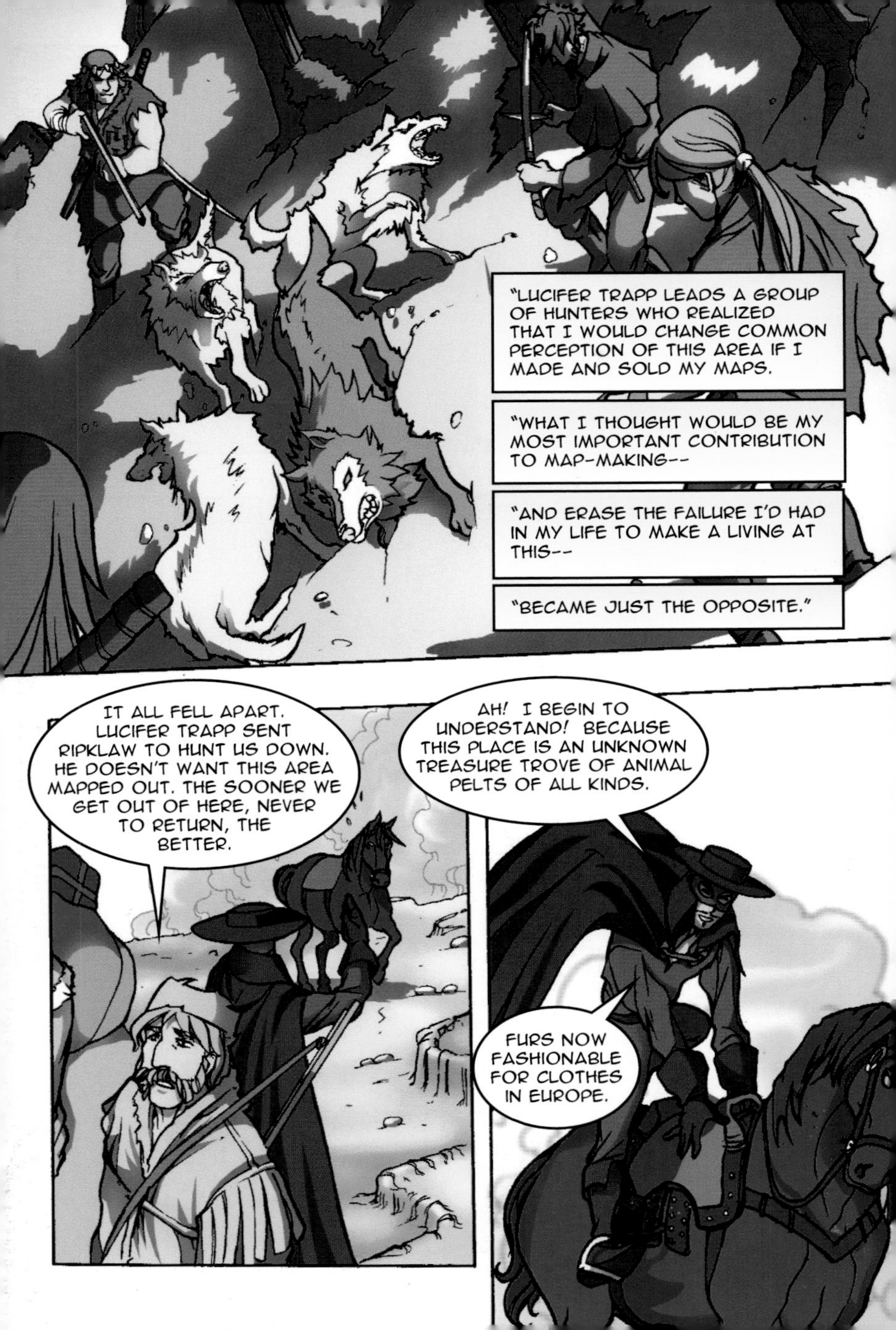
"LUCIFER TRAPP LEADS A GROUP OF HUNTERS WHO REALIZED THAT I WOULD CHANGE COMMON PERCEPTION OF THIS AREA IF I MADE AND SOLD MY MAPS.
"WHAT I THOUGHT WOULD BE MY MOST IMPORTANT CONTRIBUTION TO MAP-MAKING--
"AND ERASE THE FAILURE I'D HAD IN MY LIFE TO MAKE A LIVING AT THIS--
"BECAME JUST THE OPPOSITE."
IT ALL FELL APART. LUCIFER TRAPP SENT RIPKLAW TO HUNT US DOWN. HE DOESN'T WANT THIS AREA MAPPED OUT. THE SOONER WE GET OUT OF HERE, NEVER TO RETURN, THE BETTER.
AH! I BEGIN TO UNDERSTAND! BECAUSE THIS PLACE IS AN UNKNOWN TREASURE TROVE OF ANIMAL PELTS OF ALL KINDS.
FURS NOW FASHIONABLE FOR CLOTHES IN EUROPE.

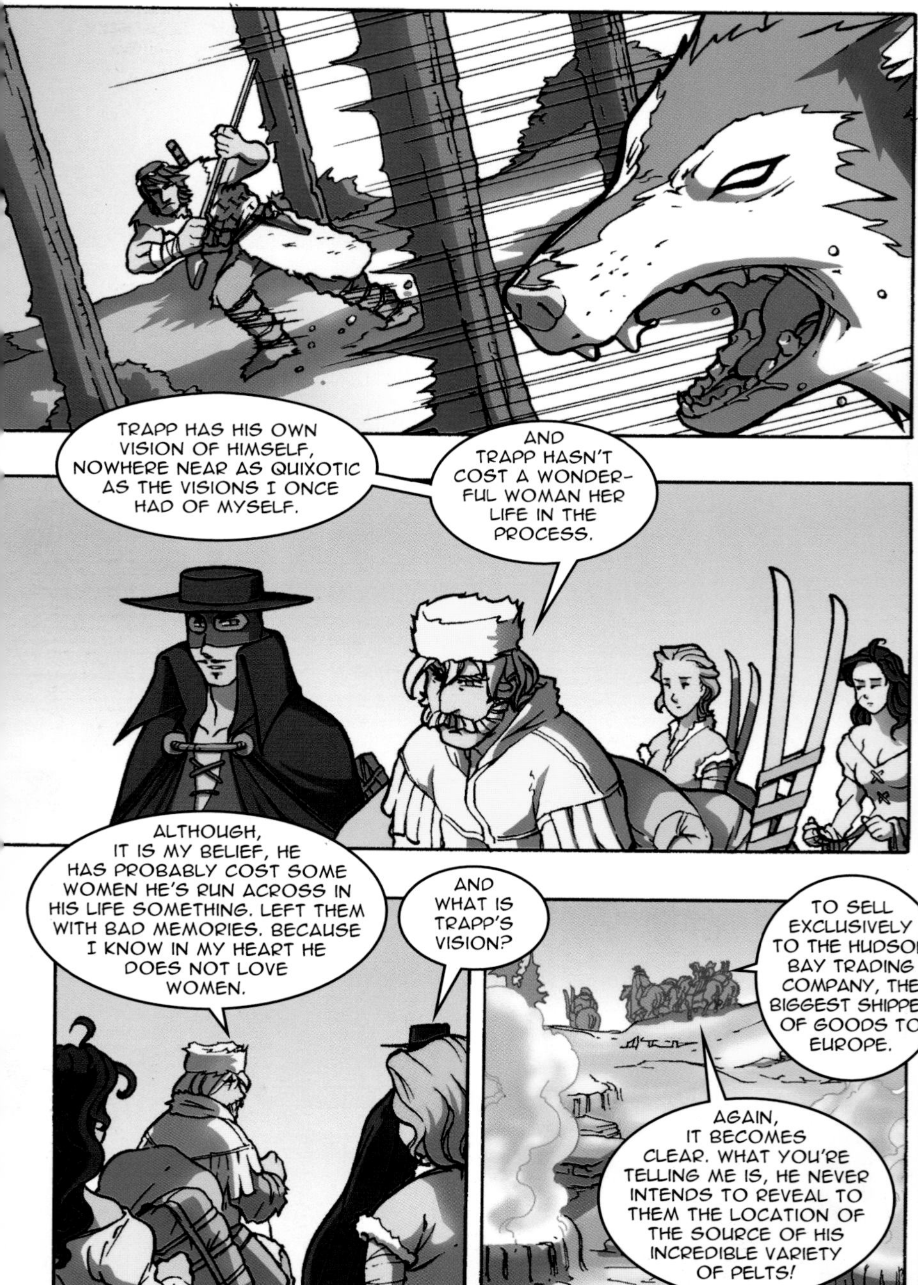
TRAPP HAS HIS OWN VISION OF HIMSELF, NOWHERE NEAR AS QUIXOTIC AS THE VISIONS I ONCE HAD OF MYSELF.
AND TRAPP HASN'T COST A WONDER-FUL WOMAN HER LIFE IN THE PROCESS.
ALTHOUGH, IT IS MY BELIEF, HE HAS PROBABLY COST SOME WOMEN HE'S RUN ACROSS IN HIS LIFE SOMETHING. LEFT THEM WITH BAD MEMORIES. BECAUSE I KNOW IN MY HEART HE DOES NOT LOVE WOMEN.
AND WHAT IS TRAPP'S VISION?
TO SELL EXCLUSIVELY TO THE HUDSON BAY TRADING COMPANY, THE BIGGEST SHIPPER OF GOODS TO EUROPE.
AGAIN, IT BECOMES CLEAR. WHAT YOU'RE TELLING ME IS, HE NEVER INTENDS TO REVEAL TO THEM THE LOCATION OF THE SOURCE OF HIS INCREDIBLE VARIETY OF PELTS!

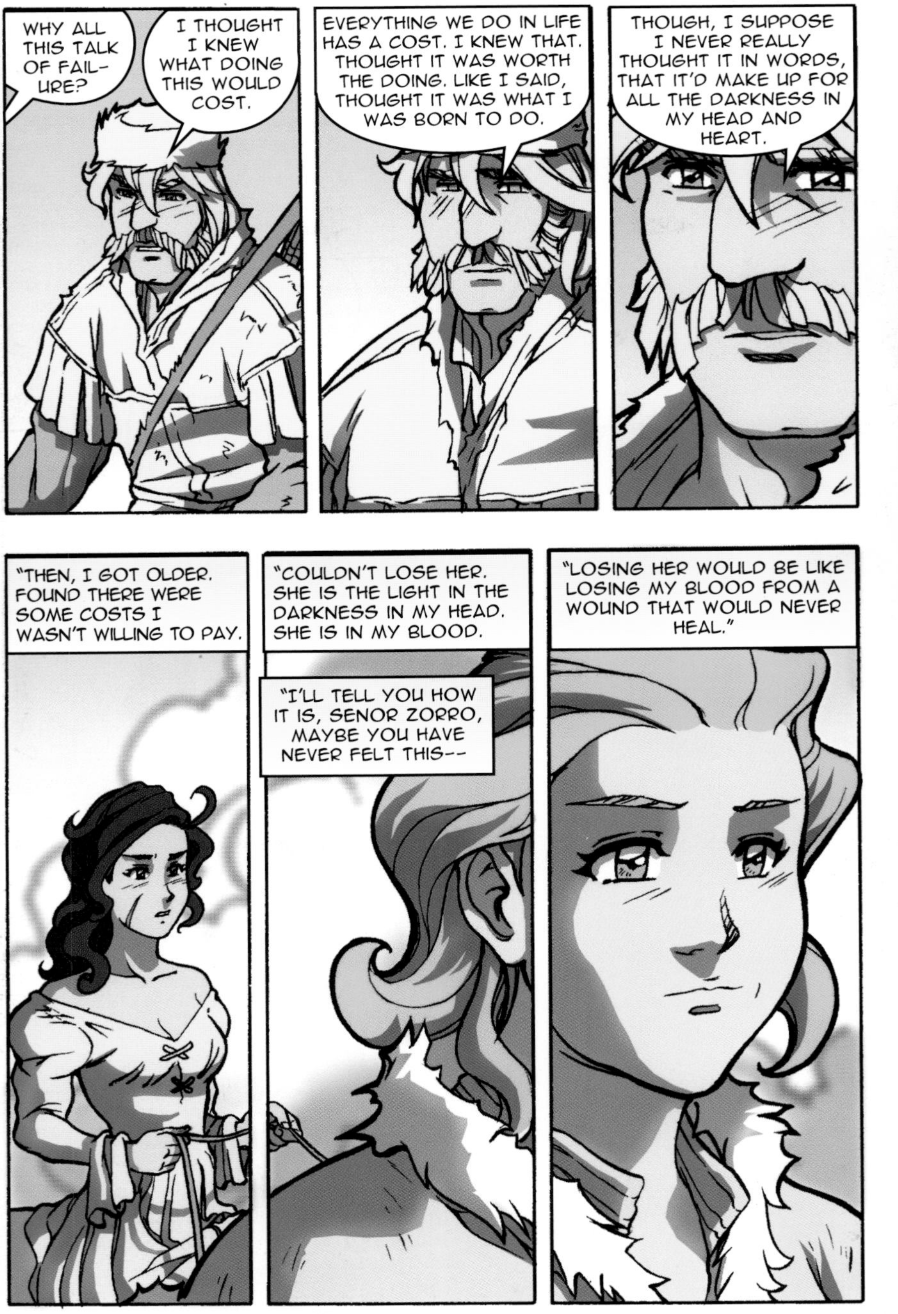
WHY ALL THIS TALK OF FAIL-URE?
I THOUGHT I KNEW WHAT DOING THIS WOULD COST.
EVERYTHING WE DO IN LIFE HAS A COST. I KNEW THAT. THOUGHT IT WAS WORTH THE DOING. LIKE I SAID, THOUGHT IT WAS WHAT I WAS BORN TO DO.
THOUGH, I SUPPOSE I NEVER REALLY THOUGHT IT IN WORDS, THAT IT'D MAKE UP FOR ALL THE DARKNESS IN MY HEAD AND HEART.
"THEN, I GOT OLDER. FOUND THERE WERE SOME COSTS I WASN'T WILLING TO PAY.
"COULDN'T LOSE HER. SHE IS THE LIGHT IN THE DARKNESS IN MY HEAD. SHE IS IN MY BLOOD.
"I'LL TELL YOU HOW IT IS, SENOR ZORRO, MAYBE YOU HAVE NEVER FELT THIS--
"LOSING HER WOULD BE LIKE LOSING MY BLOOD FROM A WOUND THAT WOULD NEVER HEAL."

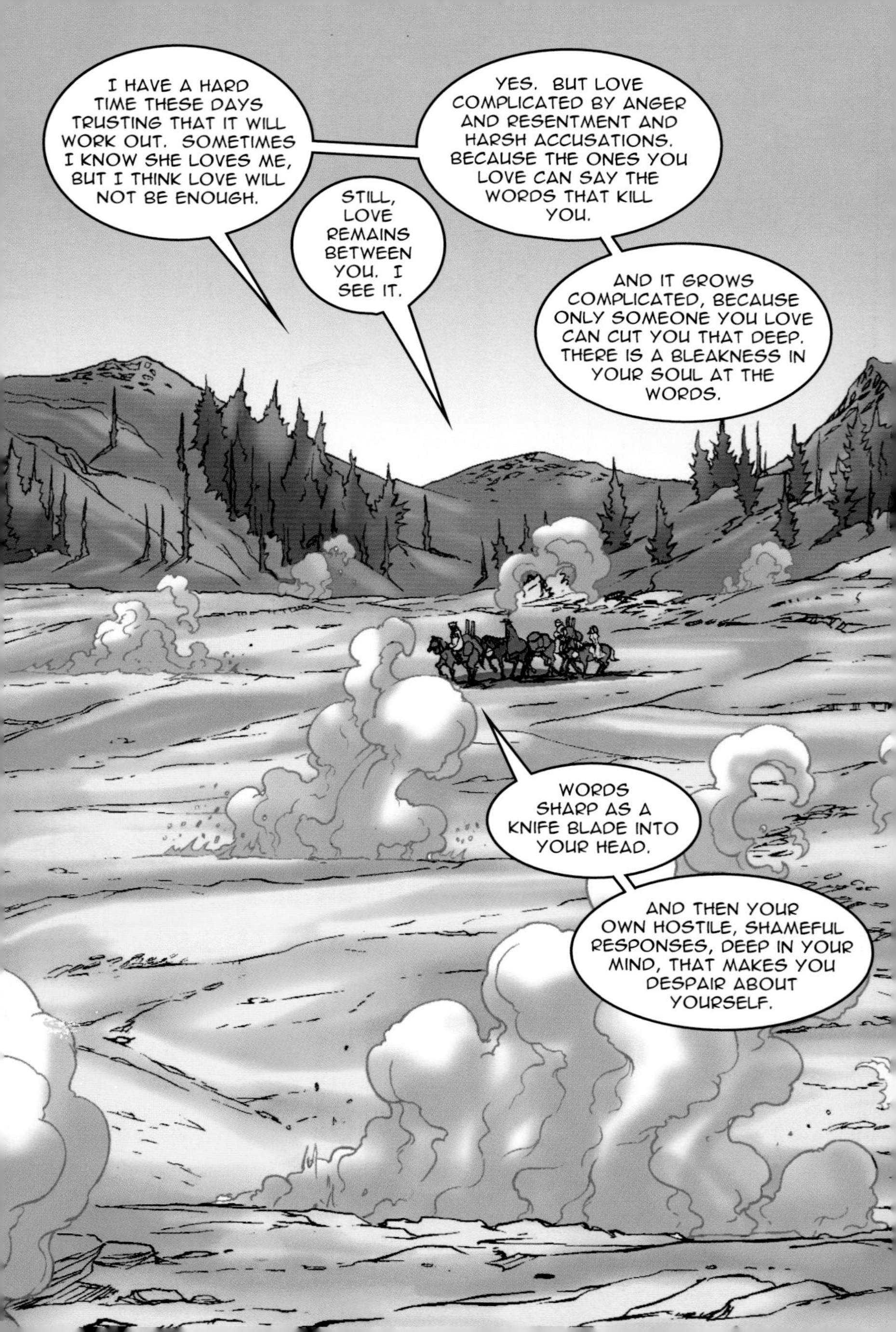
I HAVE A HARD TIME THESE DAYS TRUSTING THAT IT WILL WORK OUT. SOMETIMES I KNOW SHE LOVES ME, BUT I THINK LOVE WILL NOT BE ENOUGH.
STILL, LOVE REMAINS BETWEEN YOU. I SEE IT.
YES. BUT LOVE COMPLICATED BY ANGER AND RESENTMENT AND HARSH ACCUSATIONS. BECAUSE THE ONES YOU LOVE CAN SAY THE WORDS THAT KILL YOU.
AND IT GROWS COMPLICATED, BECAUSE ONLY SOMEONE YOU LOVE CAN CUT YOU THAT DEEP. THERE IS A BLEAKNESS IN YOUR SOUL AT THE WORDS.
WORDS SHARP AS A KNIFE BLADE INTO YOUR HEAD.
AND THEN YOUR OWN HOSTILE, SHAMEFUL RESPONSES, DEEP IN YOUR MIND, THAT MAKES YOU DESPAIR ABOUT YOURSELF.

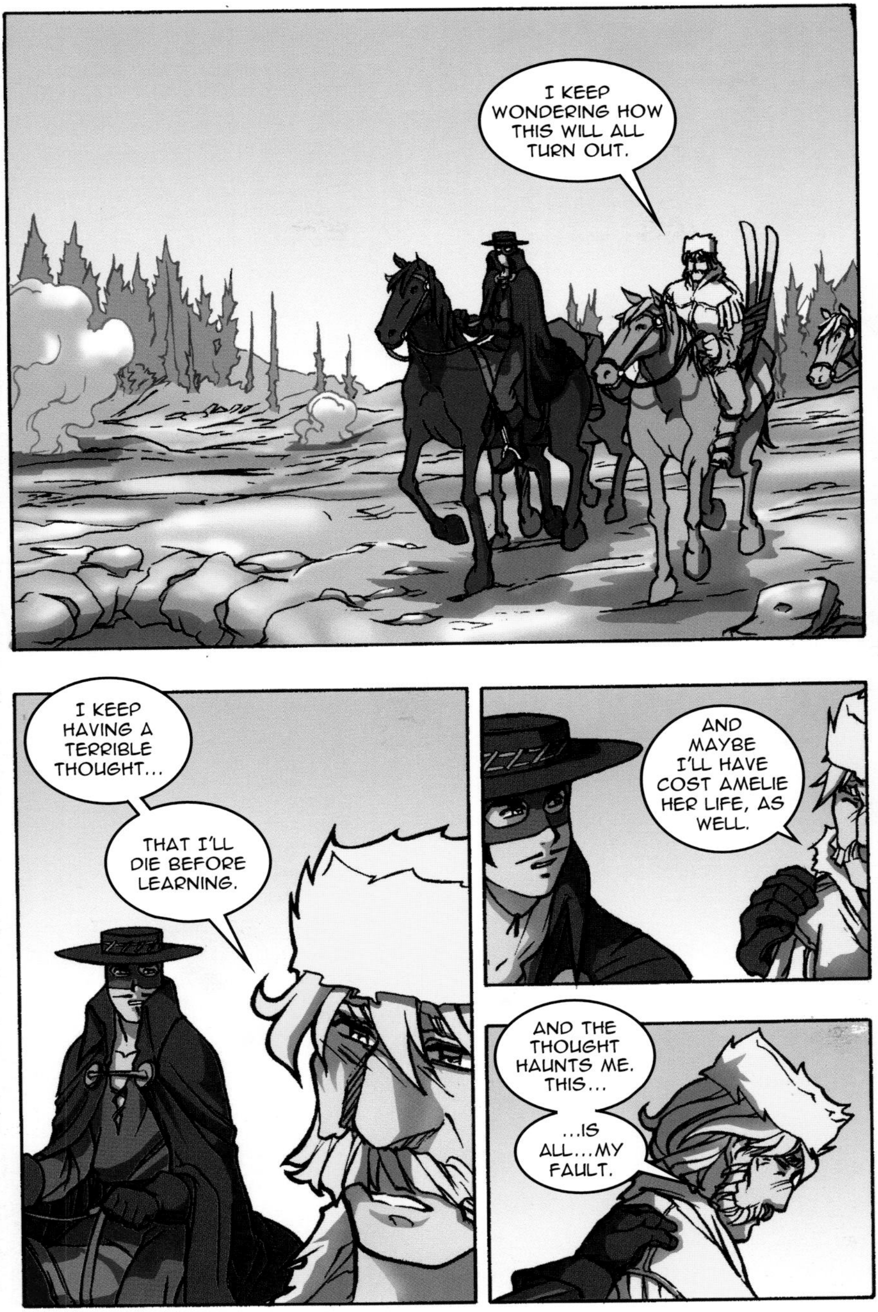
I KEEP WONDERING HOW THIS WILL ALL TURN OUT.
I KEEP HAVING A TERRIBLE THOUGHT...
THAT I'LL DIE BEFORE LEARNING.
AND MAYBE I'LL HAVE COST AMELIE HER LIFE, AS WELL.
AND THE THOUGHT HAUNTS ME. THIS...
...IS ALL...MY FAULT.

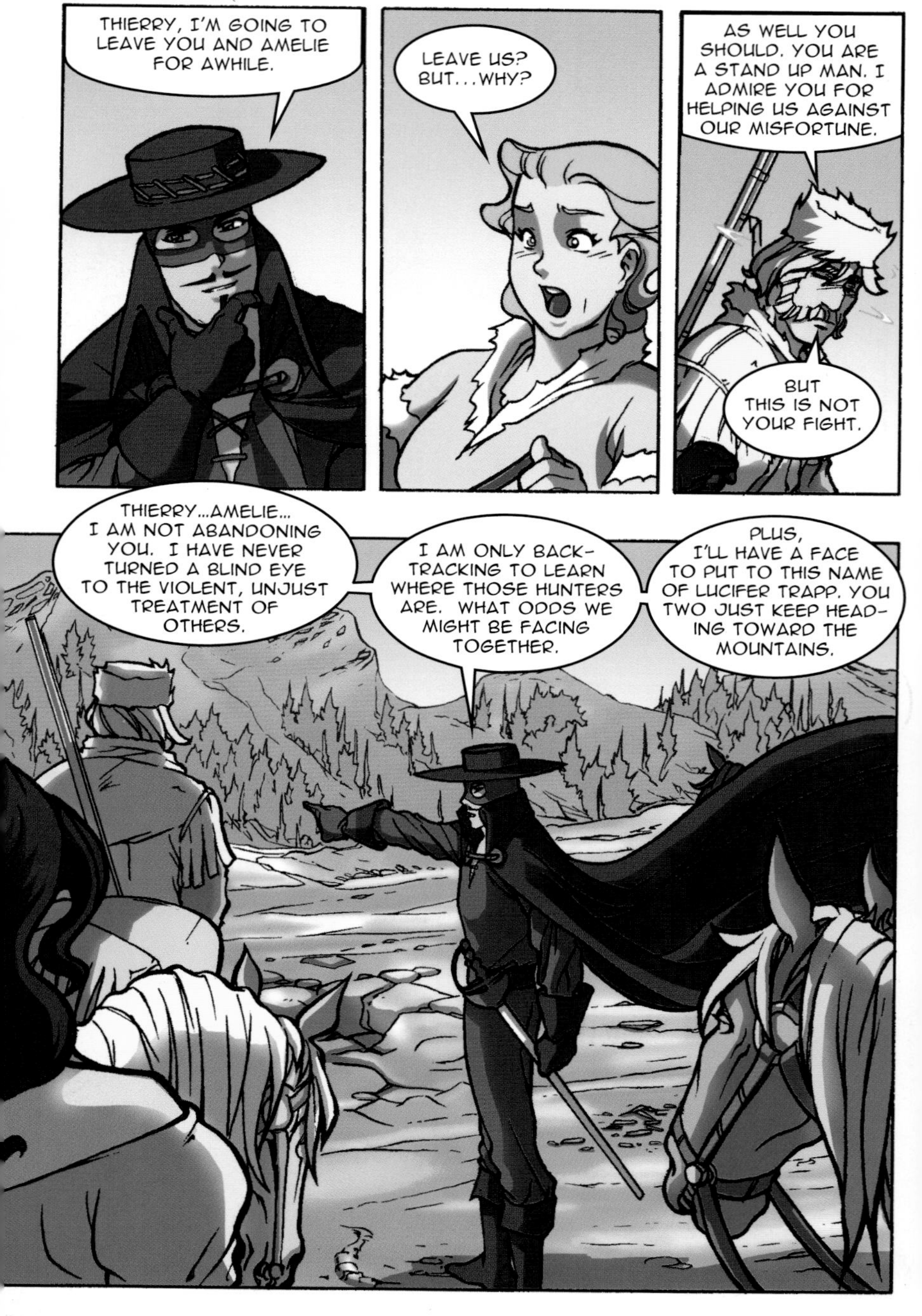
THIERRY, I'M GOING TO LEAVE YOU AND AMELIE FOR AWHILE.
LEAVE US? BUT. . . WHY?
AS WELL YOU SHOULD. YOU ARE A STAND UP MAN. I ADMIRE YOU FOR HELPING US AGAINST OUR MISFORTUNE.
BUT THIS IS NOT YOUR FIGHT.
THIERRY...AMELIE... I AM NOT ABANDONING YOU. I HAVE NEVER TURNED A BLIND EYE TO THE VIOLENT, UNJUST TREATMENT OF OTHERS.
I AM ONLY BACK-TRACKING TO LEARN WHERE THOSE HUNTERS ARE. WHAT ODDS WE MIGHT BE FACING TOGETHER.
PLUS, I'LL HAVE A FACE TO PUT TO THIS NAME OF LUCIFER TRAPP. YOU TWO JUST KEEP HEAD-ING TOWARD THE MOUNTAINS.

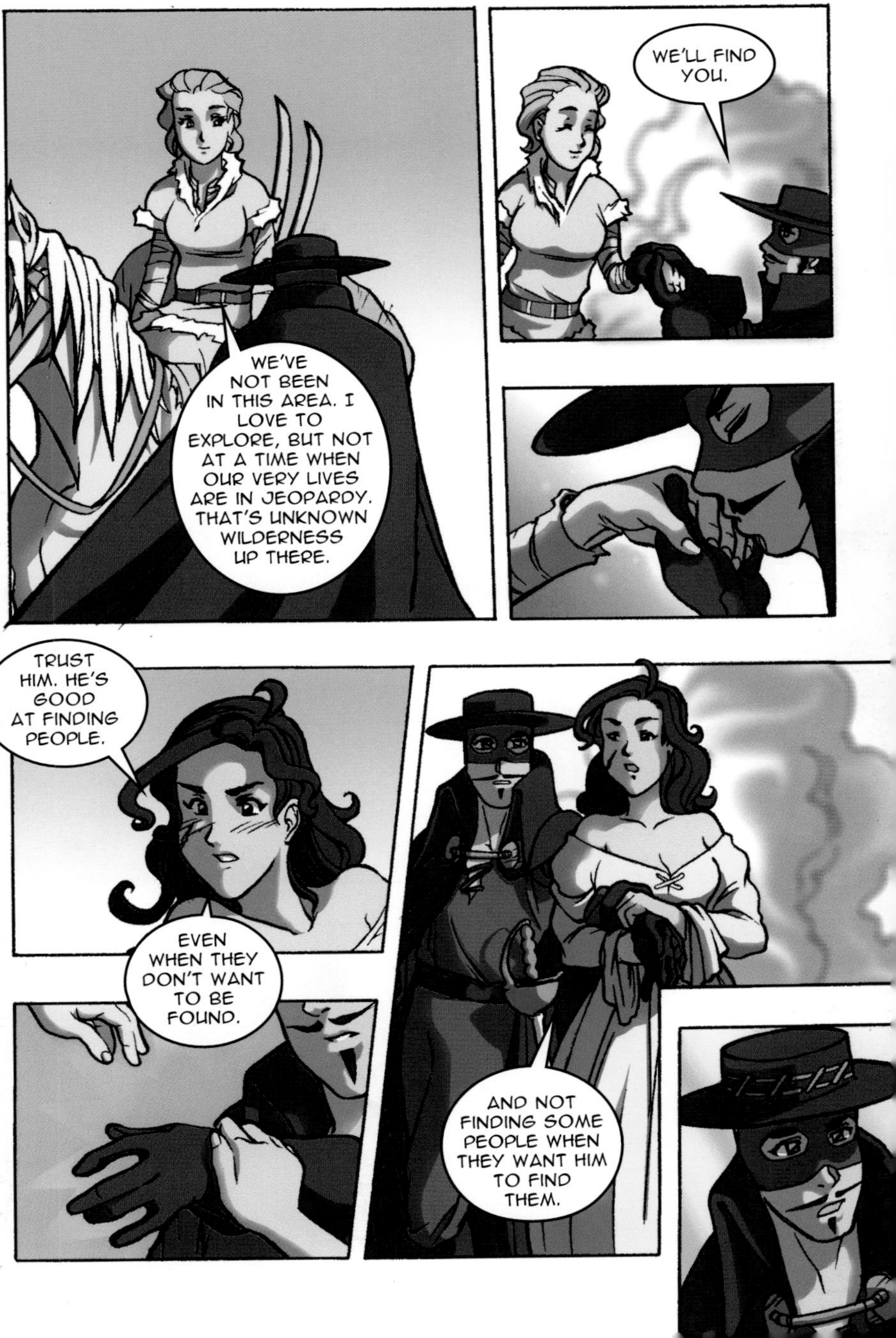
WE'VE NOT BEEN IN THIS AREA. I LOVE TO EXPLORE, BUT NOT AT A TIME WHEN OUR VERY LIVES ARE IN JEOPARDY. THAT'S UNKNOWN WILDERNESS UP THERE.
WE'LL FIND YOU.
TRUST HIM. HE'S GOOD AT FINDING PEOPLE.
EVEN WHEN THEY DON'T WANT TO BE FOUND.
AND NOT FINDING SOME PEOPLE WHEN THEY WANT HIM TO FIND THEM.

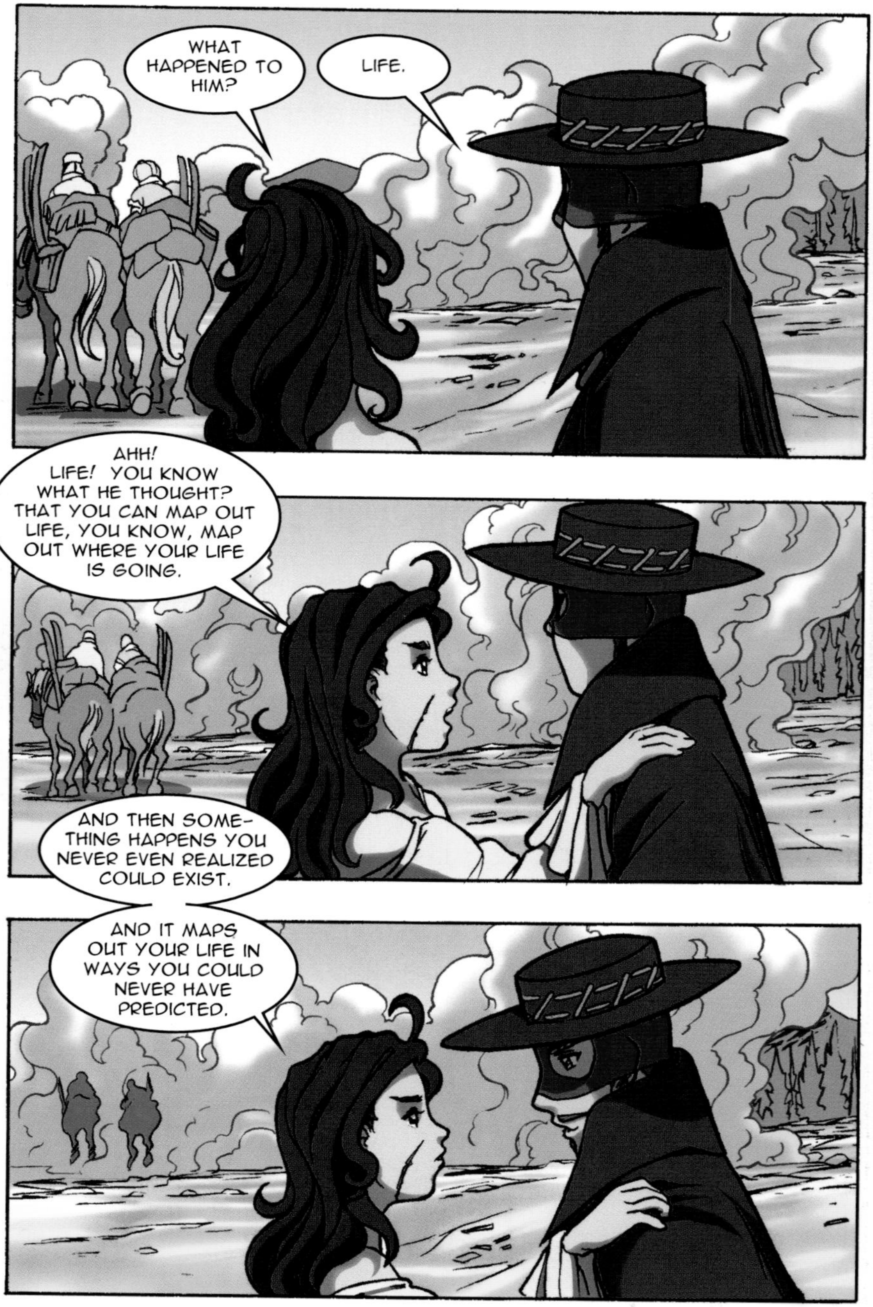
WHAT HAPPENED TO HIM?
LIFE.
AHH! LIFE! YOU KNOW WHAT HE THOUGHT? THAT YOU CAN MAP OUT LIFE, YOU KNOW, MAP OUT WHERE YOUR LIFE IS GOING.
AND THEN SOME-THING HAPPENS YOU NEVER EVEN REALIZED COULD EXIST.
AND IT MAPS OUT YOUR LIFE IN WAYS YOU COULD NEVER HAVE PREDICTED.

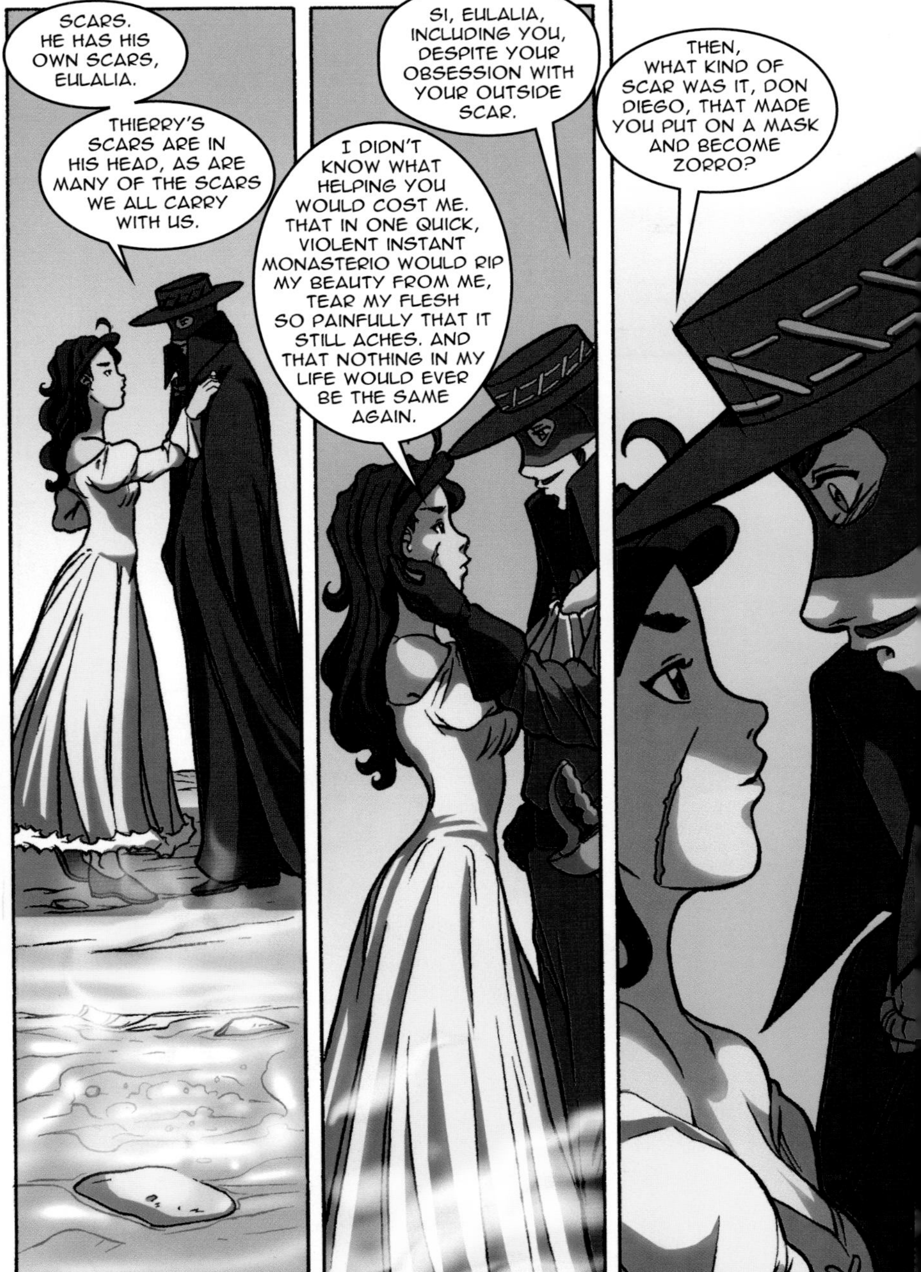
SCARS. HE HAS HIS OWN SCARS, EULALIA.
THIERRY'S SCARS ARE IN HIS HEAD, AS ARE MANY OF THE SCARS WE ALL CARRY WITH US.
SI, EULALIA, INCLUDING YOU, DESPITE YOUR OBSESSION WITH YOUR OUTSIDE SCAR.
I DIDN'T KNOW WHAT HELPING YOU WOULD COST ME. THAT IN ONE QUICK, VIOLENT INSTANT MONASTERIO WOULD RIP MY BEAUTY FROM ME, TEAR MY FLESH SO PAINFULLY THAT IT STILL ACHES. AND THAT NOTHING IN MY LIFE WOULD EVER BE THE SAME AGAIN.
THEN, WHAT KIND OF SCAR WAS IT, DON DIEGO, THAT MADE YOU PUT ON A MASK AND BECOME ZORRO?

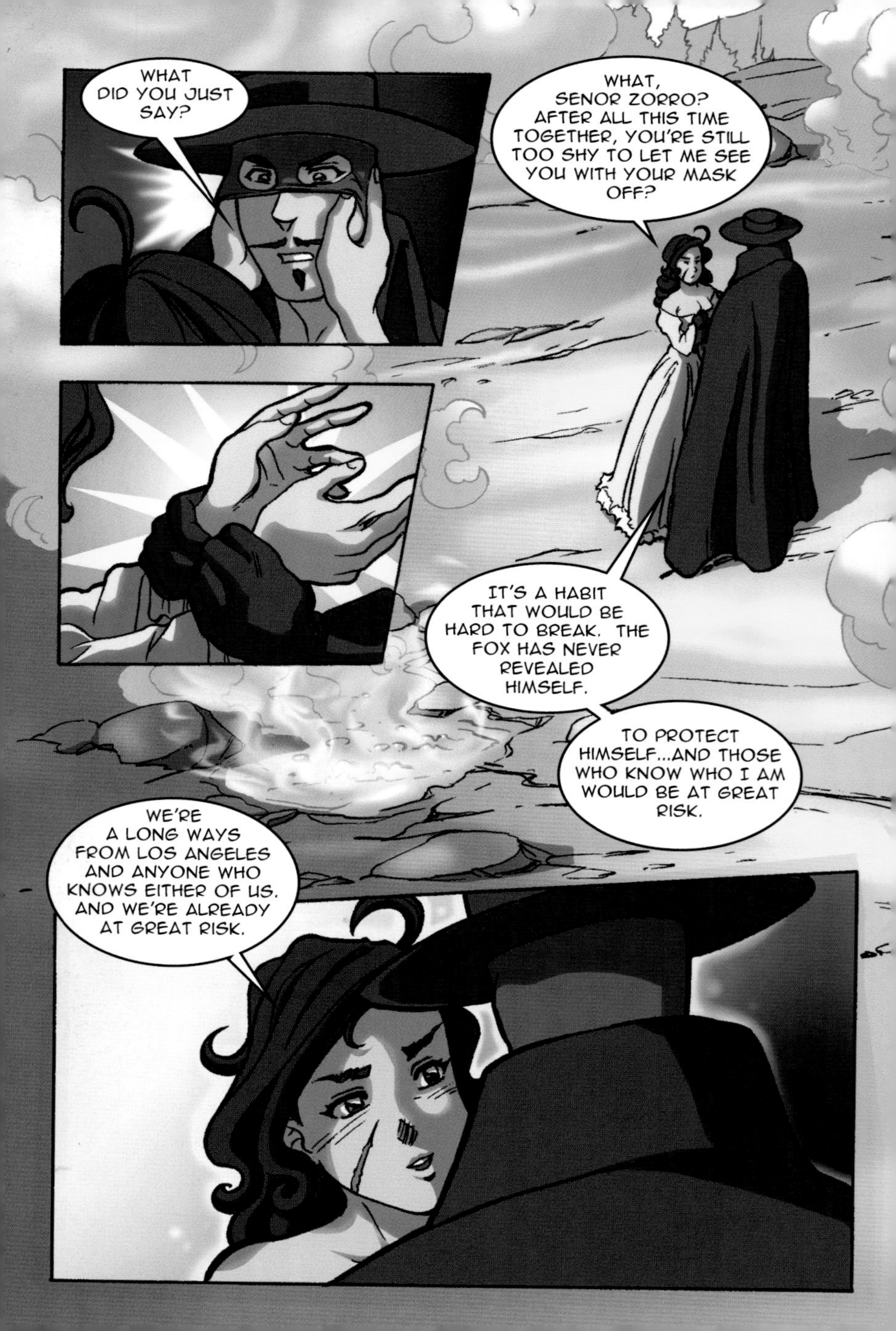
WHAT DID YOU JUST SAY?
WHAT, SENOR ZORRO? AFTER ALL THIS TIME TOGETHER, YOU'RE STILL TOO SHY TO LET ME SEE YOU WITH YOUR MASK OFF?
IT'S A HABIT THAT WOULD BE HARD TO BREAK. THE FOX HAS NEVER REVEALED HIMSELF.
TO PROTECT HIMSELF...AND THOSE WHO KNOW WHO I AM WOULD BE AT GREAT RISK.
WE'RE A LONG WAYS FROM LOS ANGELES AND ANYONE WHO KNOWS EITHER OF US. AND WE'RE ALREADY AT GREAT RISK.

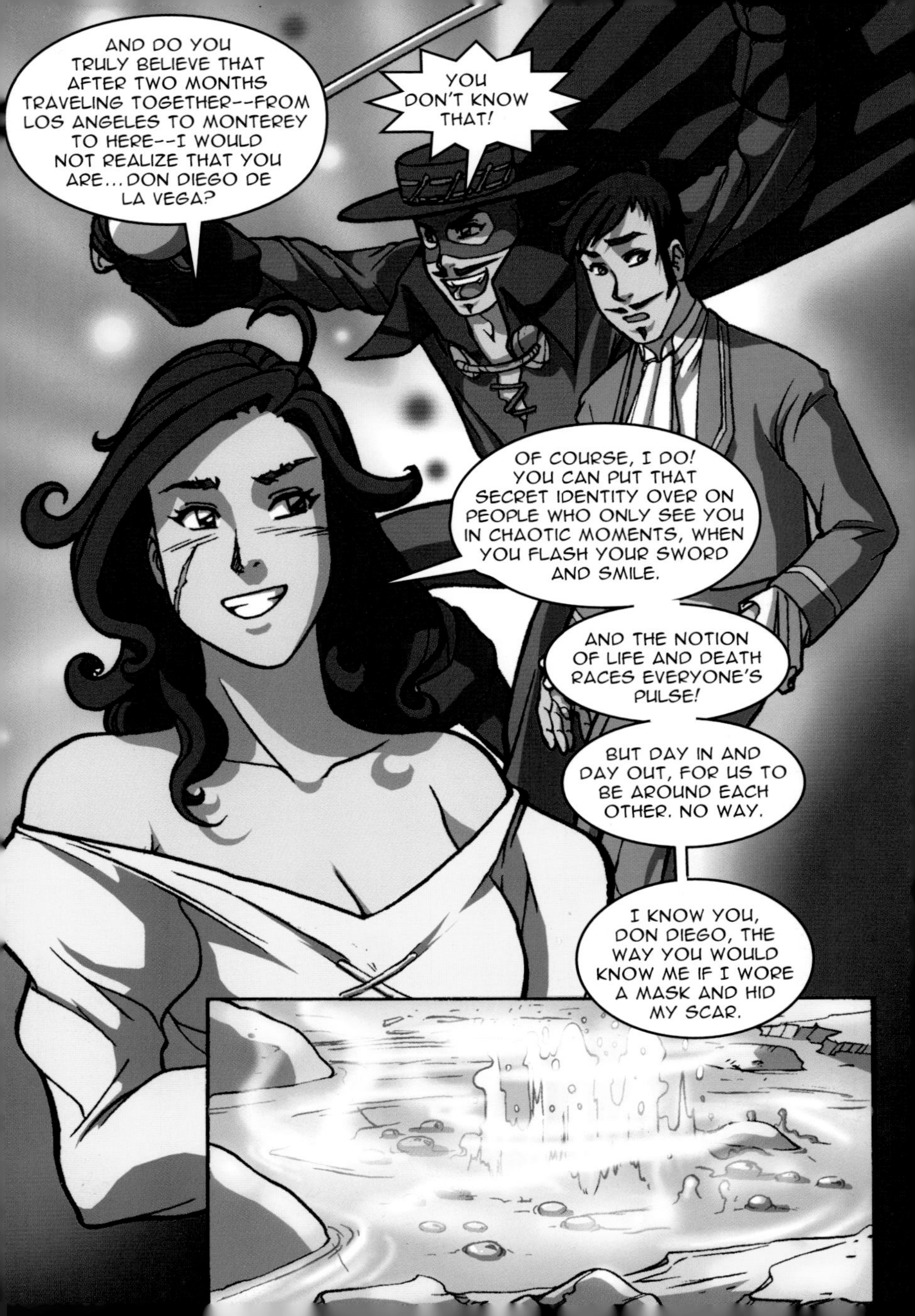
AND DO YOU TRULY BELIEVE THAT AFTER TWO MONTHS TRAVELING TOGETHER--FROM LOS ANGELES TO MONTEREY TO HERE--I WOULD NOT REALIZE THAT YOU ARE...DON DIEGO DE LA VEGA?
YOU DON'T KNOW THAT!
OF COURSE, I DO! YOU CAN PUT THAT SECRET IDENTITY OVER ON PEOPLE WHO ONLY SEE YOU IN CHAOTIC MOMENTS, WHEN YOU FLASH YOUR SWORD AND SMILE.
AND THE NOTION OF LIFE AND DEATH RACES EVERYONE'S PULSE!
BUT DAY IN AND DAY OUT, FOR US TO BE AROUND EACH OTHER. NO WAY.
I KNOW YOU, DON DIEGO, THE WAY YOU WOULD KNOW ME IF I WORE A MASK AND HID MY SCAR.

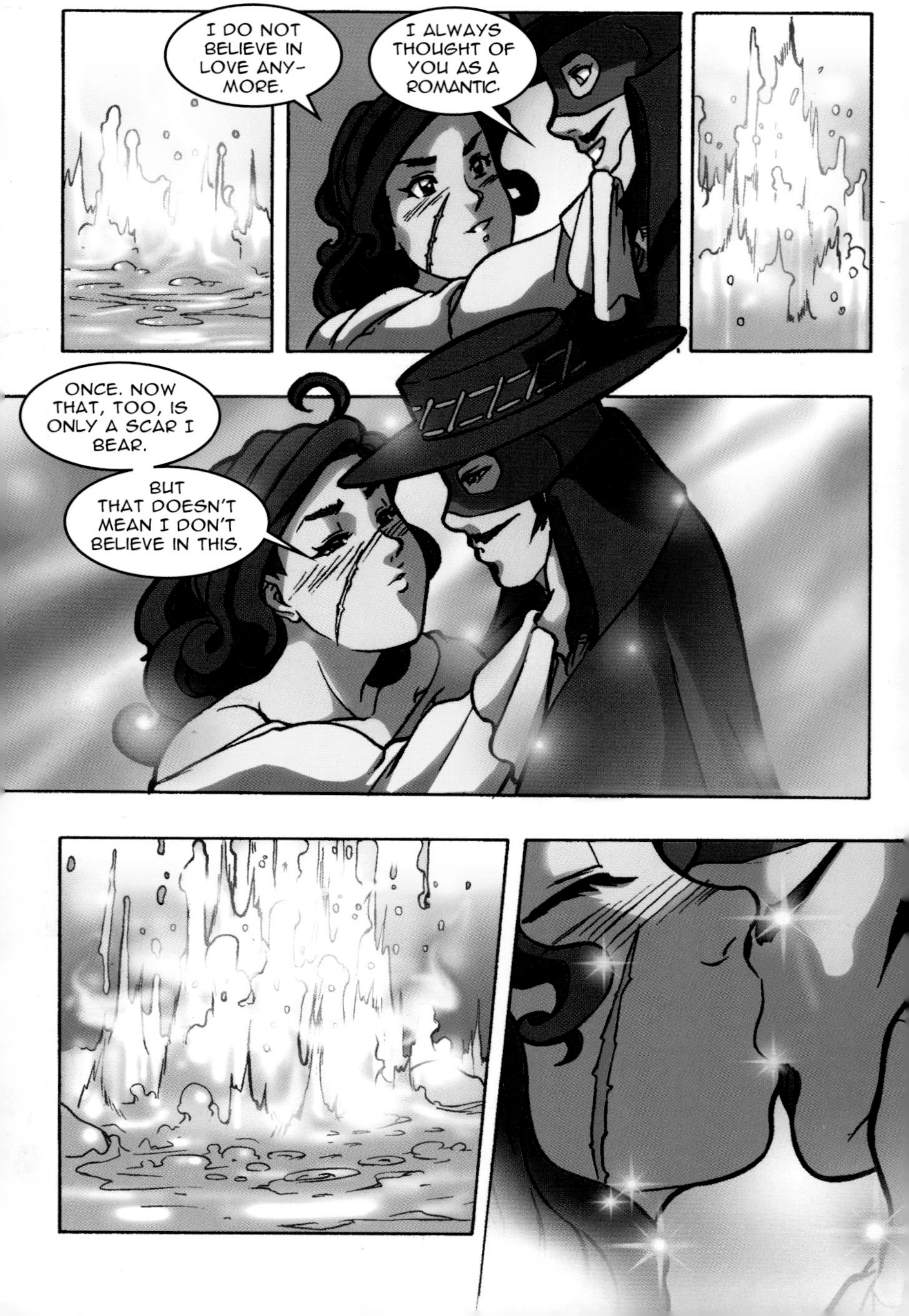
I DO NOT BELIEVE IN LOVE ANY-MORE.
I ALWAYS THOUGHT OF YOU AS A ROMANTIC.
ONCE. NOW THAT, TOO, IS ONLY A SCAR I BEAR.
BUT THAT DOESN'T MEAN I DON'T BELIEVE IN THIS.

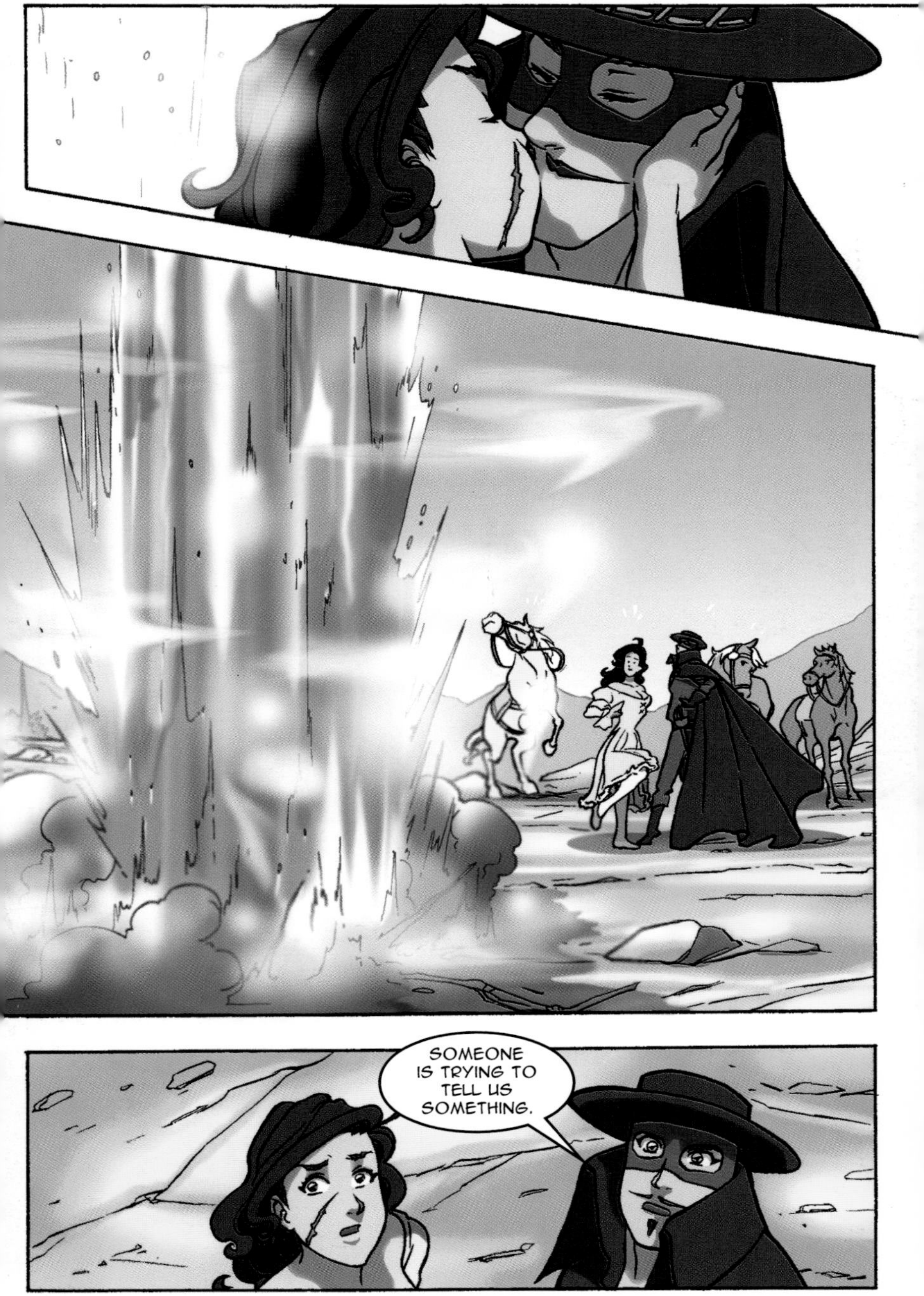
SOMEONE IS TRYING TO TELL US SOMETHING.

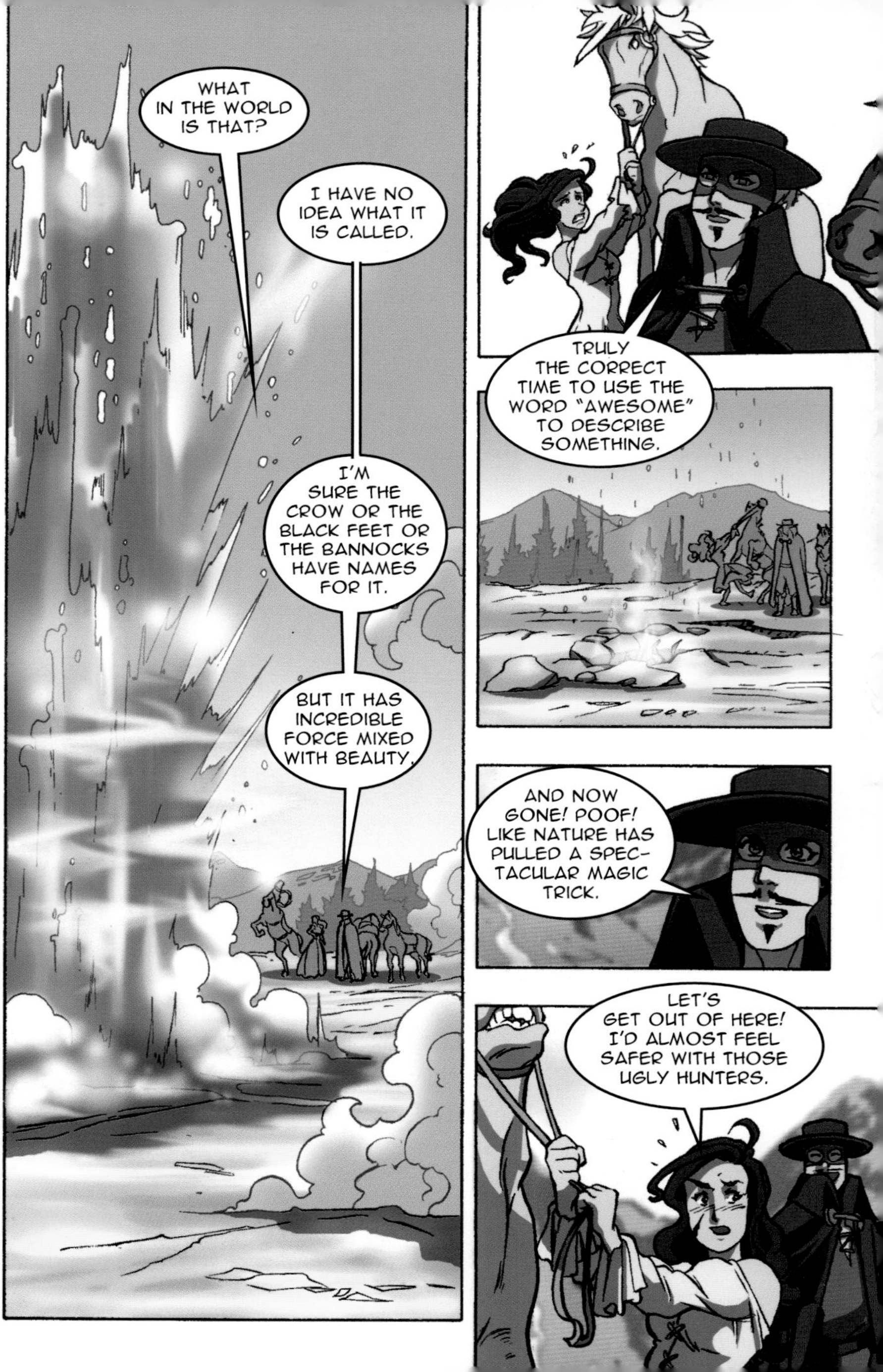
WHAT IN THE WORLD IS THAT?
I HAVE NO IDEA WHAT IT IS CALLED.
I'M SURE THE CROW OR THE BLACK FEET OR THE BANNOCKS HAVE NAMES FOR IT.
BUT IT HAS INCREDIBLE FORCE MIXED WITH BEAUTY.
TRULY THE CORRECT TIME TO USE THE WORD "AWESOME" TO DESCRIBE SOMETHING.
AND NOW GONE! POOF! LIKE NATURE HAS PULLED A SPEC-TACULAR MAGIC TRICK.
LET'S GET OUT OF HERE! I'D ALMOST FEEL SAFER WITH THOSE UGLY HUNTERS.

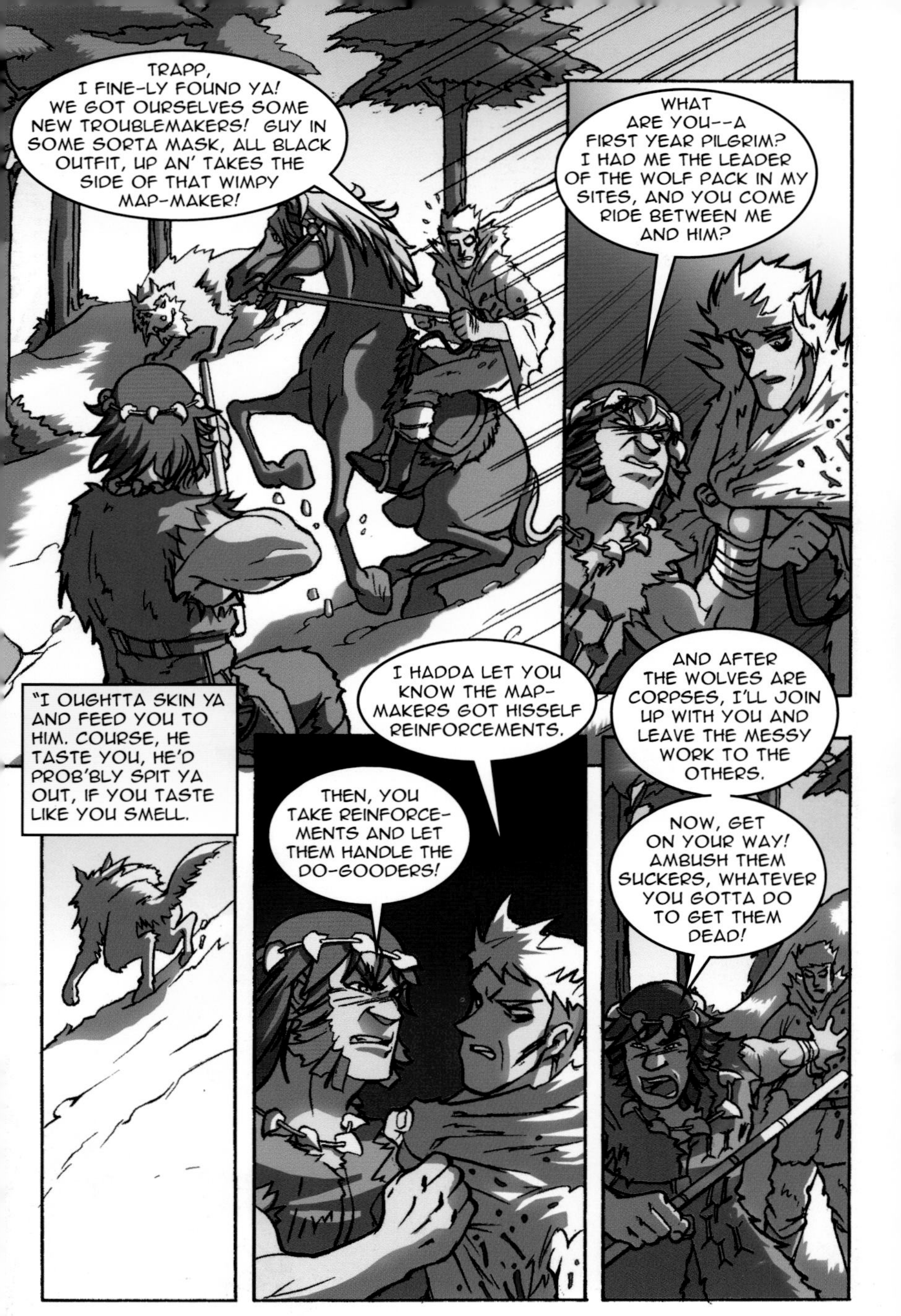
TRAPP, I FINE-LY FOUND YA! WE GOT OURSELVES SOME NEW TROUBLEMAKERS! GUY IN SOME SORTA MASK, ALL BLACK OUTFIT, UP AN' TAKES THE SIDE OF THAT WIMPY MAP-MAKER!
WHAT ARE YOU--A FIRST YEAR PILGRIM? I HAD ME THE LEADER OF THE WOLF PACK IN MY SITES, AND YOU COME RIDE BETWEEN ME AND HIM?
"I OUGHTTA SKIN YA AND FEED YOU TO HIM. COURSE, HE TASTE YOU, HE'D PROB'BLY SPIT YA OUT, IF YOU TASTE LIKE YOU SMELL.
I HADDA LET YOU KNOW THE MAP-MAKERS GOT HISSELF REINFORCEMENTS.
THEN, YOU TAKE REINFORCE-MENTS AND LET THEM HANDLE THE DO-GOODERS!
AND AFTER THE WOLVES ARE CORPSES, I'LL JOIN UP WITH YOU AND LEAVE THE MESSY WORK TO THE OTHERS.
NOW, GET ON YOUR WAY! AMBUSH THEM SUCKERS, WHATEVER YOU GOTTA DO TO GET THEM DEAD!

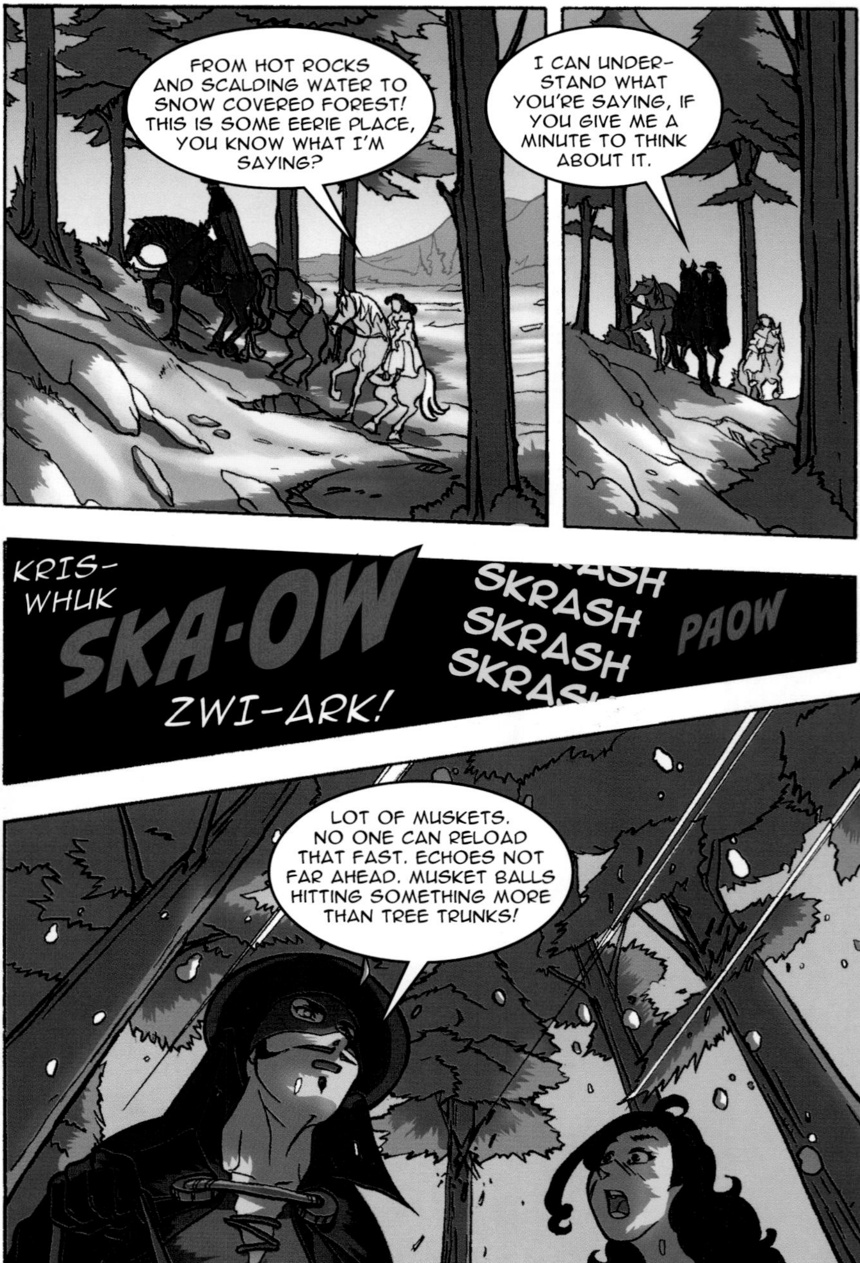
FROM HOT ROCKS AND SCALDING WATER TO SNOW COVERED FOREST! THIS IS SOME EERIE PLACE, YOU KNOW WHAT I'M SAYING?
I CAN UNDER-STAND WHAT YOU'RE SAYING, IF YOU GIVE ME A MINUTE TO THINK ABOUT IT.
KRIS-WHUK
SKA-OW
ZWI-ARK!
SKRASH
SKRASH
SKRASH
PAOW
LOT OF MUSKETS. NO ONE CAN RELOAD THAT FAST. ECHOES NOT FAR AHEAD. MUSKET BALLS HITTING SOMETHING MORE THAN TREE TRUNKS!

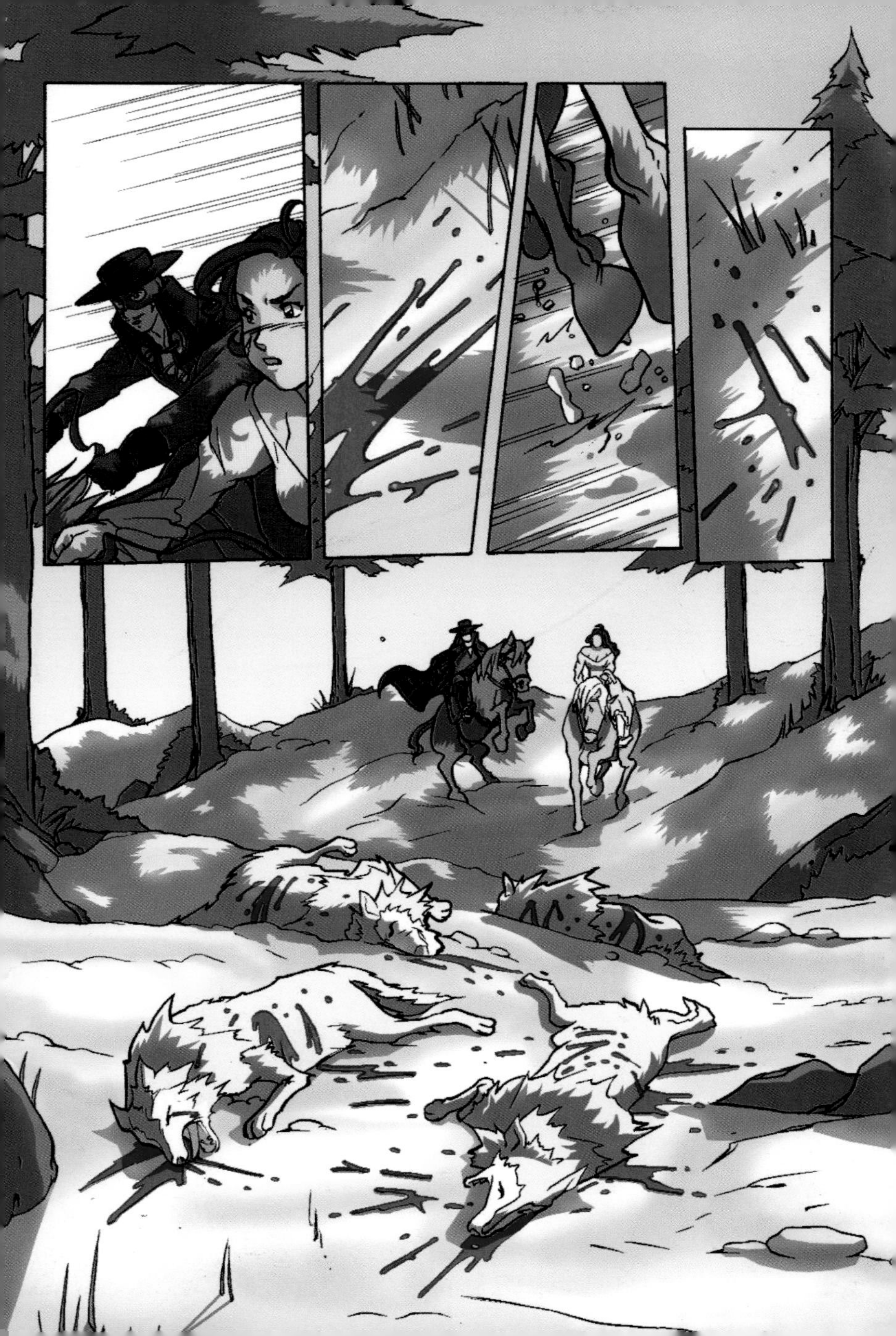

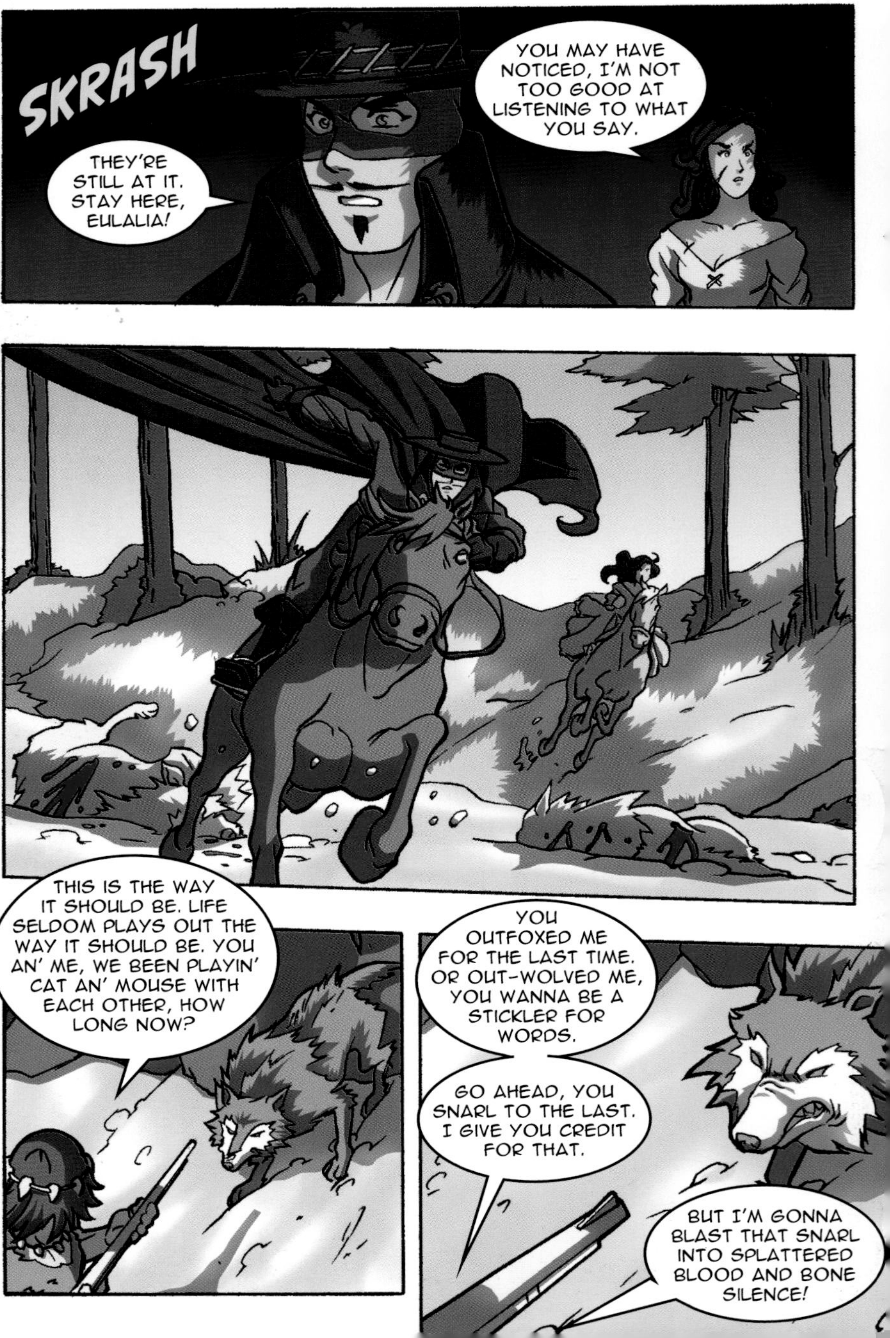
SKRASH
THEY'RE STILL AT IT. STAY HERE, EULALIA!
YOU MAY HAVE NOTICED, I'M NOT TOO GOOD AT LISTENING TO WHAT YOU SAY.
THIS IS THE WAY IT SHOULD BE. LIFE SELDOM PLAYS OUT THE WAY IT SHOULD BE. YOU AN' ME, WE BEEN PLAYIN' CAT AN' MOUSE WITH EACH OTHER, HOW LONG NOW?
YOU OUTFOXED ME FOR THE LAST TIME. OR OUT-WOLVED ME, YOU WANNA BE A STICKLER FOR WORDS.
GO AHEAD, YOU SNARL TO THE LAST. I GIVE YOU CREDIT FOR THAT.
BUT I'M GONNA BLAST THAT SNARL INTO SPLATTERED BLOOD AND BONE SILENCE!

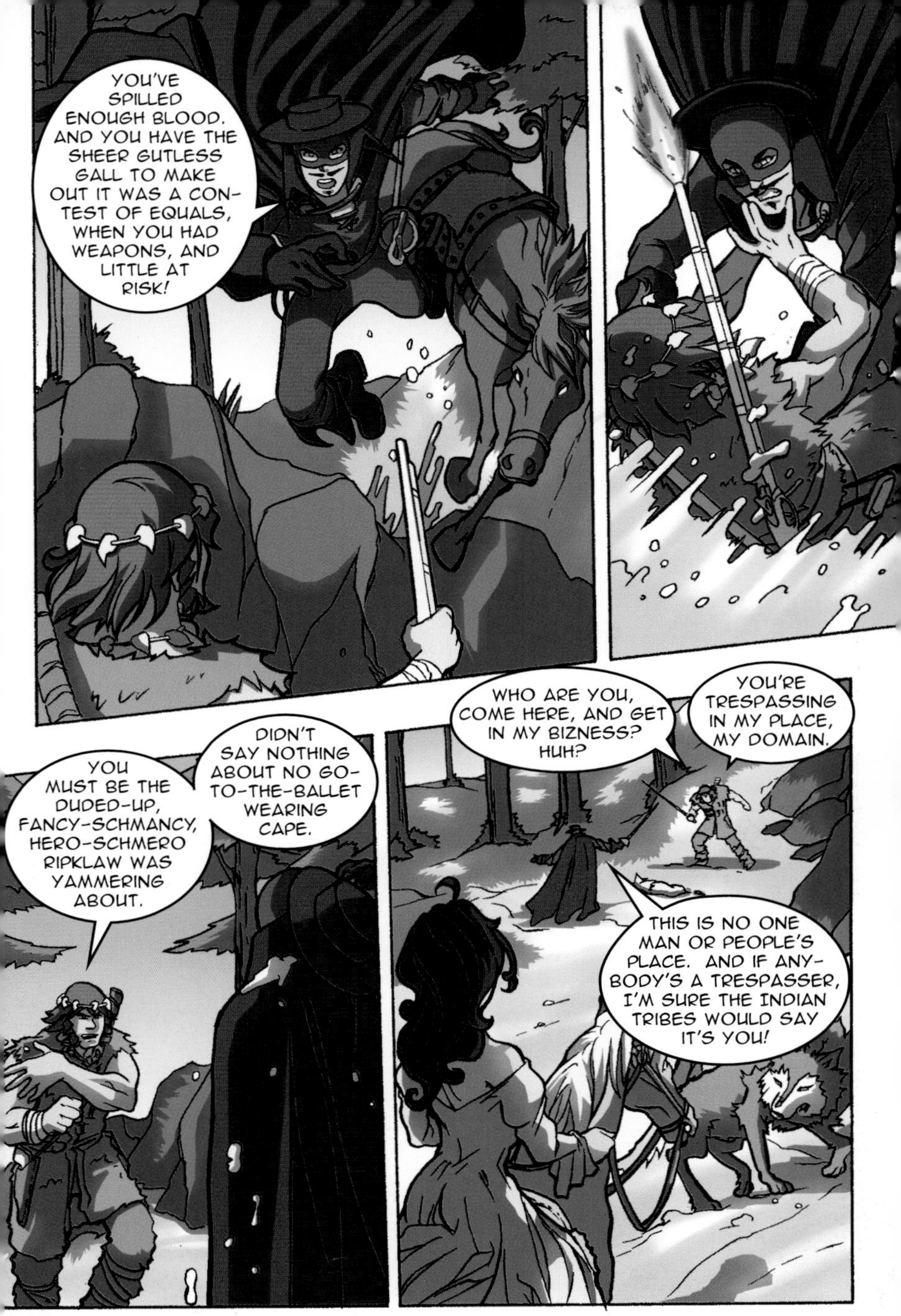
YOU'VE SPILLED ENOUGH BLOOD. AND YOU HAVE THE SHEER GUTLESS GALL TO MAKE OUT IT WAS A CONTEST OF EQUALS, WHEN YOU HAD WEAPONS, AND LITTLE AT RISK!
YOU MUST BE THE DUDED-UP, FANCY-SCHMANCY, HERO-SCHMERO RIPKLAW WAS YAMMERING ABOUT.
DIDN'T SAY NOTHING ABOUT NO GO-TO-THE-BALLET WEARING CAPE.
WHO ARE YOU, COME HERE, AND GET IN MY BIZNESS? HUH?
YOU'RE TRESPASSING IN MY PLACE, MY DOMAIN.
THIS IS NO ONE MAN OR PEOPLE'S PLACE. AND IF ANYBODY'S A TRESPASSER, I'M SURE THE INDIAN TRIBES WOULD SAY IT'S YOU!

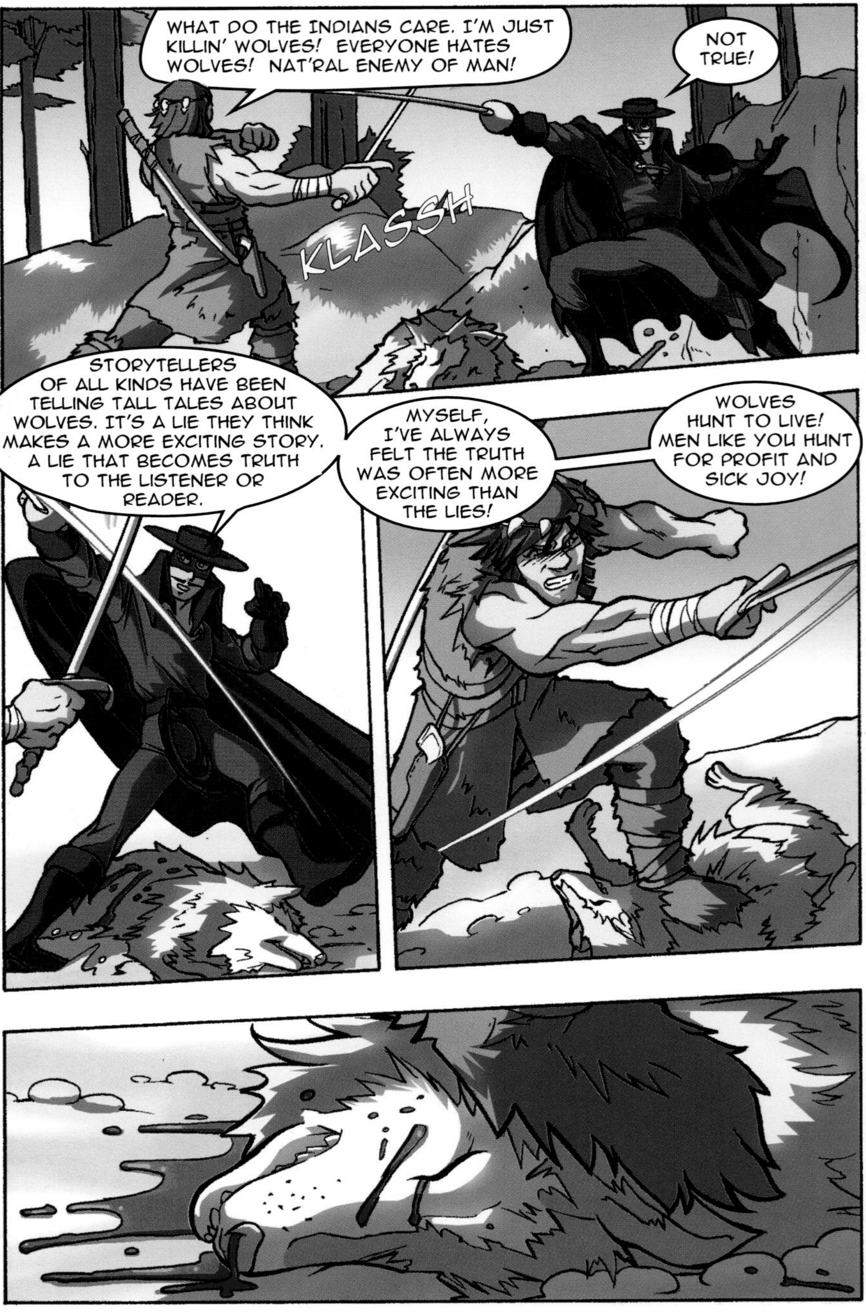
WHAT DO THE INDIANS CARE. I'M JUST KILLIN' WOLVES! EVERYONE HATES WOLVES! NAT'RAL ENEMY OF MAN!
NOT TRUE!
KLASSH
STORYTELLERS OF ALL KINDS HAVE BEEN TELLING TALL TALES ABOUT WOLVES. IT'S A LIE THEY THINK MAKES A MORE EXCITING STORY. A LIE THAT BECOMES TRUTH TO THE LISTENER OR READER.
MYSELF, I'VE ALWAYS FELT THE TRUTH WAS OFTEN MORE EXCITING THAN THE LIES!
WOLVES HUNT TO LIVE! MEN LIKE YOU HUNT FOR PROFIT AND SICK JOY!

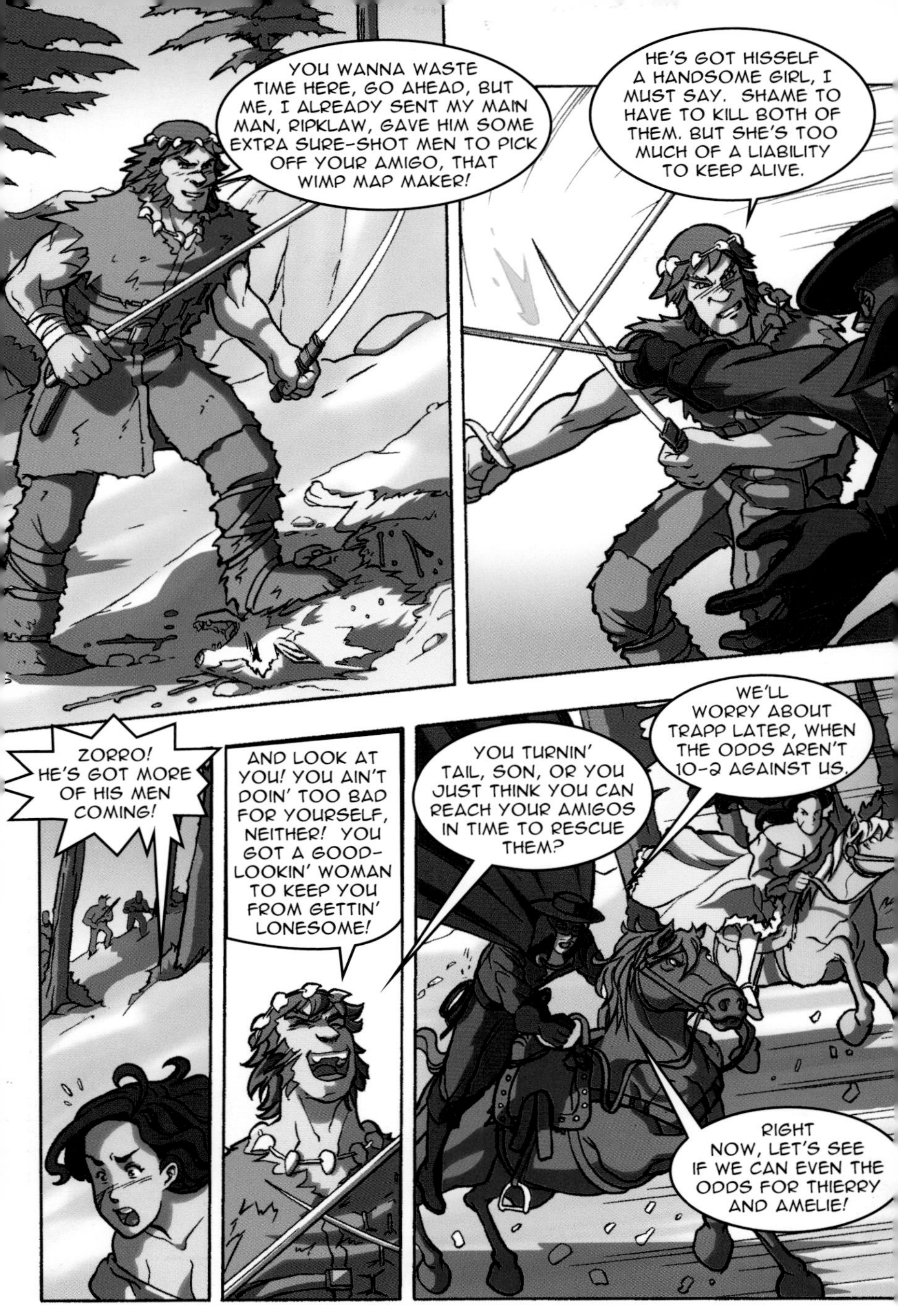
YOU WANNA WASTE TIME HERE, GO AHEAD, BUT ME, I ALREADY SENT MY MAIN MAN, RIPKLAW, GAVE HIM SOME EXTRA SURE-SHOT MEN TO PICK OFF YOUR AMIGO, THAT WIMP MAP MAKER!
HE'S GOT HISSELF A HANDSOME GIRL, I MUST SAY. SHAME TO HAVE TO KILL BOTH OF THEM. BUT SHE'S TOO MUCH OF A LIABILITY TO KEEP ALIVE.
ZORRO! HE'S GOT MORE OF HIS MEN COMING!
AND LOOK AT YOU! YOU AIN'T DOIN' TOO BAD FOR YOURSELF, NEITHER! YOU GOT A GOOD-LOOKIN' WOMAN TO KEEP YOU FROM GETTIN' LONESOME!
YOU TURNIN' TAIL, SON, OR YOU JUST THINK YOU CAN REACH YOUR AMIGOS IN TIME TO RESCUE THEM?
WE'LL WORRY ABOUT TRAPP LATER, WHEN THE ODDS AREN'T 10-2 AGAINST US.
RIGHT NOW, LET'S SEE IF WE CAN EVEN THE ODDS FOR THIERRY AND AMELIE!

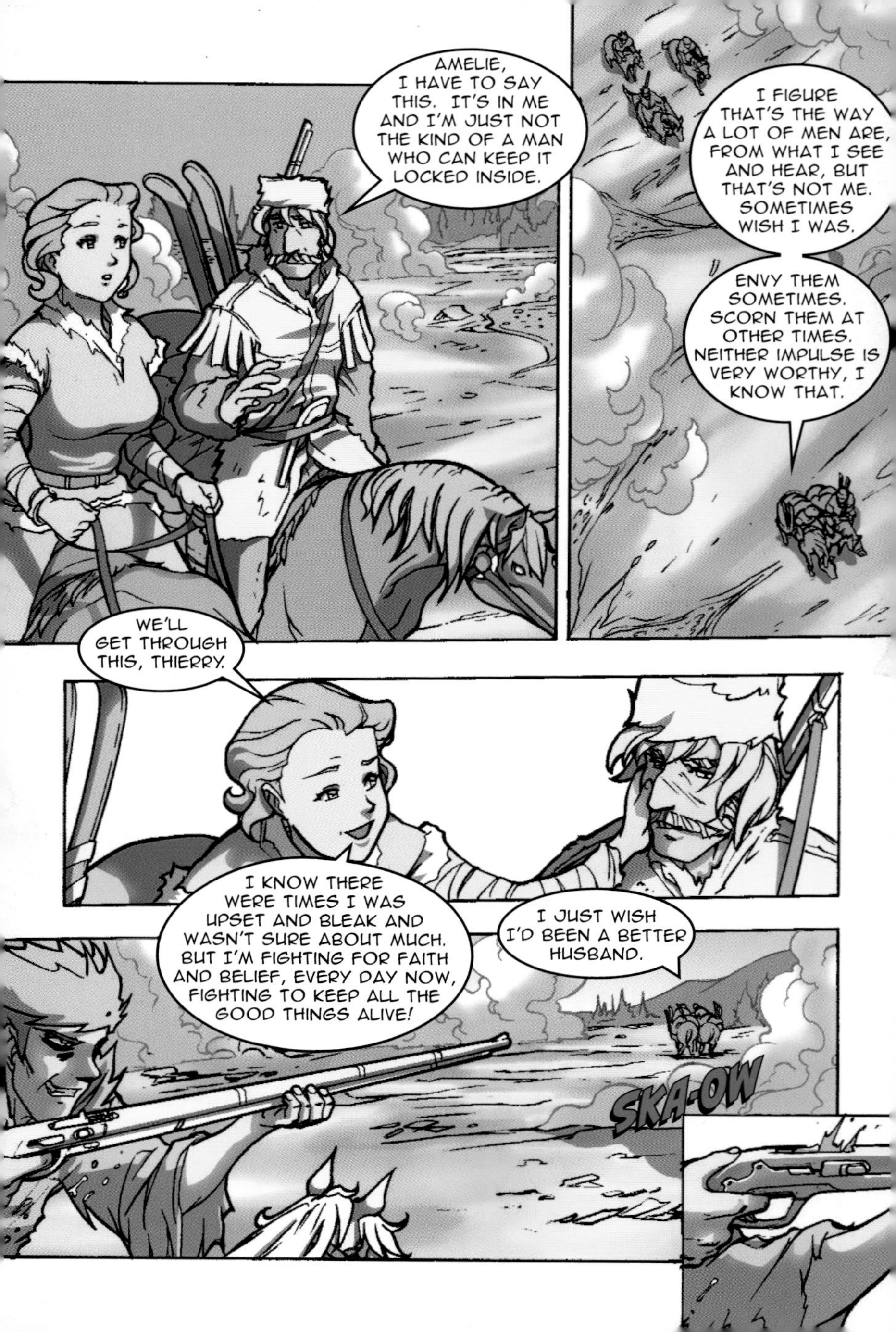
AMELIE, I HAVE TO SAY THIS. IT'S IN ME AND I'M JUST NOT THE KIND OF A MAN WHO CAN KEEP IT LOCKED INSIDE.
I FIGURE THAT'S THE WAY A LOT OF MEN ARE, FROM WHAT I SEE AND HEAR, BUT THAT'S NOT ME. SOMETIMES WISH I WAS.
ENVY THEM SOMETIMES. SCORN THEM AT OTHER TIMES. NEITHER IMPULSE IS VERY WORTHY, I KNOW THAT.
WE'LL GET THROUGH THIS, THIERRY.
I KNOW THERE WERE TIMES I WAS UPSET AND BLEAK AND WASN'T SURE ABOUT MUCH. BUT I'M FIGHTING FOR FAITH AND BELIEF, EVERY DAY NOW, FIGHTING TO KEEP ALL THE GOOD THINGS ALIVE!
I JUST WISH I'D BEEN A BETTER HUSBAND.
SKA-OW

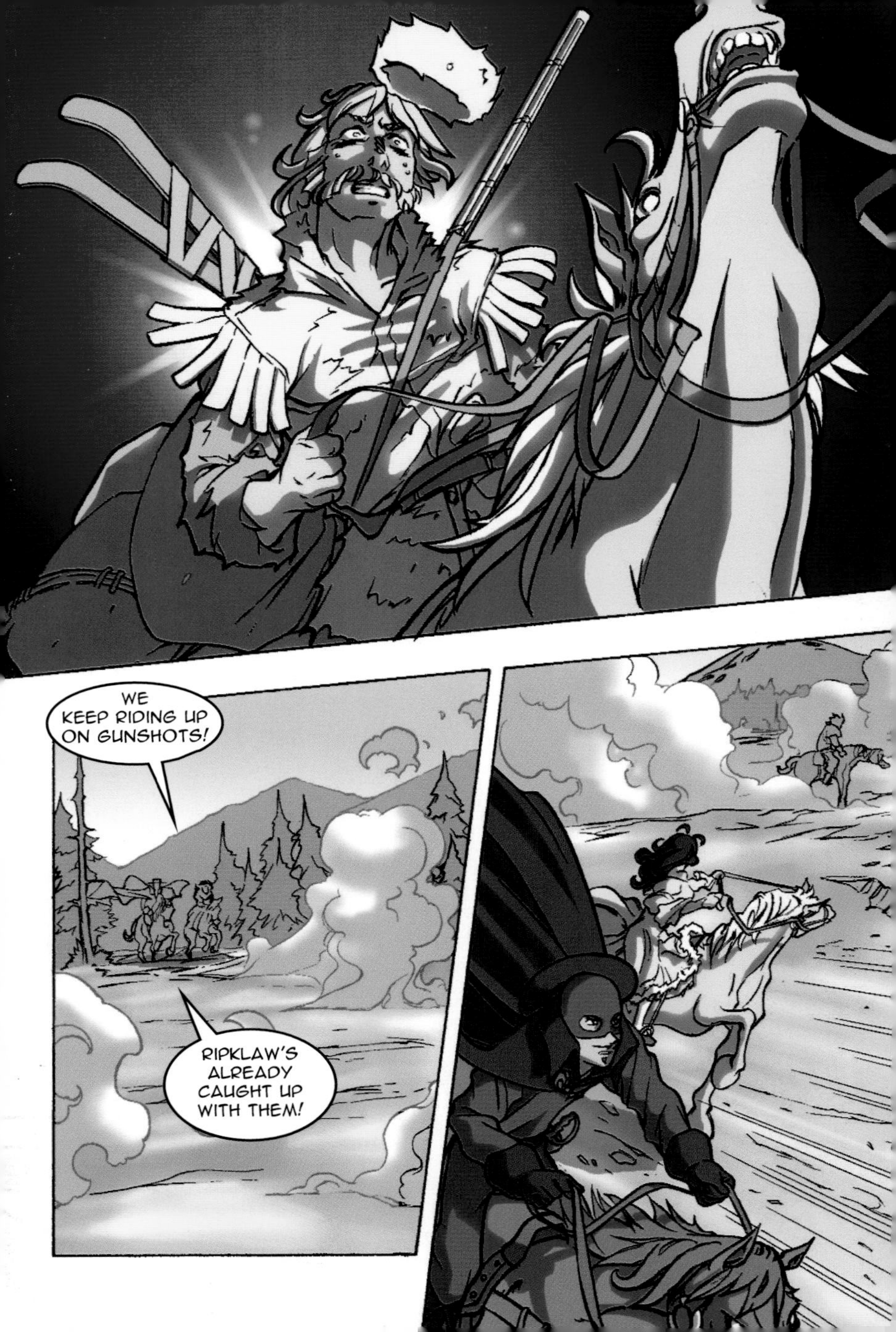
WE KEEP RIDING UP ON GUNSHOTS!
RIPKLAW'S ALREADY CAUGHT UP WITH THEM!

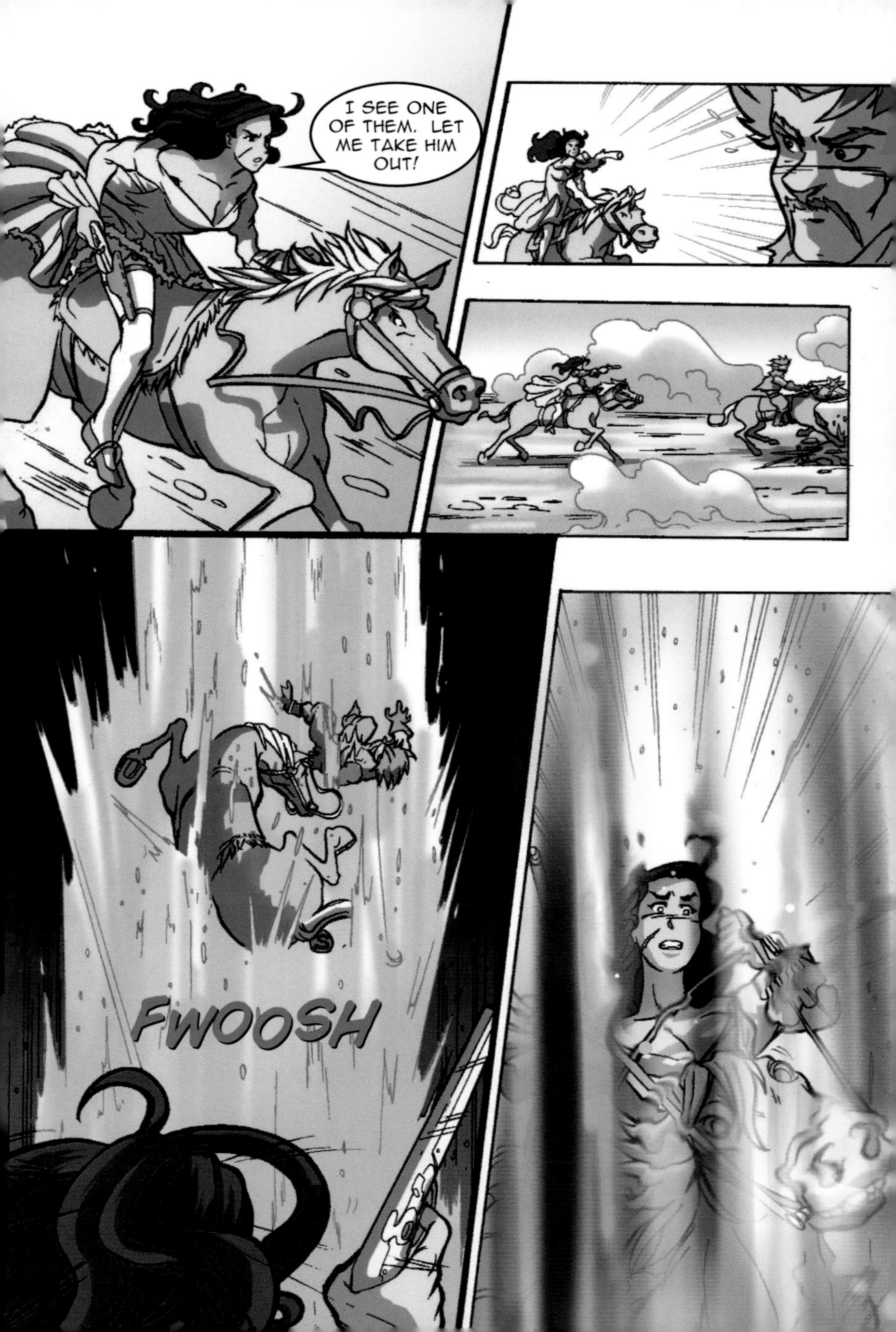
I SEE ONE OF THEM. LET ME TAKE HIM OUT!
FWOOSH

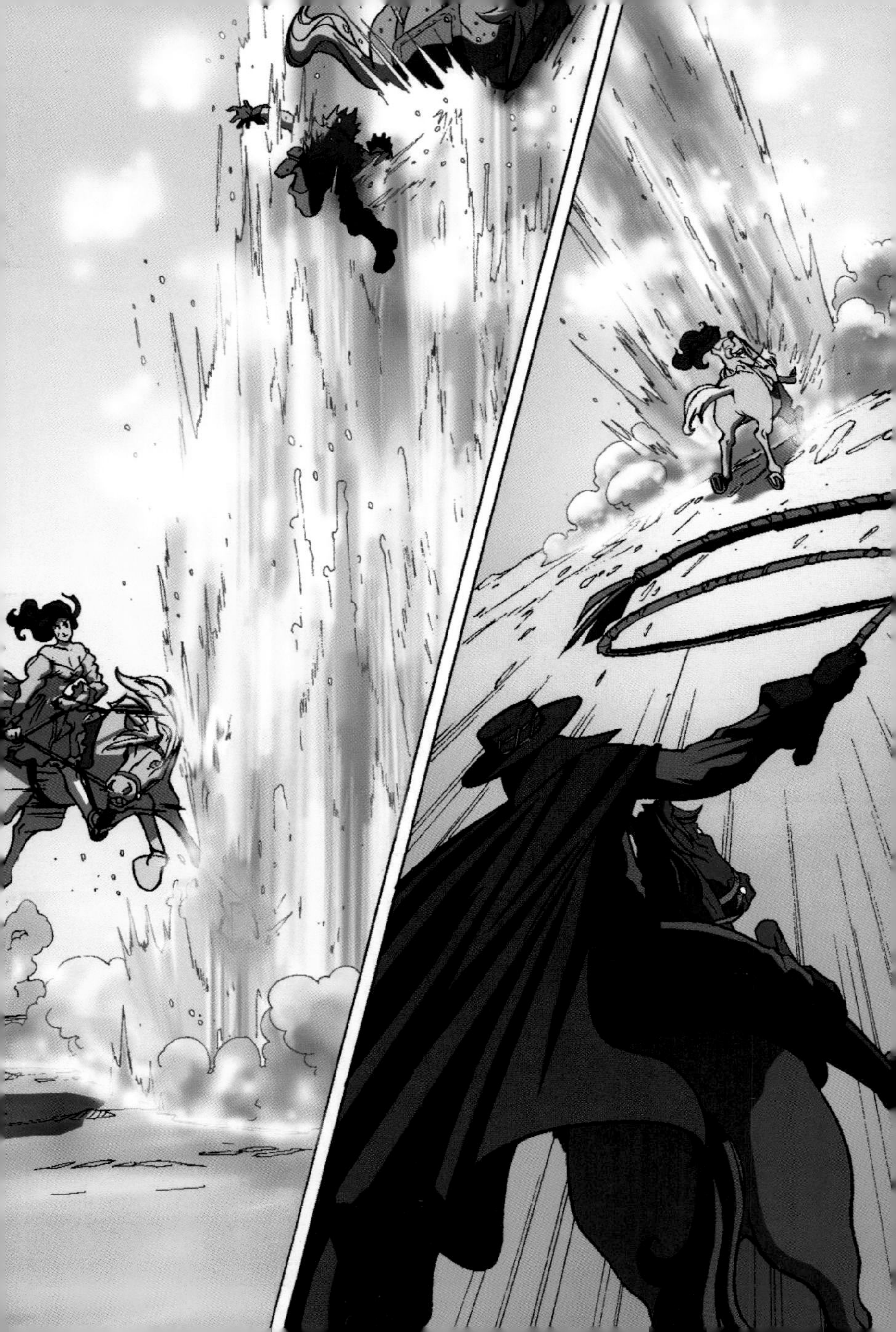

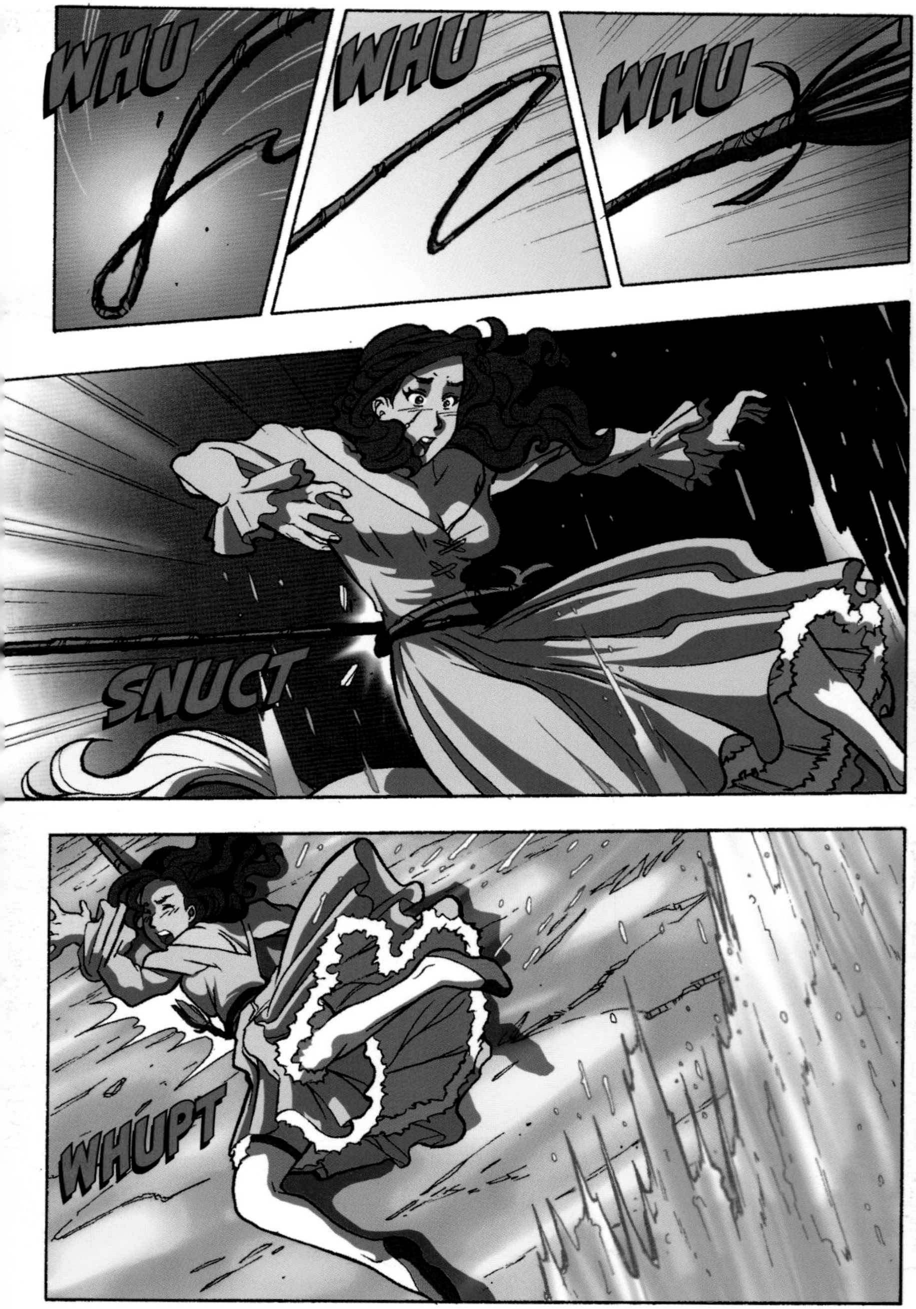
WHU
WHU
WHU
SNUCT
WHUPT

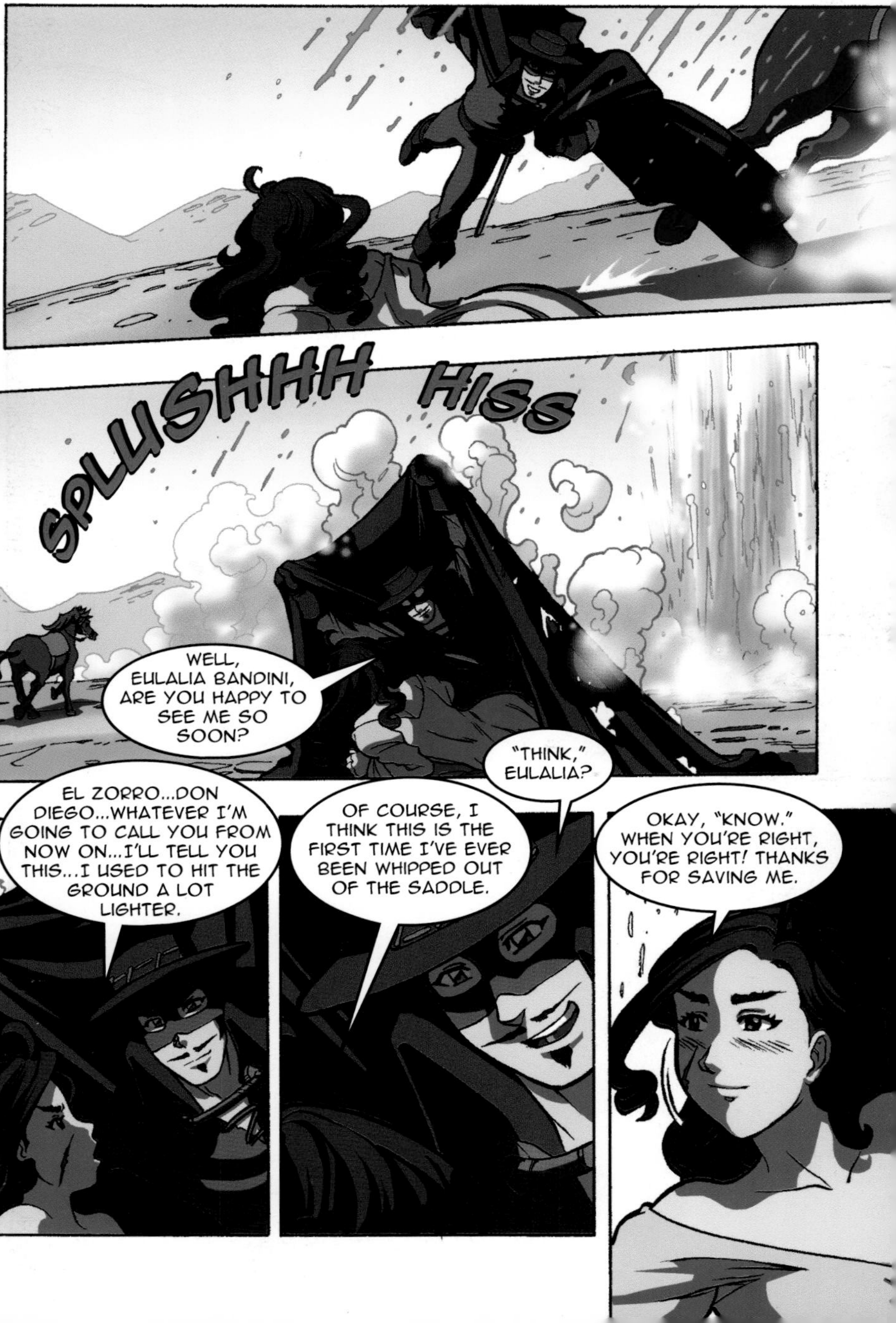
SPLUSHHH HISS
WELL, EULALIA BANDINI, ARE YOU HAPPY TO SEE ME SO SOON?
EL ZORRO...DON DIEGO...WHATEVER I'M GOING TO CALL YOU FROM NOW ON...I'LL TELL YOU THIS...I USED TO HIT THE GROUND A LOT LIGHTER.
OF COURSE, I THINK THIS IS THE FIRST TIME I'VE EVER BEEN WHIPPED OUT OF THE SADDLE.
"THINK," EULALIA?
OKAY, "KNOW." WHEN YOU'RE RIGHT, YOU'RE RIGHT! THANKS FOR SAVING ME.

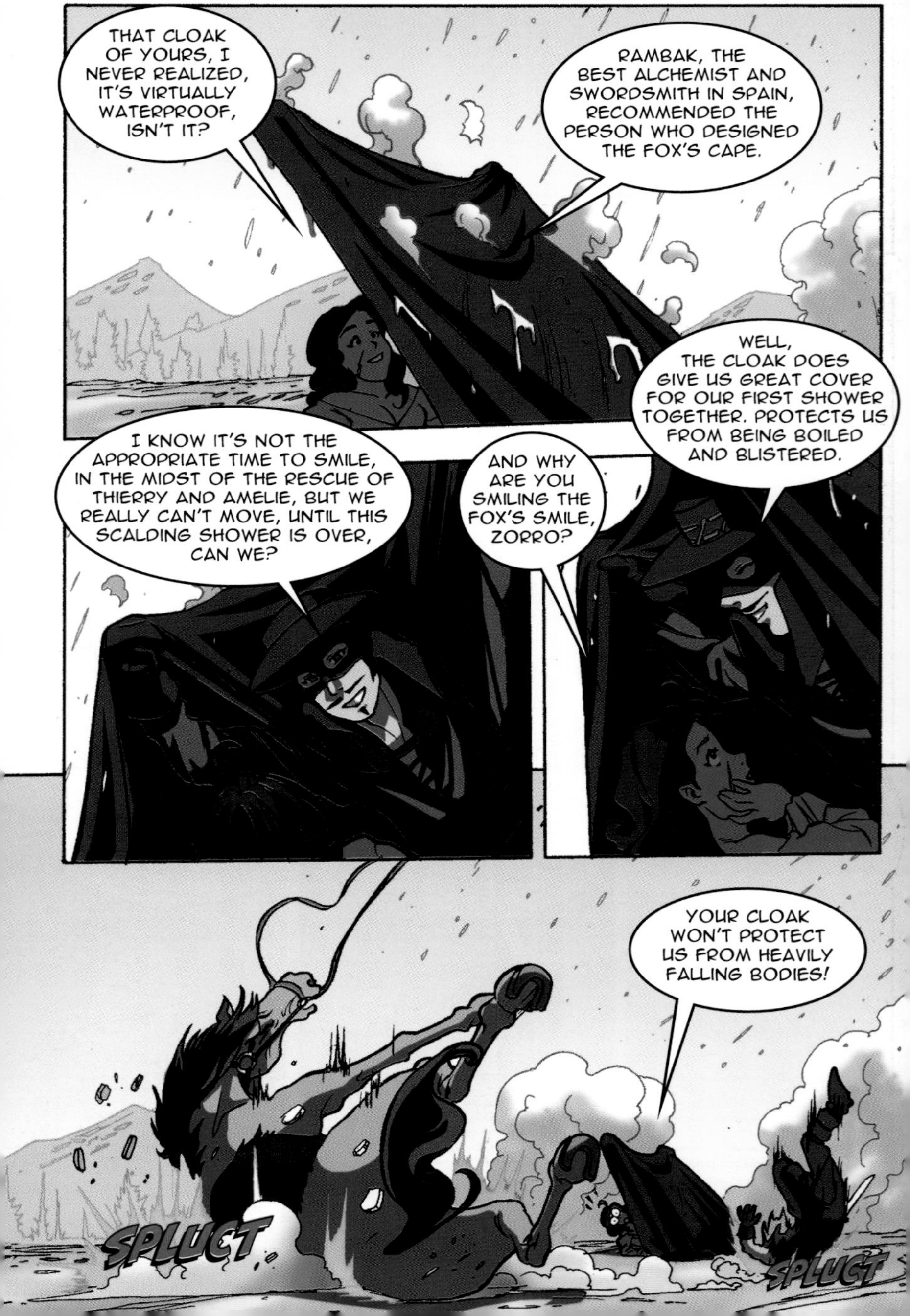
THAT CLOAK OF YOURS, I NEVER REALIZED, IT'S VIRTUALLY WATERPROOF, ISN'T IT?
RAMBAK, THE BEST ALCHEMIST AND SWORDSMITH IN SPAIN, RECOMMENDED THE PERSON WHO DESIGNED THE FOX'S CAPE.
WELL, THE CLOAK DOES GIVE US GREAT COVER FOR OUR FIRST SHOWER TOGETHER. PROTECTS US FROM BEING BOILED AND BLISTERED.
I KNOW IT'S NOT THE APPROPRIATE TIME TO SMILE, IN THE MIDST OF THE RESCUE OF THIERRY AND AMELIE, BUT WE REALLY CAN'T MOVE, UNTIL THIS SCALDING SHOWER IS OVER, CAN WE?
AND WHY ARE YOU SMILING THE FOX'S SMILE, ZORRO?
YOUR CLOAK WON'T PROTECT US FROM HEAVILY FALLING BODIES!
SPLUCT
SPLUCT

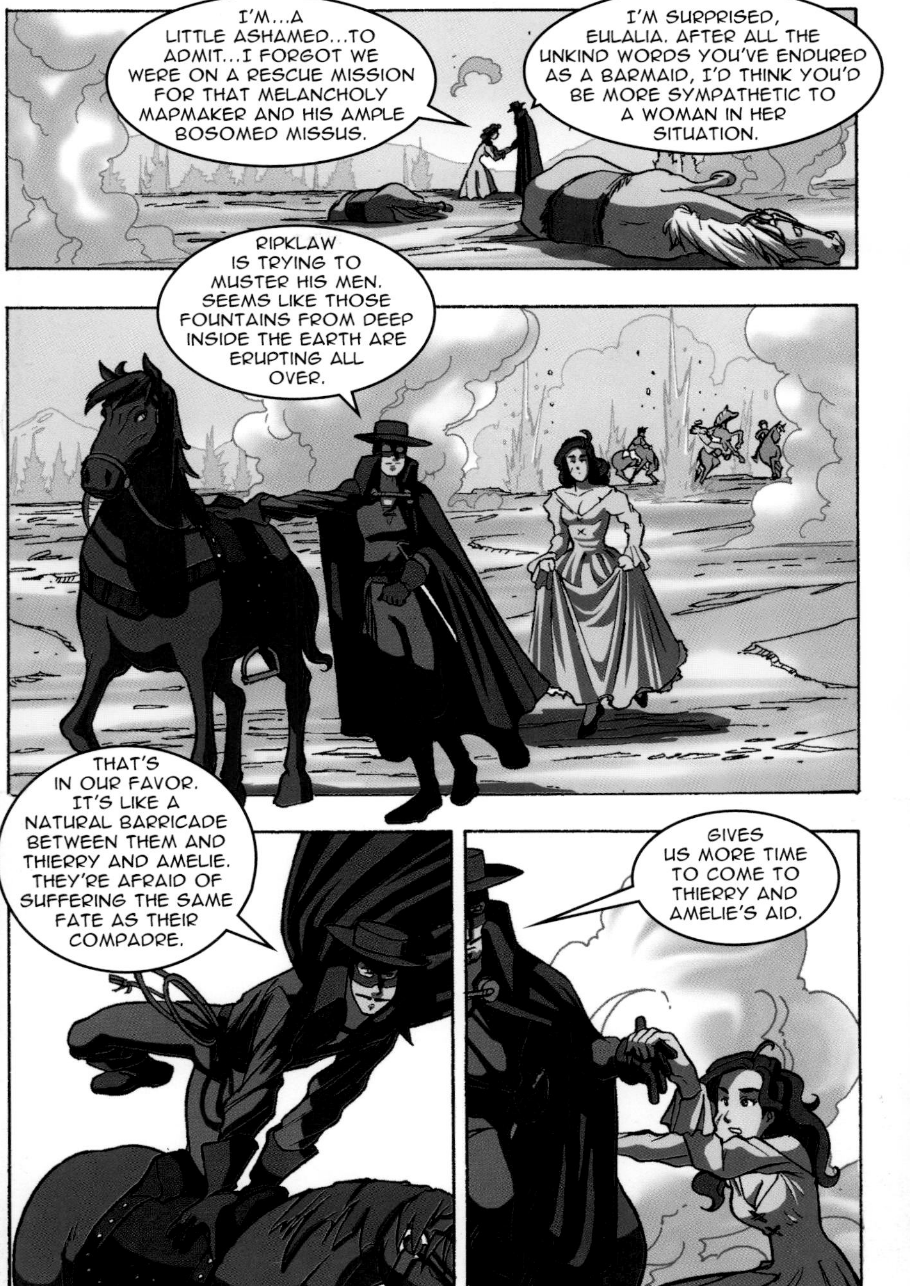
I'M...A LITTLE ASHAMED...TO ADMIT...I FORGOT WE WERE ON A RESCUE MISSION FOR THAT MELANCHOLY MAPMAKER AND HIS AMPLE BOSOMED MISSUS.
I'M SURPRISED, EULALIA. AFTER ALL THE UNKIND WORDS YOU'VE ENDURED AS A BARMAID, I'D THINK YOU'D BE MORE SYMPATHETIC TO A WOMAN IN HER SITUATION.
RIPKLAW IS TRYING TO MUSTER HIS MEN. SEEMS LIKE THOSE FOUNTAINS FROM DEEP INSIDE THE EARTH ARE ERUPTING ALL OVER.
THAT'S IN OUR FAVOR. IT'S LIKE A NATURAL BARRICADE BETWEEN THEM AND THIERRY AND AMELIE. THEY'RE AFRAID OF SUFFERING THE SAME FATE AS THEIR COMPADRE.
GIVES US MORE TIME TO COME TO THIERRY AND AMELIE'S AID.

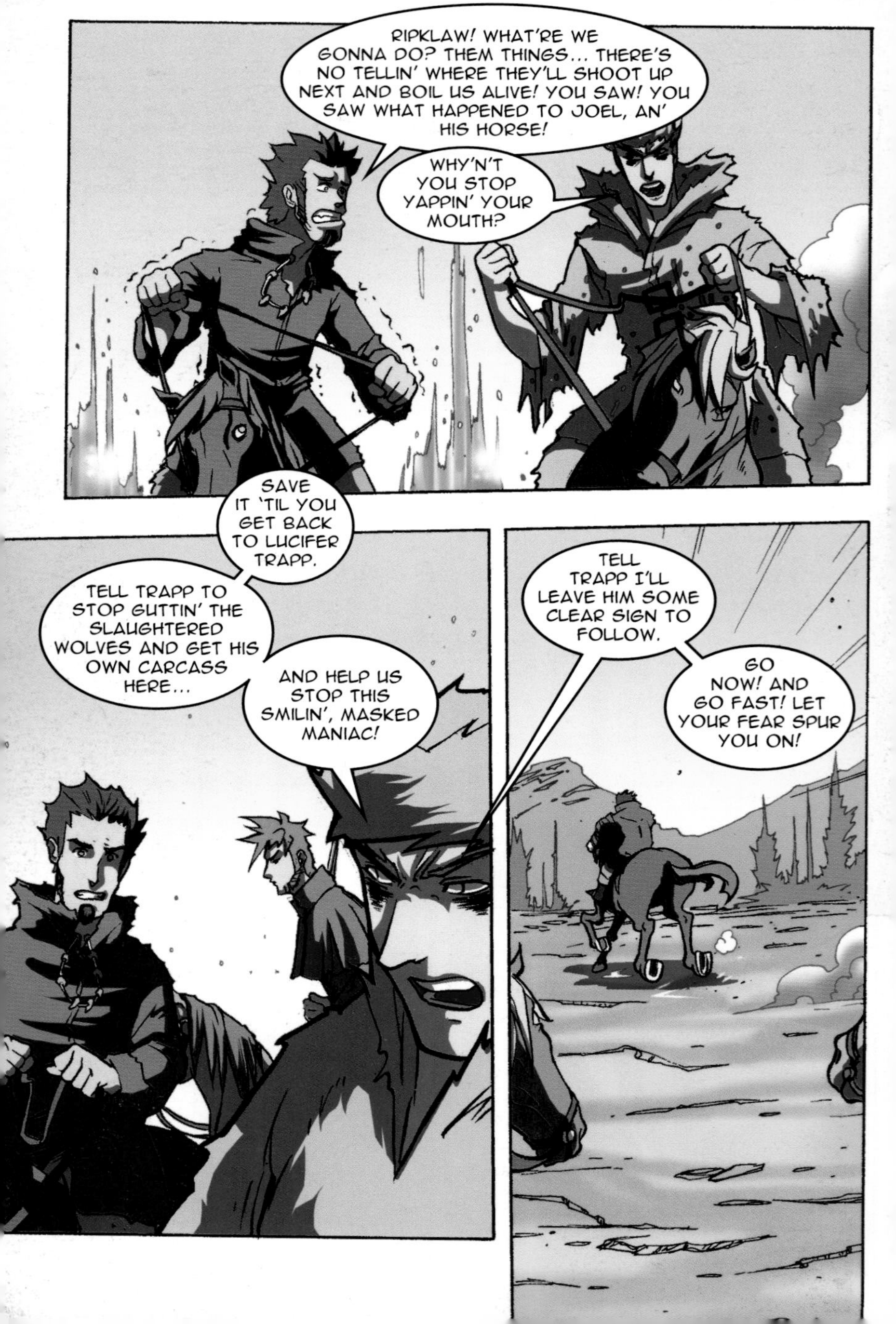
RIPKLAW! WHAT'RE WE GONNA DO? THEM THINGS... THERE'S NO TELLIN' WHERE THEY'LL SHOOT UP NEXT AND BOIL US ALIVE! YOU SAW! YOU SAW WHAT HAPPENED TO JOEL, AN' HIS HORSE!
WHY'N'T YOU STOP YAPPIN' YOUR MOUTH?
SAVE IT 'TIL YOU GET BACK TO LUCIFER TRAPP.
TELL TRAPP TO STOP GUTTIN' THE SLAUGHTERED WOLVES AND GET HIS OWN CARCASS HERE...
AND HELP US STOP THIS SMILIN', MASKED MANIAC!
TELL TRAPP I'LL LEAVE HIM SOME CLEAR SIGN TO FOLLOW.
GO NOW! AND GO FAST! LET YOUR FEAR SPUR YOU ON!

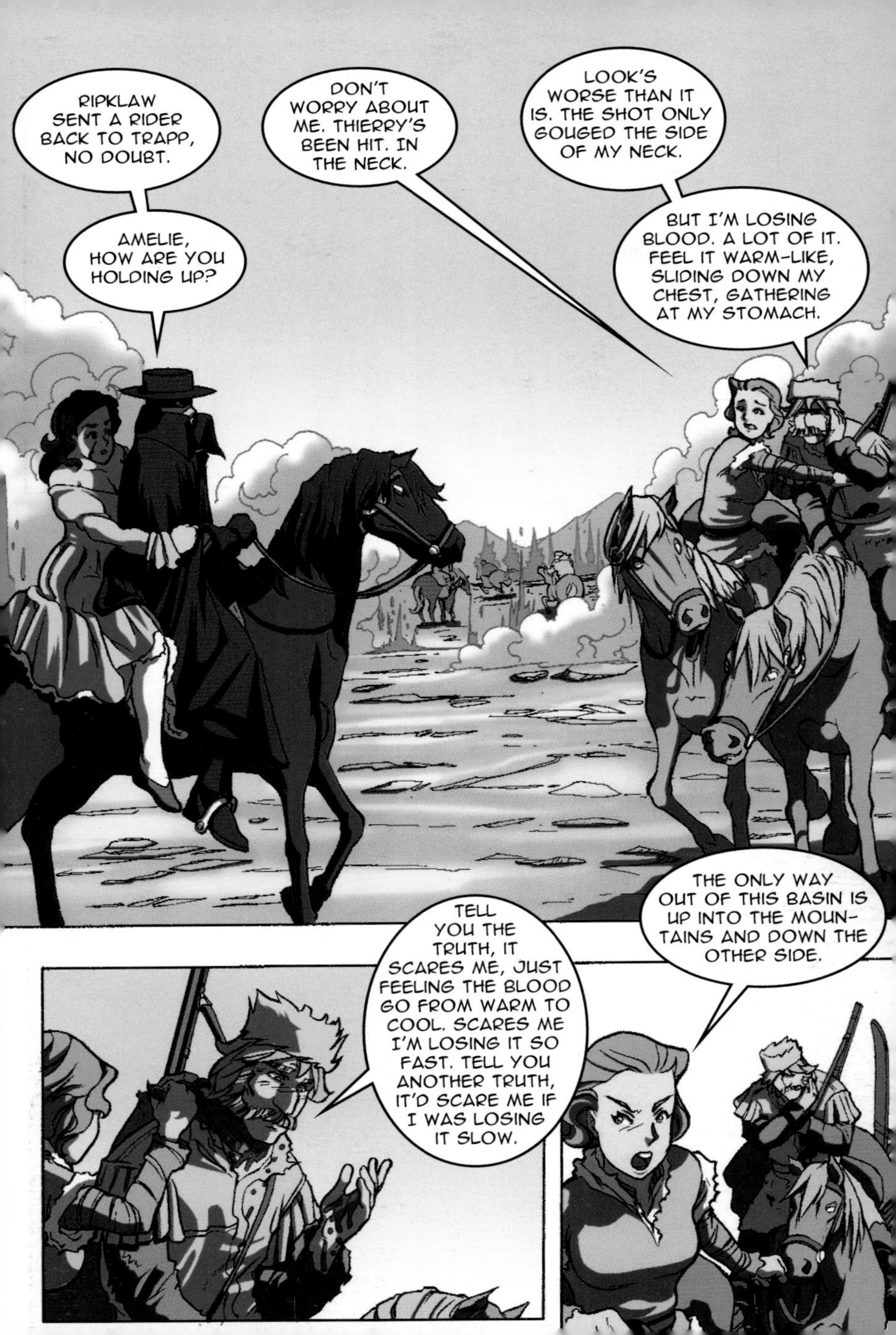
RIPKLAW SENT A RIDER BACK TO TRAPP, NO DOUBT.
AMELIE, HOW ARE YOU HOLDING UP?
DON'T WORRY ABOUT ME. THIERRY'S BEEN HIT. IN THE NECK.
LOOK'S WORSE THAN IT IS. THE SHOT ONLY GOUGED THE SIDE OF MY NECK.
BUT I'M LOSING BLOOD. A LOT OF IT. FEEL IT WARM-LIKE, SLIDING DOWN MY CHEST, GATHERING AT MY STOMACH.
TELL YOU THE TRUTH, IT SCARES ME, JUST FEELING THE BLOOD GO FROM WARM TO COOL. SCARES ME I'M LOSING IT SO FAST. TELL YOU ANOTHER TRUTH, IT'D SCARE ME IF I WAS LOSING IT SLOW.
THE ONLY WAY OUT OF THIS BASIN IS UP INTO THE MOUN-TAINS AND DOWN THE OTHER SIDE.

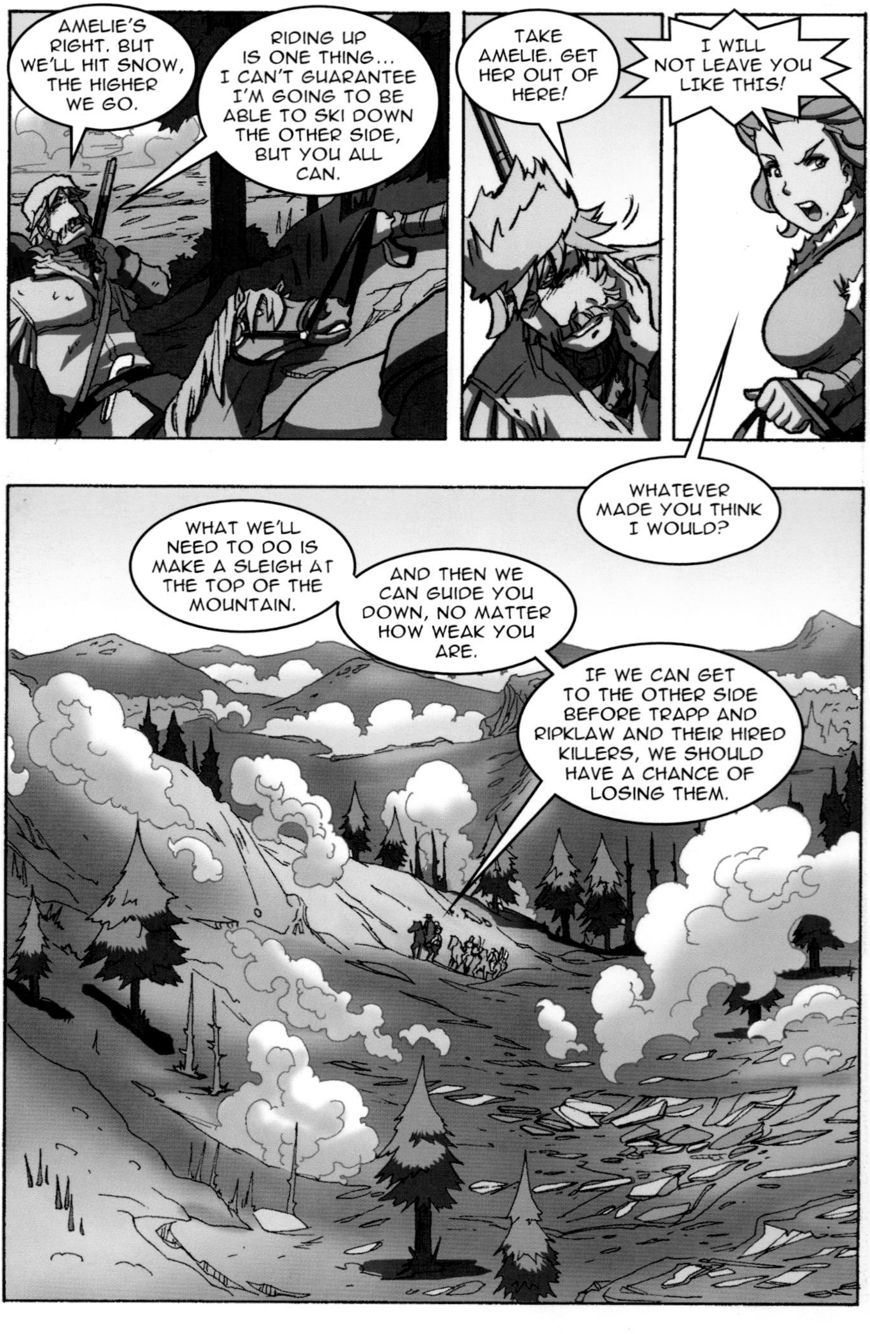
AMELIE'S RIGHT. BUT WE'LL HIT SNOW, THE HIGHER WE GO.
RIDING UP IS ONE THING... I CAN'T GUARANTEE I'M GOING TO BE ABLE TO SKI DOWN THE OTHER SIDE, BUT YOU ALL CAN.
TAKE AMELIE. GET HER OUT OF HERE!
I WILL NOT LEAVE YOU LIKE THIS!
WHATEVER MADE YOU THINK I WOULD?
WHAT WE'LL NEED TO DO IS MAKE A SLEIGH AT THE TOP OF THE MOUNTAIN.
AND THEN WE CAN GUIDE YOU DOWN, NO MATTER HOW WEAK YOU ARE.
IF WE CAN GET TO THE OTHER SIDE BEFORE TRAPP AND RIPKLAW AND THEIR HIRED KILLERS, WE SHOULD HAVE A CHANCE OF LOSING THEM.

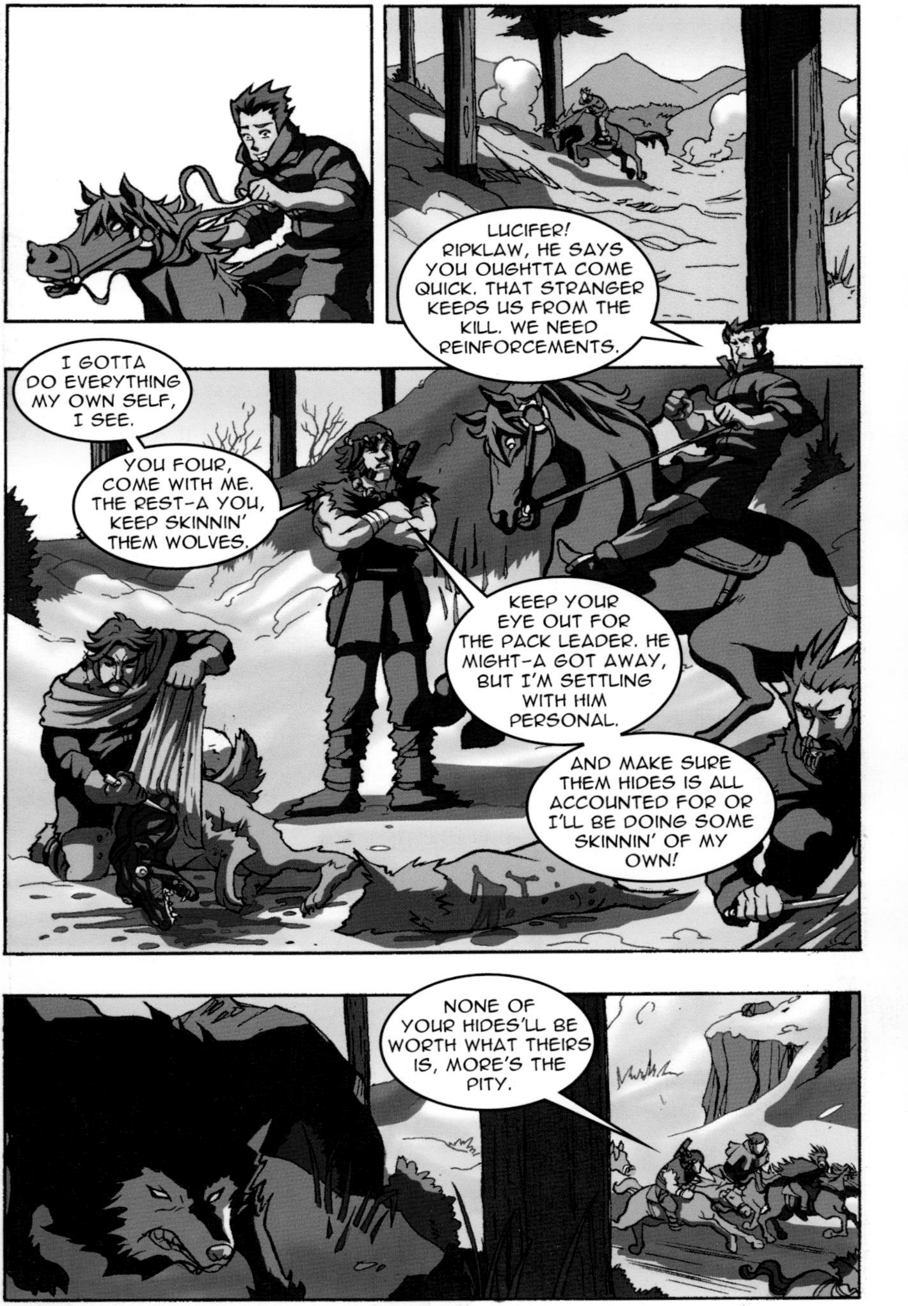
LUCIFER! RIPKLAW, HE SAYS YOU OUGHTTA COME QUICK. THAT STRANGER KEEPS US FROM THE KILL. WE NEED REINFORCEMENTS.
I GOTTA DO EVERYTHING MY OWN SELF, I SEE.
YOU FOUR, COME WITH ME. THE REST-A YOU, KEEP SKINNIN' THEM WOLVES.
KEEP YOUR EYE OUT FOR THE PACK LEADER. HE MIGHT-A GOT AWAY, BUT I'M SETTLING WITH HIM PERSONAL.
AND MAKE SURE THEM HIDES IS ALL ACCOUNTED FOR OR I'LL BE DOING SOME SKINNIN' OF MY OWN!
NONE OF YOUR HIDES'LL BE WORTH WHAT THEIRS IS, MORE'S THE PITY.

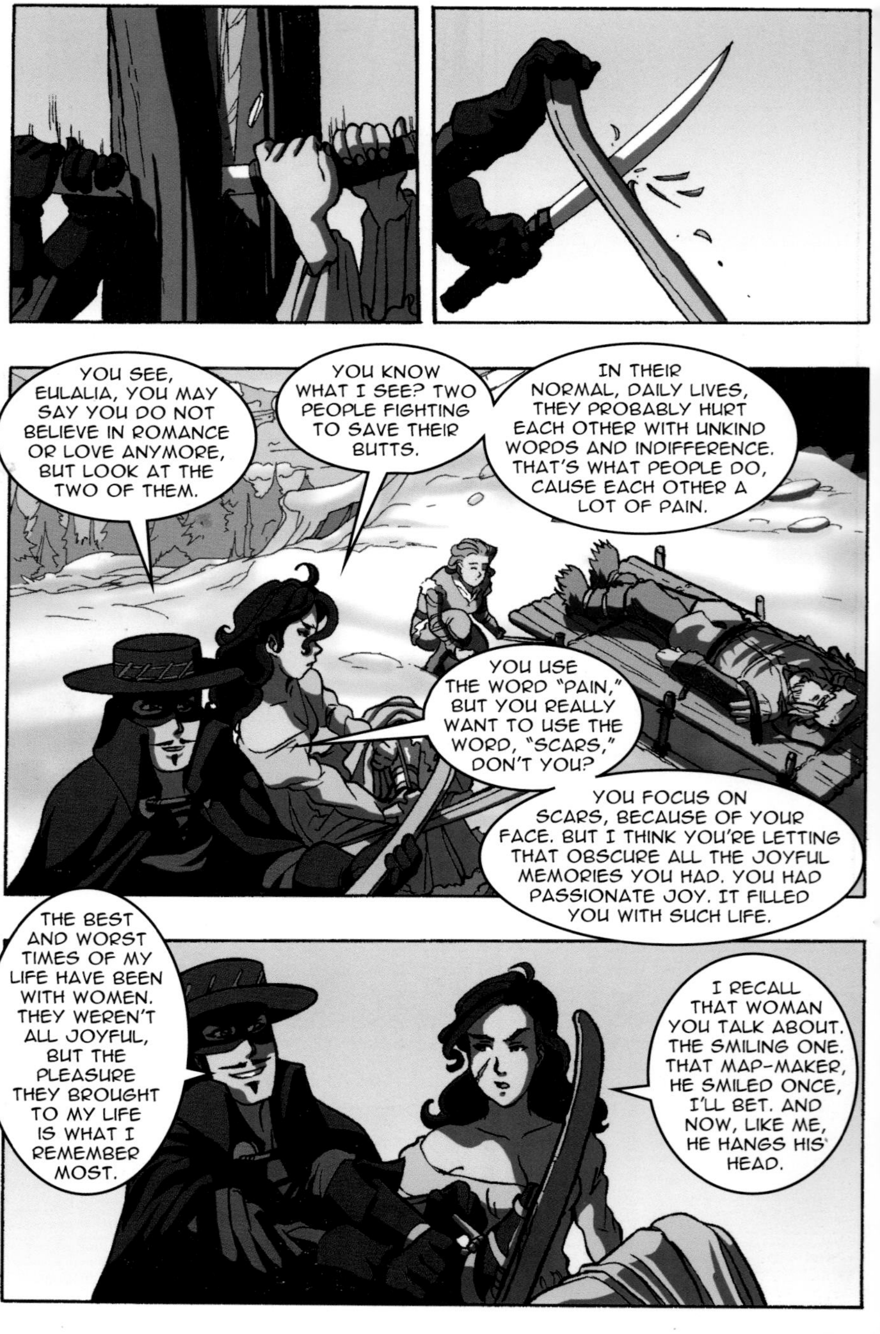
YOU SEE, EULALIA, YOU MAY SAY YOU DO NOT BELIEVE IN ROMANCE OR LOVE ANYMORE, BUT LOOK AT THE TWO OF THEM.
YOU KNOW WHAT I SEE? TWO PEOPLE FIGHTING TO SAVE THEIR BUTTS.
IN THEIR NORMAL, DAILY LIVES, THEY PROBABLY HURT EACH OTHER WITH UNKIND WORDS AND INDIFFERENCE. THAT'S WHAT PEOPLE DO, CAUSE EACH OTHER A LOT OF PAIN.
YOU USE THE WORD "PAIN," BUT YOU REALLY WANT TO USE THE WORD, "SCARS," DON'T YOU?
YOU FOCUS ON SCARS, BECAUSE OF YOUR FACE. BUT I THINK YOU'RE LETTING THAT OBSCURE ALL THE JOYFUL MEMORIES YOU HAD. YOU HAD PASSIONATE JOY. IT FILLED YOU WITH SUCH LIFE.
THE BEST AND WORST TIMES OF MY LIFE HAVE BEEN WITH WOMEN. THEY WEREN'T ALL JOYFUL, BUT THE PLEASURE THEY BROUGHT TO MY LIFE IS WHAT I REMEMBER MOST.
I RECALL THAT WOMAN YOU TALK ABOUT. THE SMILING ONE. THAT MAP-MAKER, HE SMILED ONCE, I'LL BET. AND NOW, LIKE ME, HE HANGS HIS HEAD.

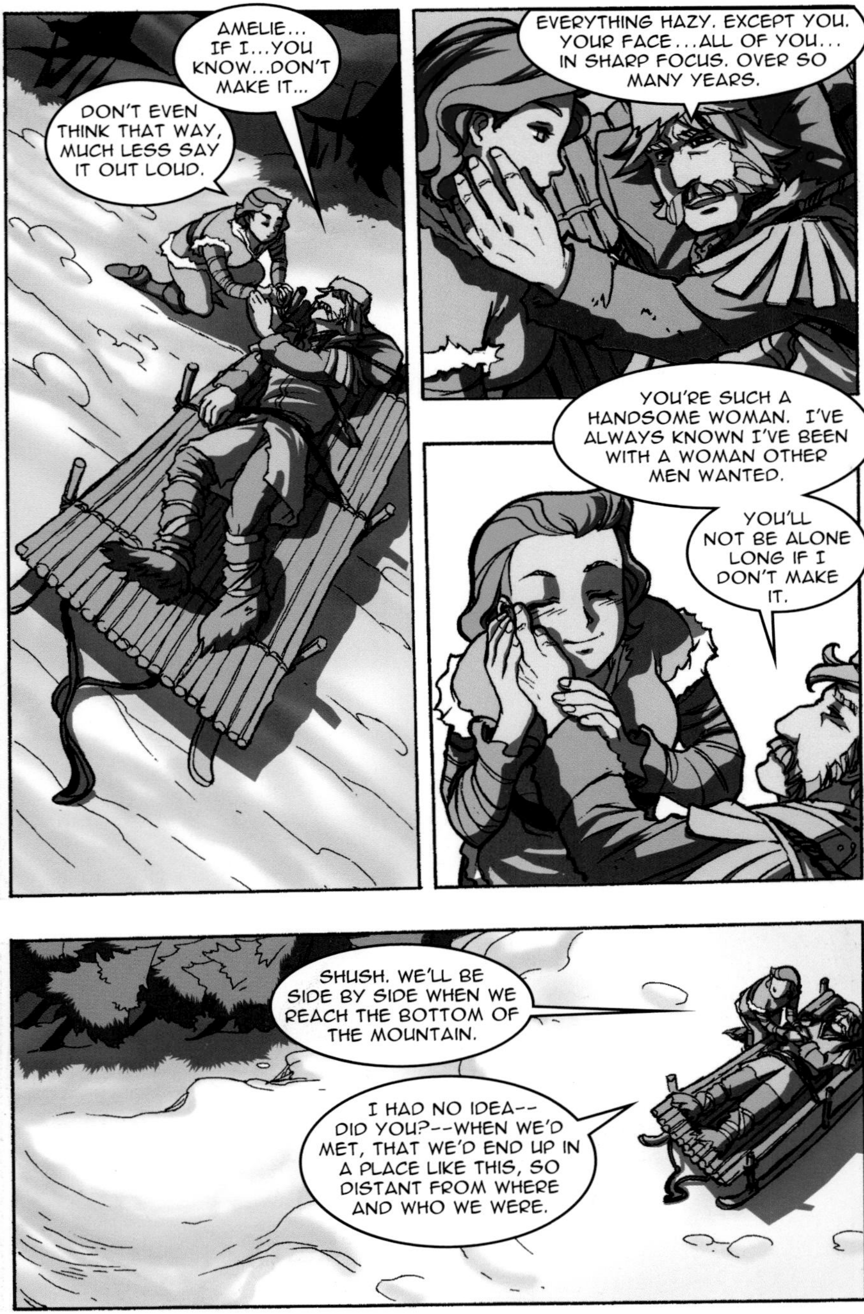
AMELIE... IF I...YOU KNOW...DON'T MAKE IT...
DON'T EVEN THINK THAT WAY, MUCH LESS SAY IT OUT LOUD.
EVERYTHING HAZY. EXCEPT YOU. YOUR FACE...ALL OF YOU... IN SHARP FOCUS. OVER SO MANY YEARS.
YOU'RE SUCH A HANDSOME WOMAN. I'VE ALWAYS KNOWN I'VE BEEN WITH A WOMAN OTHER MEN WANTED.
YOU'LL NOT BE ALONE LONG IF I DON'T MAKE IT.
SHUSH. WE'LL BE SIDE BY SIDE WHEN WE REACH THE BOTTOM OF THE MOUNTAIN.
I HAD NO IDEA--DID YOU?--WHEN WE'D MET, THAT WE'D END UP IN A PLACE LIKE THIS, SO DISTANT FROM WHERE AND WHO WE WERE.

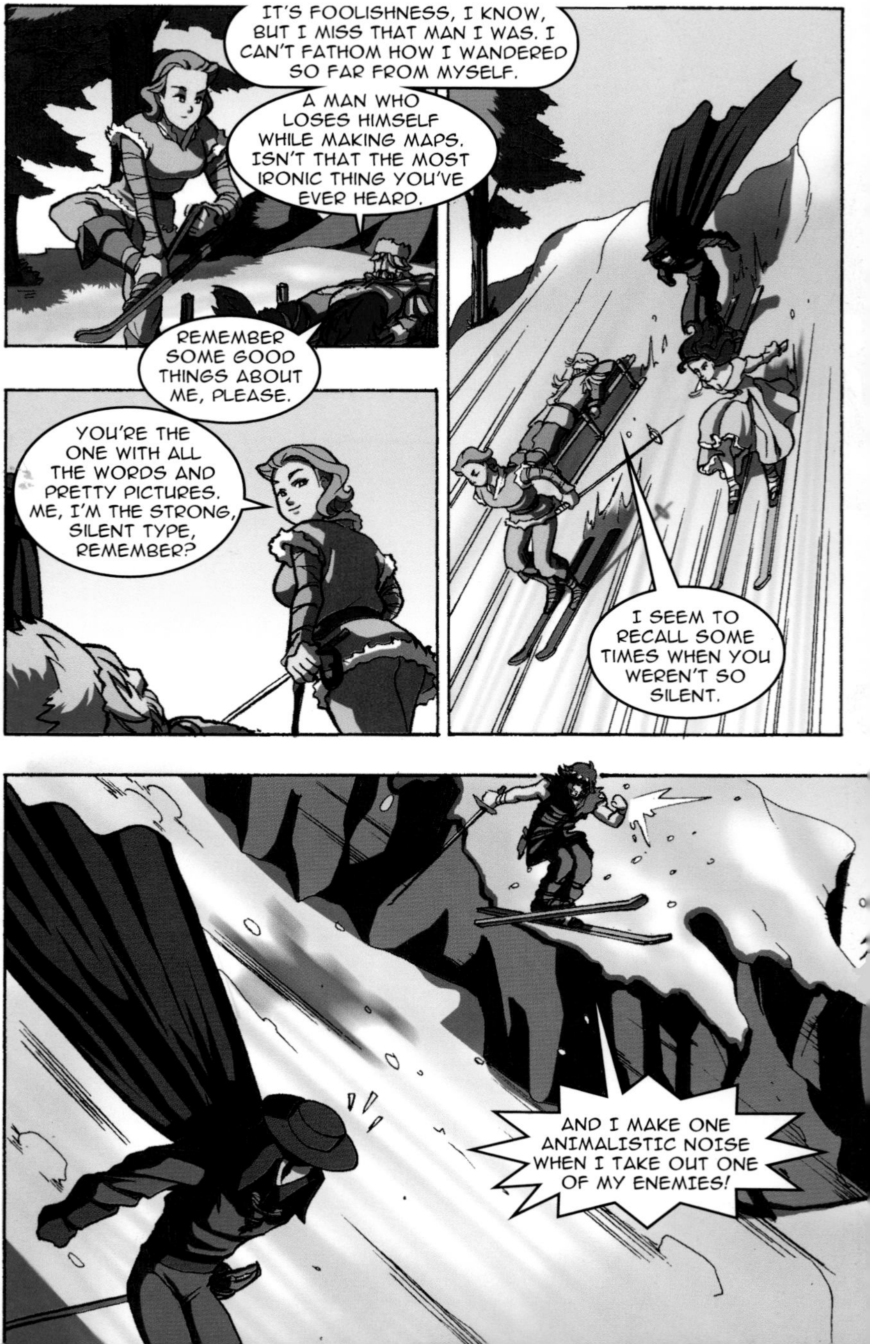
IT'S FOOLISHNESS, I KNOW, BUT I MISS THAT MAN I WAS. I CAN'T FATHOM HOW I WANDERED SO FAR FROM MYSELF.
A MAN WHO LOSES HIMSELF WHILE MAKING MAPS. ISN'T THAT THE MOST IRONIC THING YOU'VE EVER HEARD.
REMEMBER SOME GOOD THINGS ABOUT ME, PLEASE.
YOU'RE THE ONE WITH ALL THE WORDS AND PRETTY PICTURES. ME, I'M THE STRONG, SILENT TYPE, REMEMBER?
I SEEM TO RECALL SOME TIMES WHEN YOU WEREN'T SO SILENT.
AND I MAKE ONE ANIMALISTIC NOISE WHEN I TAKE OUT ONE OF MY ENEMIES!

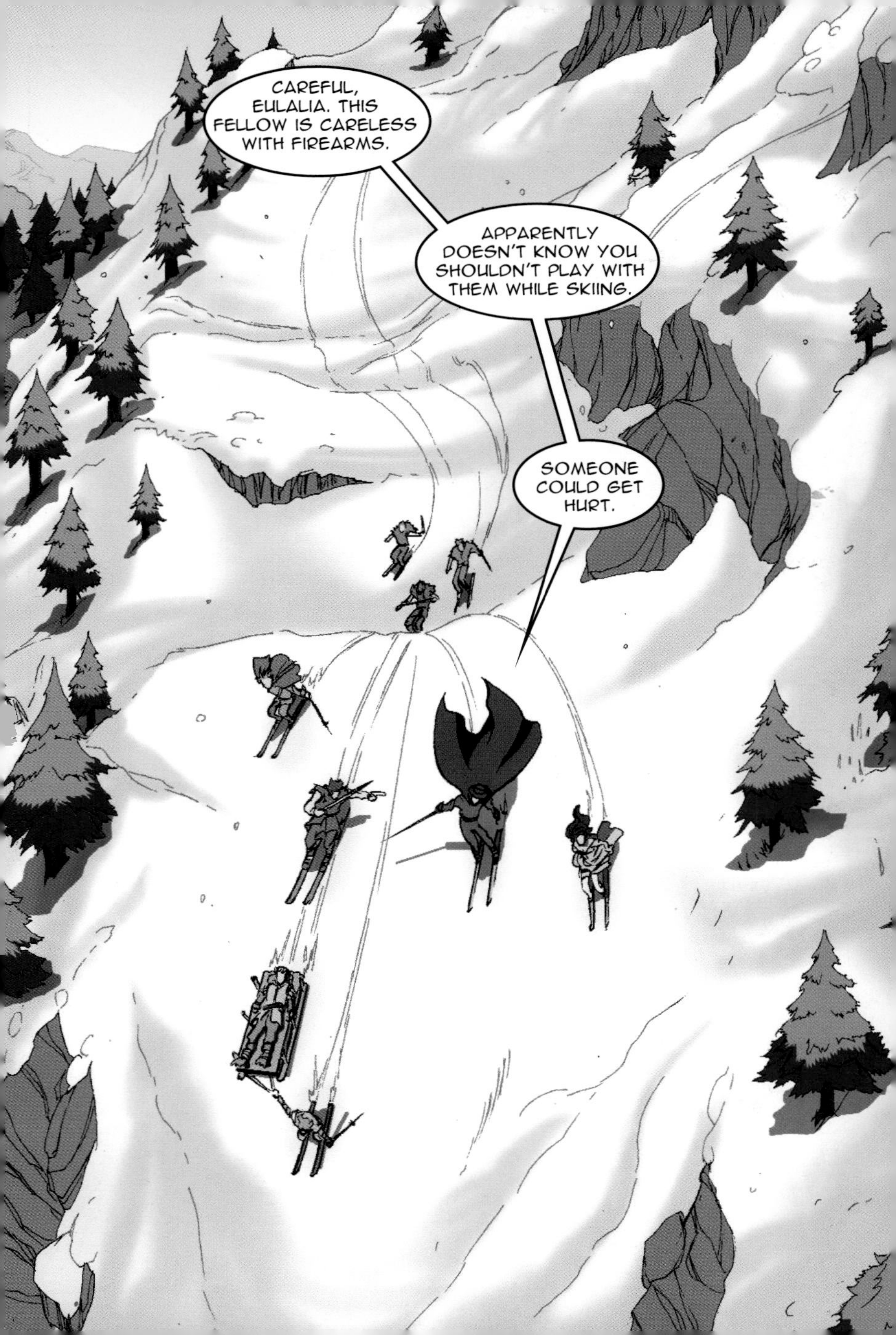
CAREFUL, EULALIA. THIS FELLOW IS CARELESS WITH FIREARMS.
APPARENTLY DOESN'T KNOW YOU SHOULDN'T PLAY WITH THEM WHILE SKIING.
SOMEONE COULD GET HURT.

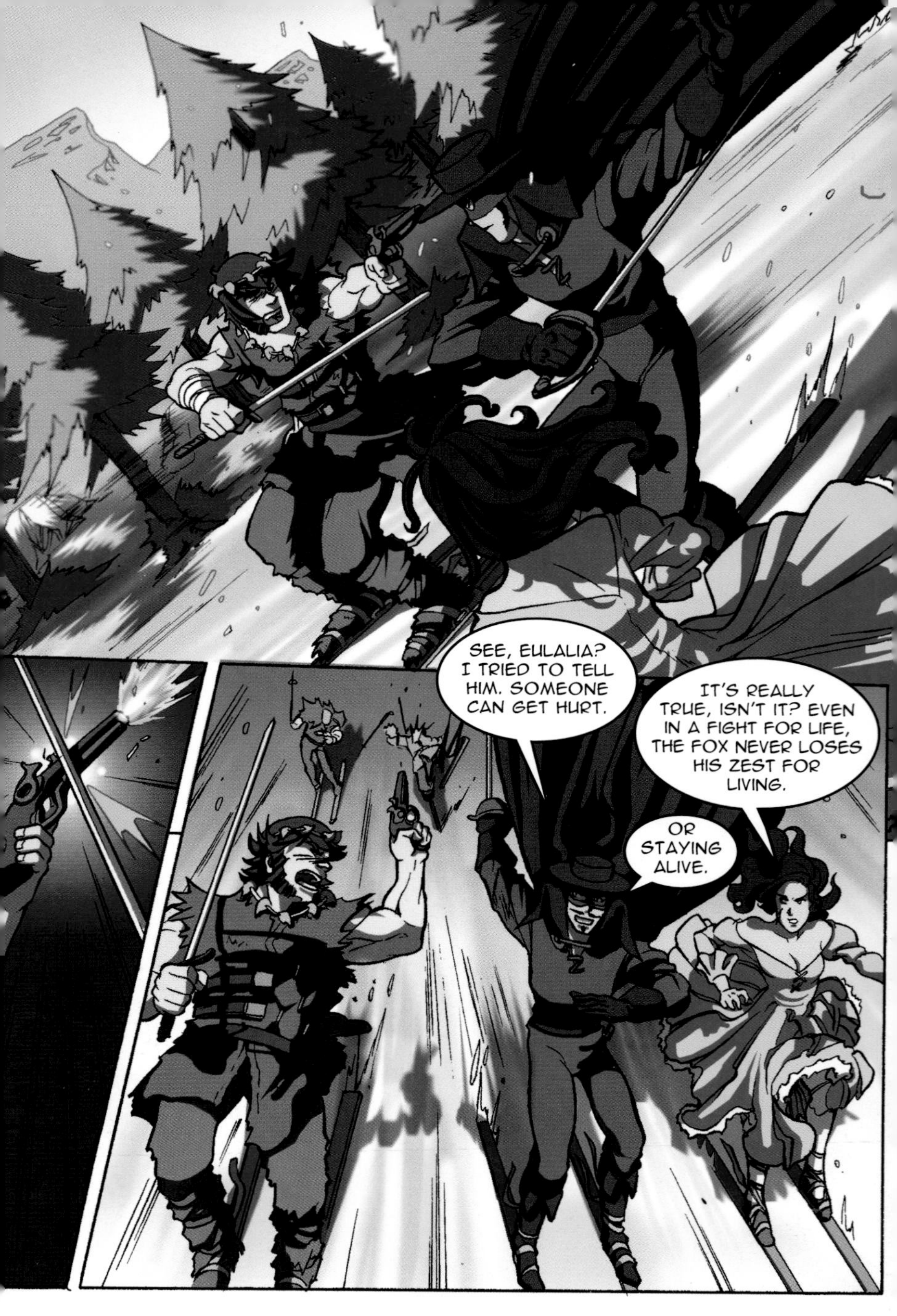
SEE, EULALIA? I TRIED TO TELL HIM. SOMEONE CAN GET HURT.
IT'S REALLY TRUE, ISN'T IT? EVEN IN A FIGHT FOR LIFE, THE FOX NEVER LOSES HIS ZEST FOR LIVING.
OR STAYING ALIVE.

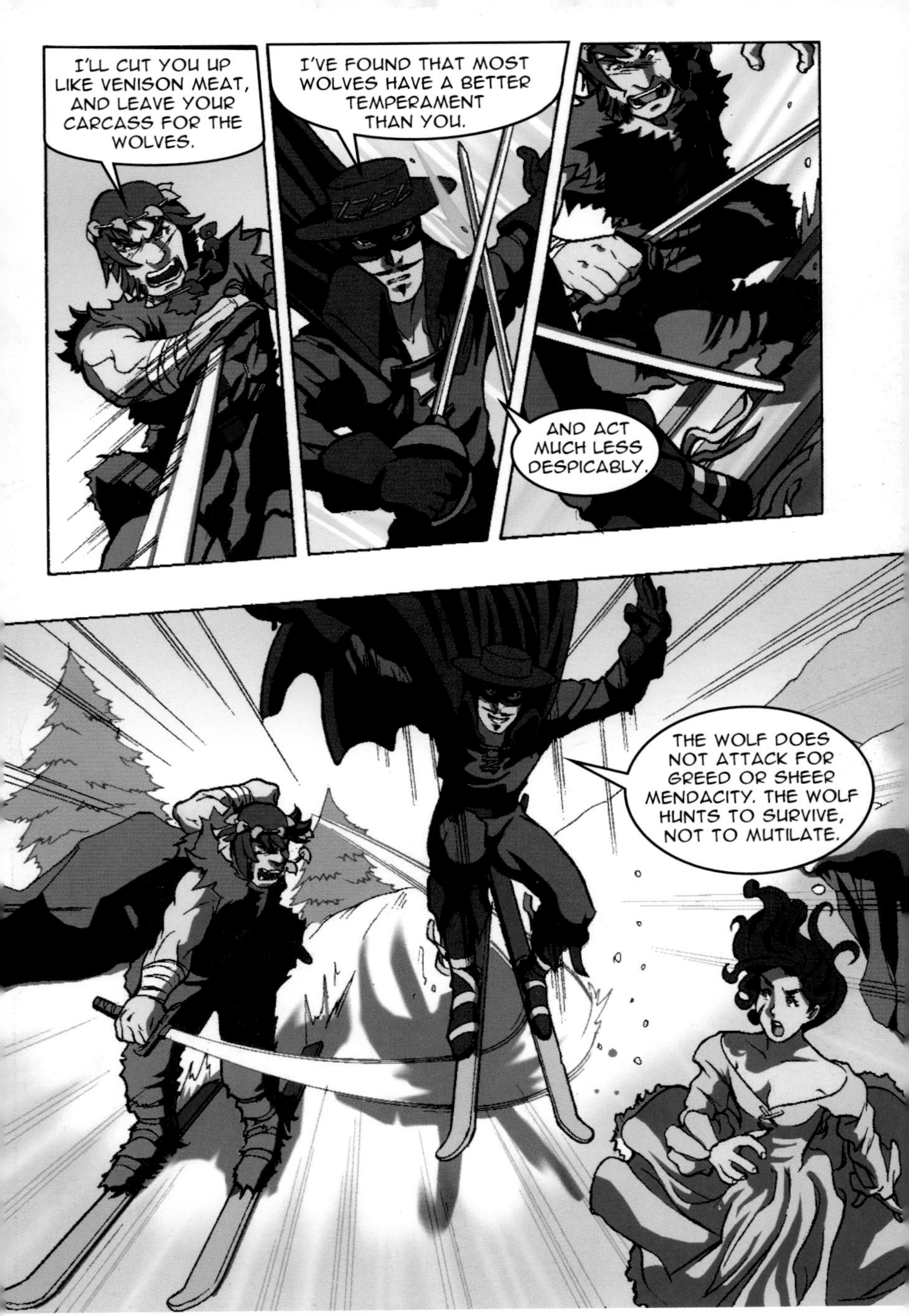
I'LL CUT YOU UP LIKE VENISON MEAT, AND LEAVE YOUR CARCASS FOR THE WOLVES.
I'VE FOUND THAT MOST WOLVES HAVE A BETTER TEMPERAMENT THAN YOU.
AND ACT MUCH LESS DESPICABLY.
THE WOLF DOES NOT ATTACK FOR GREED OR SHEER MENDACITY. THE WOLF HUNTS TO SURVIVE, NOT TO MUTILATE.

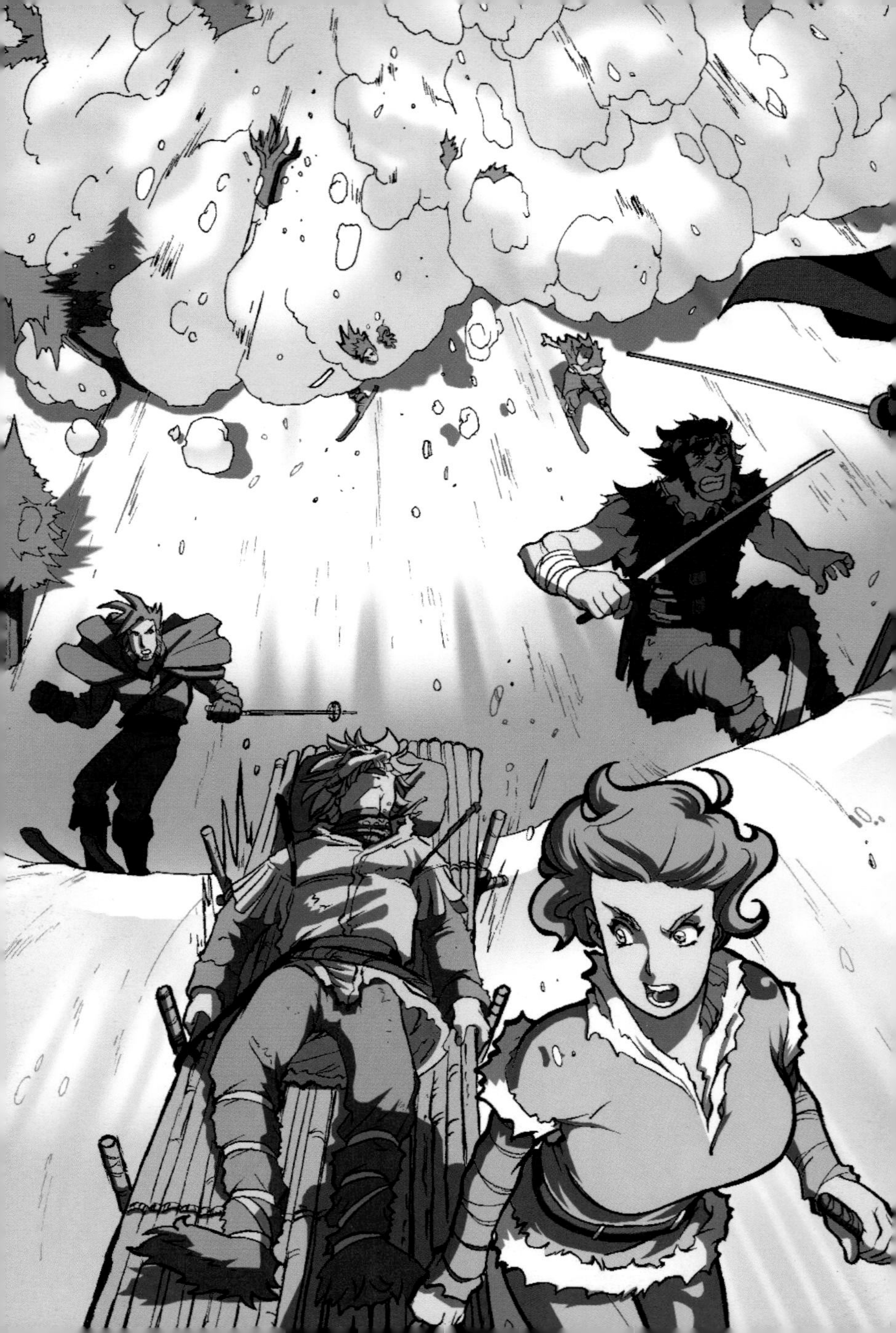

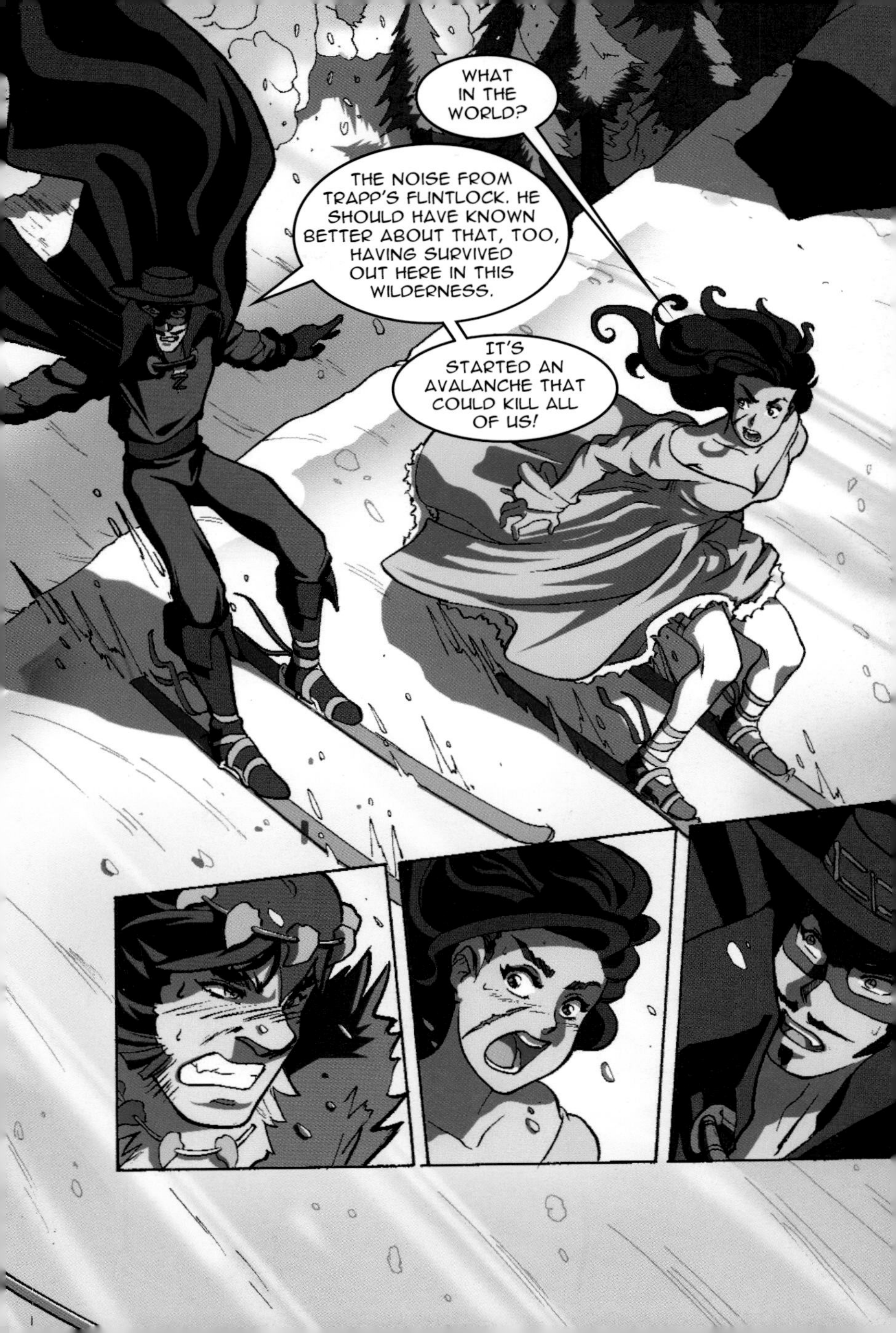
WHAT IN THE WORLD?
THE NOISE FROM TRAPP'S FLINTLOCK. HE SHOULD HAVE KNOWN BETTER ABOUT THAT, TOO, HAVING SURVIVED OUT HERE IN THIS WILDERNESS.
IT'S STARTED AN AVALANCHE THAT COULD KILL ALL OF US!

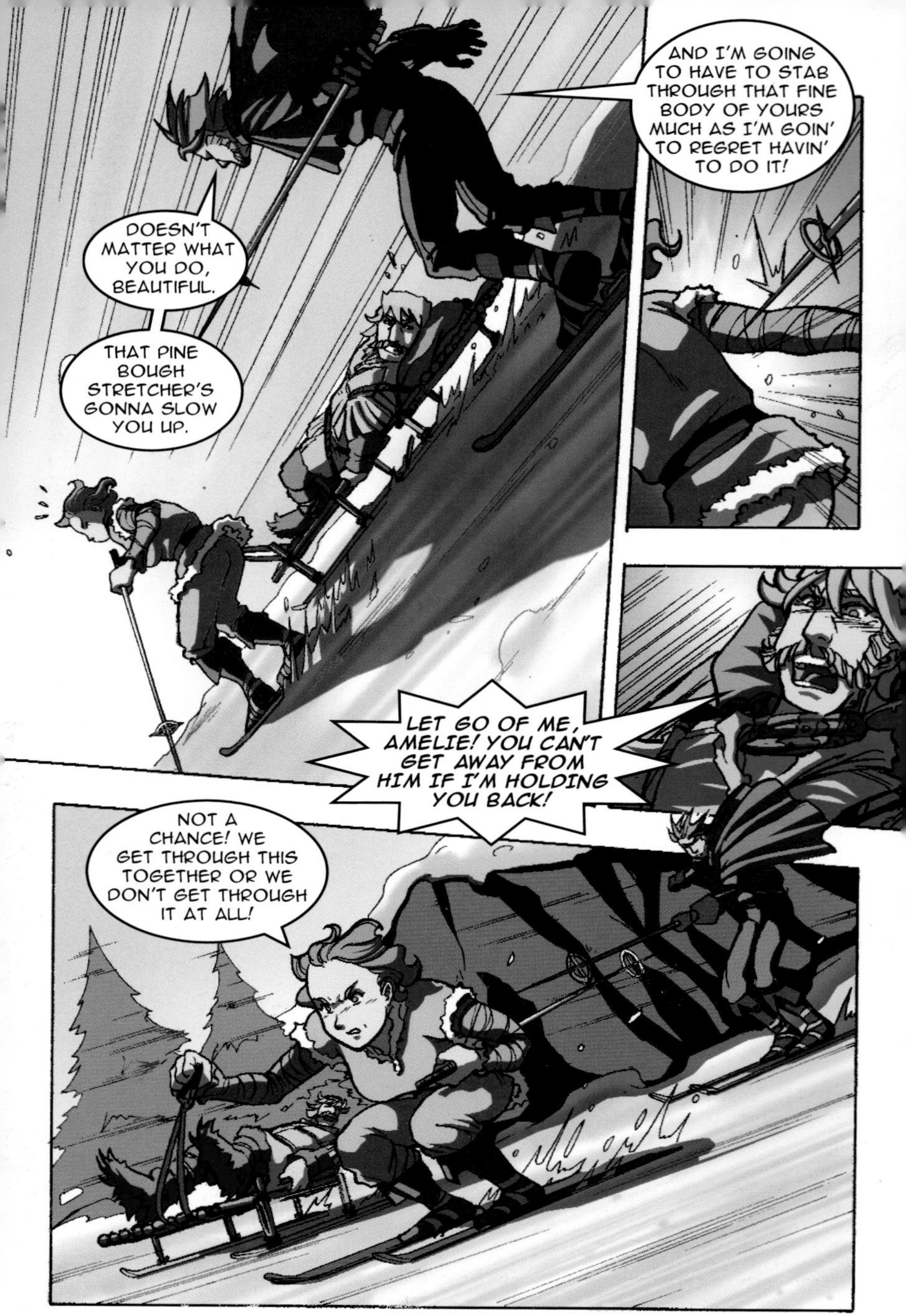
DOESN'T MATTER WHAT YOU DO, BEAUTIFUL.
THAT PINE BOUGH STRETCHER'S GONNA SLOW YOU UP.
AND I'M GOING TO HAVE TO STAB THROUGH THAT FINE BODY OF YOURS MUCH AS I'M GOIN' TO REGRET HAVIN' TO DO IT!
LET GO OF ME, AMELIE! YOU CAN'T GET AWAY FROM HIM IF I'M HOLDING YOU BACK!
NOT A CHANCE! WE GET THROUGH THIS TOGETHER OR WE DON'T GET THROUGH IT AT ALL!

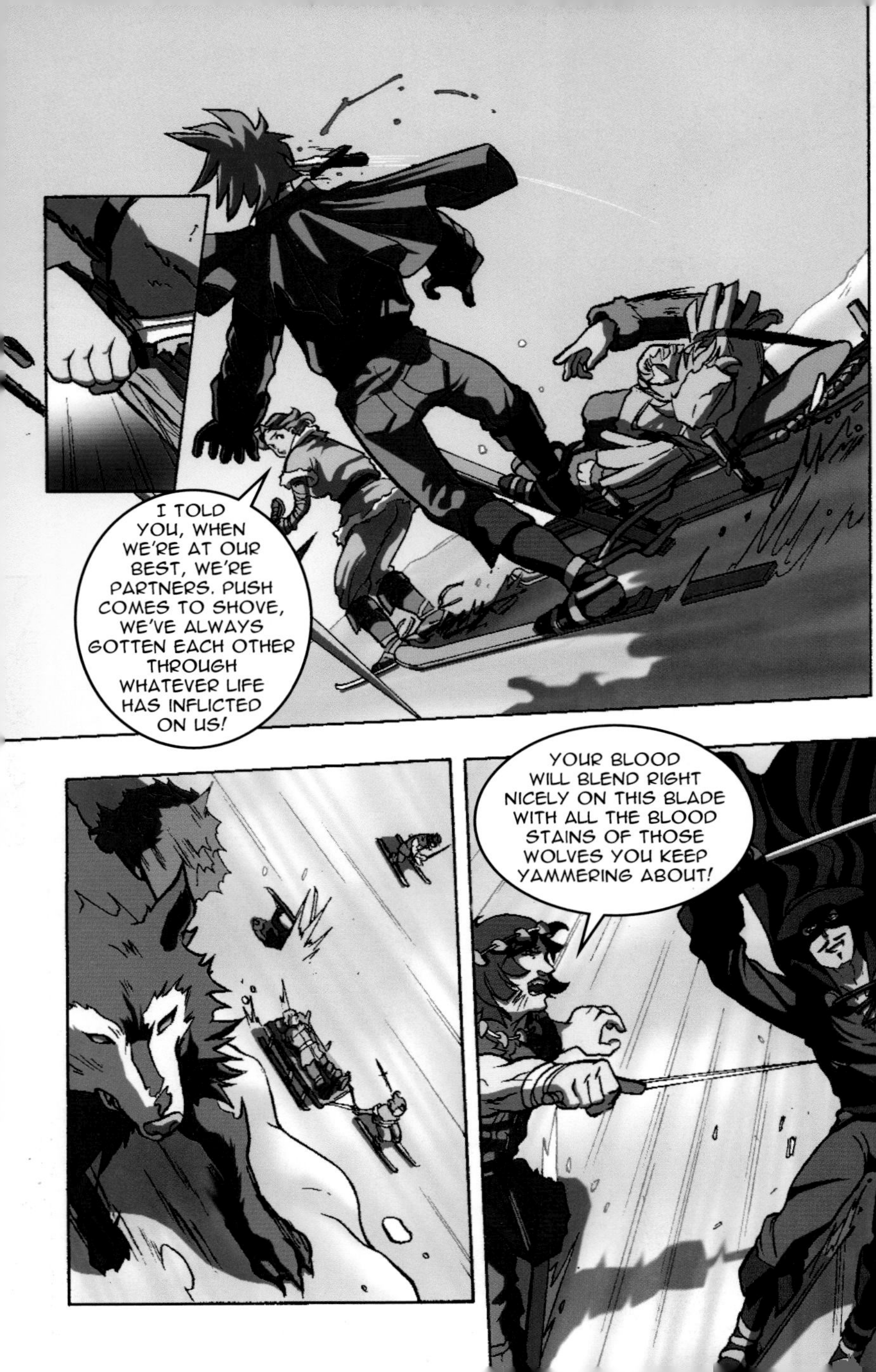
I TOLD YOU, WHEN WE'RE AT OUR BEST, WE'RE PARTNERS. PUSH COMES TO SHOVE, WE'VE ALWAYS GOTTEN EACH OTHER THROUGH WHATEVER LIFE HAS INFLICTED ON US!
YOUR BLOOD WILL BLEND RIGHT NICELY ON THIS BLADE WITH ALL THE BLOOD STAINS OF THOSE WOLVES YOU KEEP YAMMERING ABOUT!

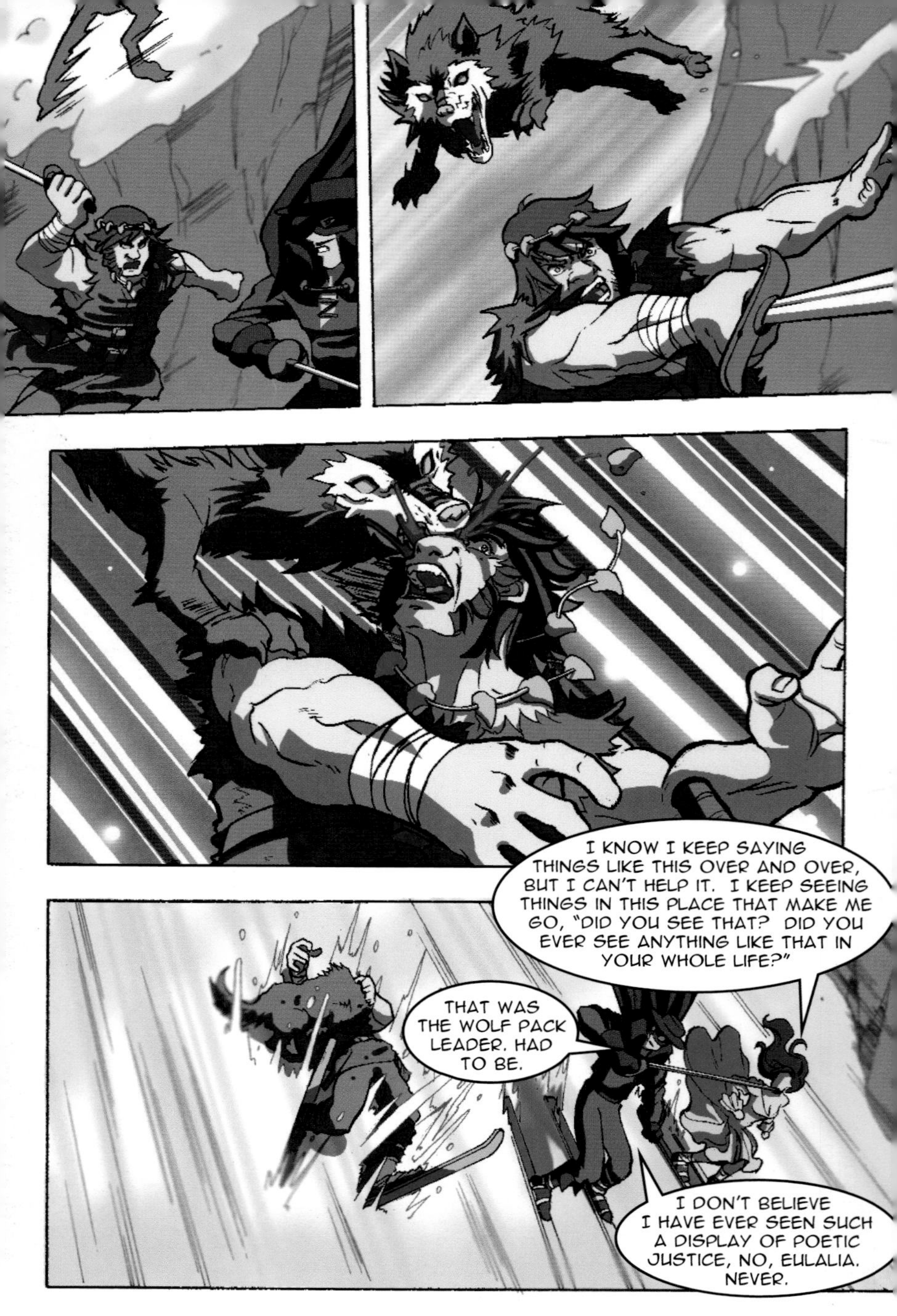
I KNOW I KEEP SAYING THINGS LIKE THIS OVER AND OVER, BUT I CAN'T HELP IT. I KEEP SEEING THINGS IN THIS PLACE THAT MAKE ME GO, "DID YOU SEE THAT? DID YOU EVER SEE ANYTHING LIKE THAT IN YOUR WHOLE LIFE?"
THAT WAS THE WOLF PACK LEADER. HAD TO BE.
I DON'T BELIEVE I HAVE EVER SEEN SUCH A DISPLAY OF POETIC JUSTICE, NO, EULALIA. NEVER.

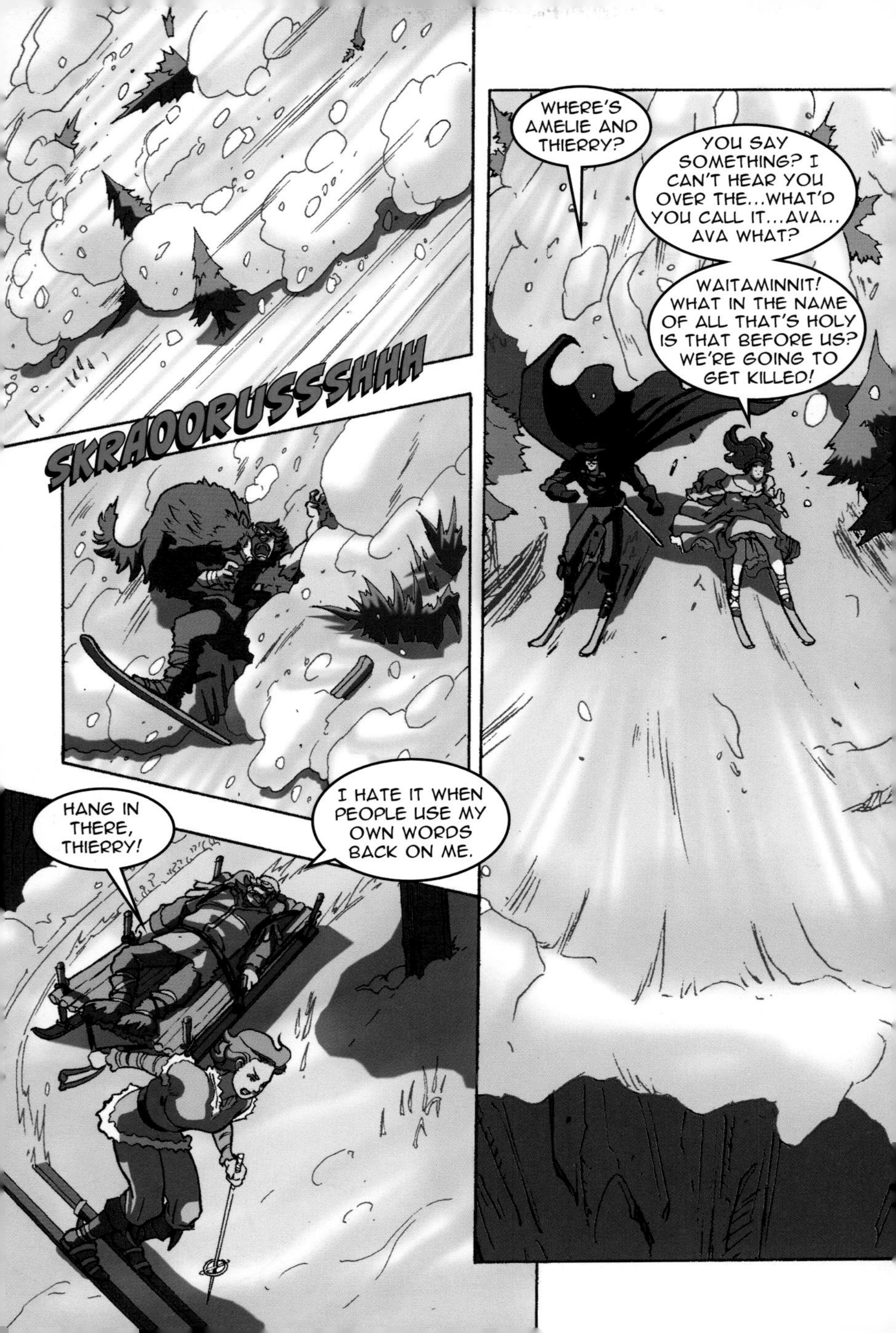
SKRAOORUSSSHHH
WHERE'S AMELIE AND THIERRY?
YOU SAY SOMETHING? I CAN'T HEAR YOU OVER THE...WHAT'D YOU CALL IT...AVA... AVA WHAT?
WAITAMINNIT! WHAT IN THE NAME OF ALL THAT'S HOLY IS THAT BEFORE US? WE'RE GOING TO GET KILLED!
HANG IN THERE, THIERRY!
I HATE IT WHEN PEOPLE USE MY OWN WORDS BACK ON ME.

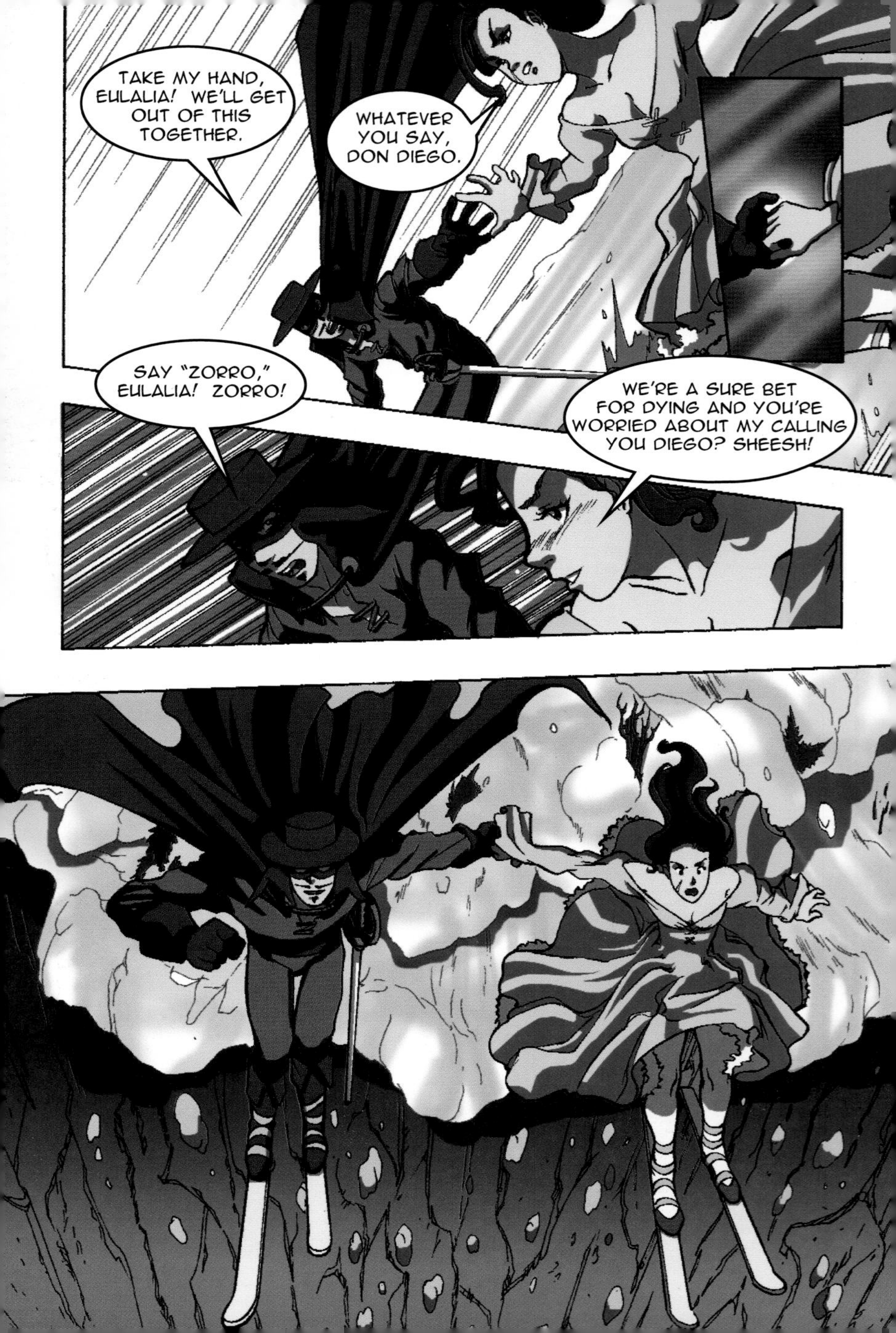
TAKE MY HAND, EULALIA! WE'LL GET OUT OF THIS TOGETHER.
WHATEVER YOU SAY, DON DIEGO.
SAY "ZORRO," EULALIA! ZORRO!
WE'RE A SURE BET FOR DYING AND YOU'RE WORRIED ABOUT MY CALLING YOU DIEGO? SHEESH!

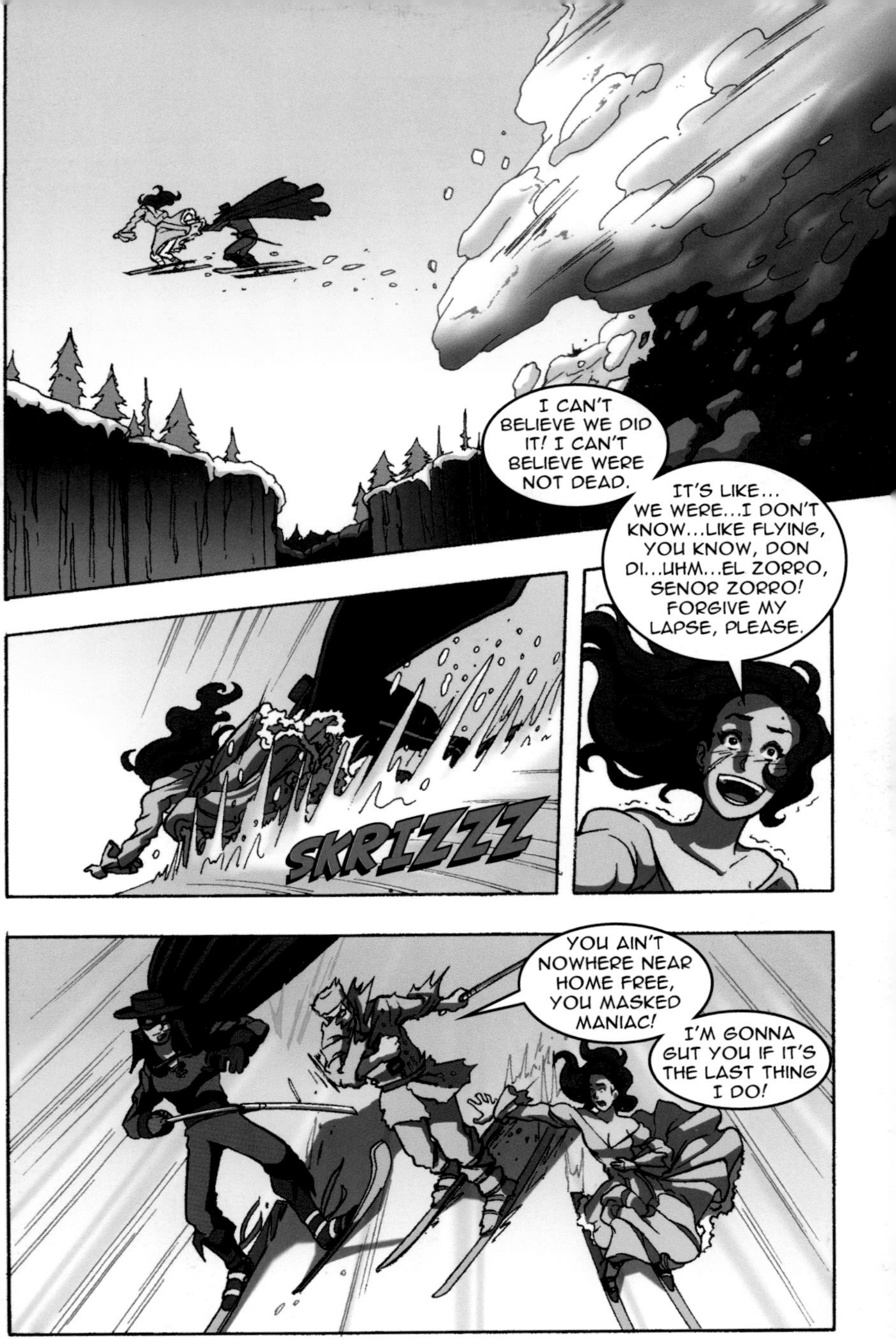
I CAN'T BELIEVE WE DID IT! I CAN'T BELIEVE WERE NOT DEAD.
IT'S LIKE... WE WERE...I DON'T KNOW...LIKE FLYING, YOU KNOW, DON DI...UHM...EL ZORRO, SENOR ZORRO! FORGIVE MY LAPSE, PLEASE.
SKRIZZZ
YOU AIN'T NOWHERE NEAR HOME FREE, YOU MASKED MANIAC!
I'M GONNA GUT YOU IF IT'S THE LAST THING I DO!

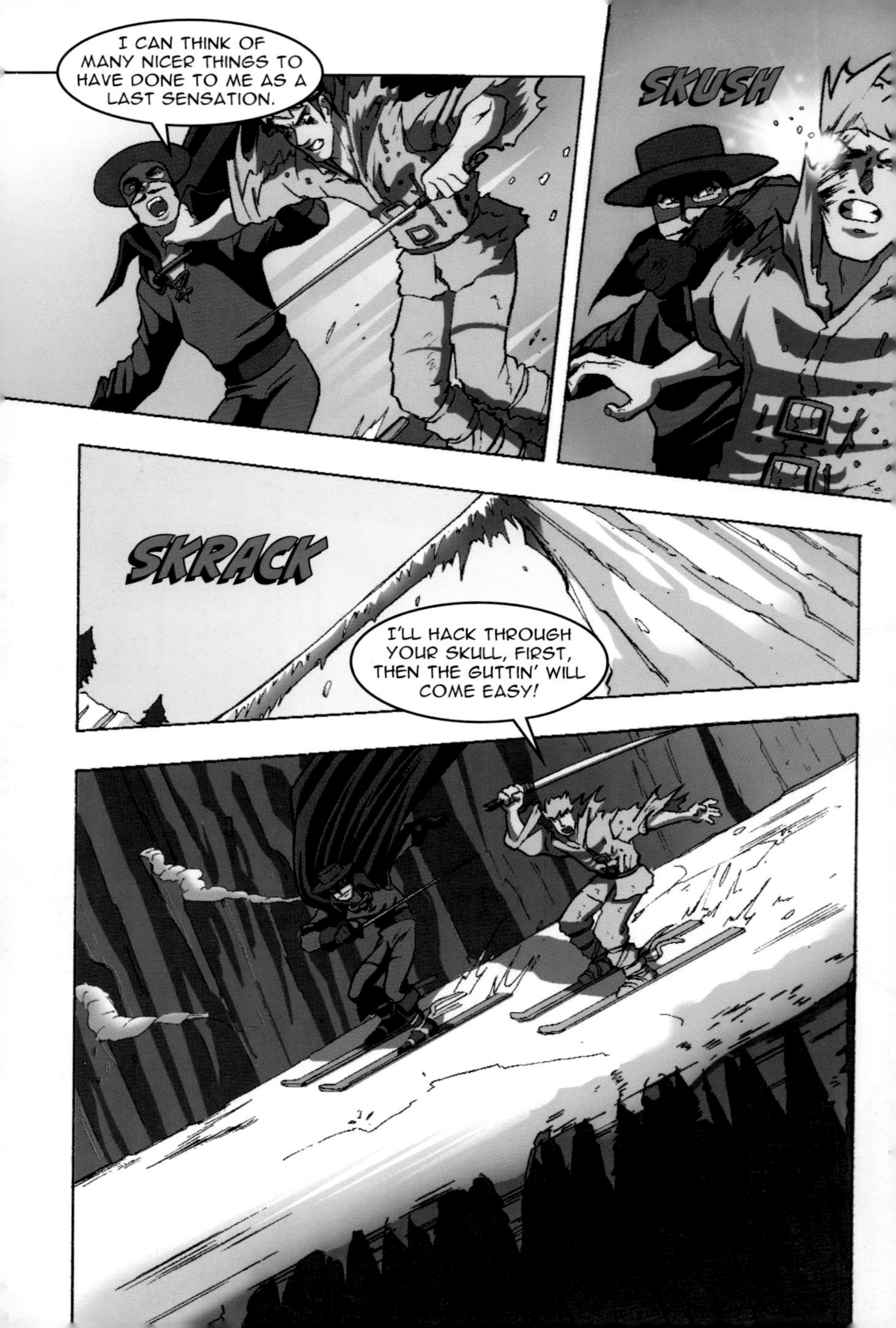
I CAN THINK OF MANY NICER THINGS TO HAVE DONE TO ME AS A LAST SENSATION.
SKUSH
SKRACK
I'LL HACK THROUGH YOUR SKULL, FIRST, THEN THE GUTTIN' WILL COME EASY!

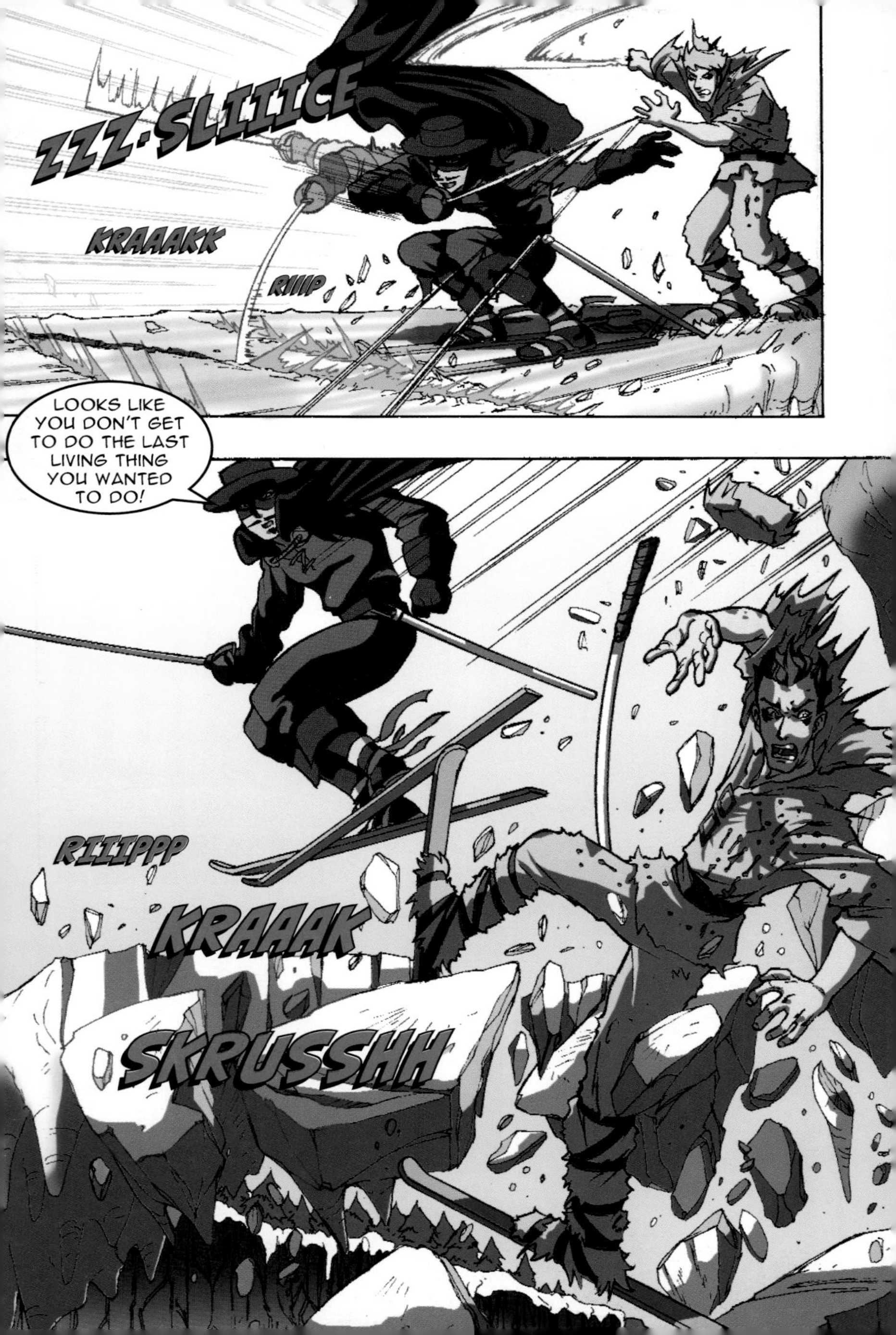
ZZZ-SLIIICE
KRAAAKK
RIIIP
LOOKS LIKE YOU DON'T GET TO DO THE LAST LIVING THING YOU WANTED TO DO!
RIIIPPP
KRAAAK
SKRUSSHH

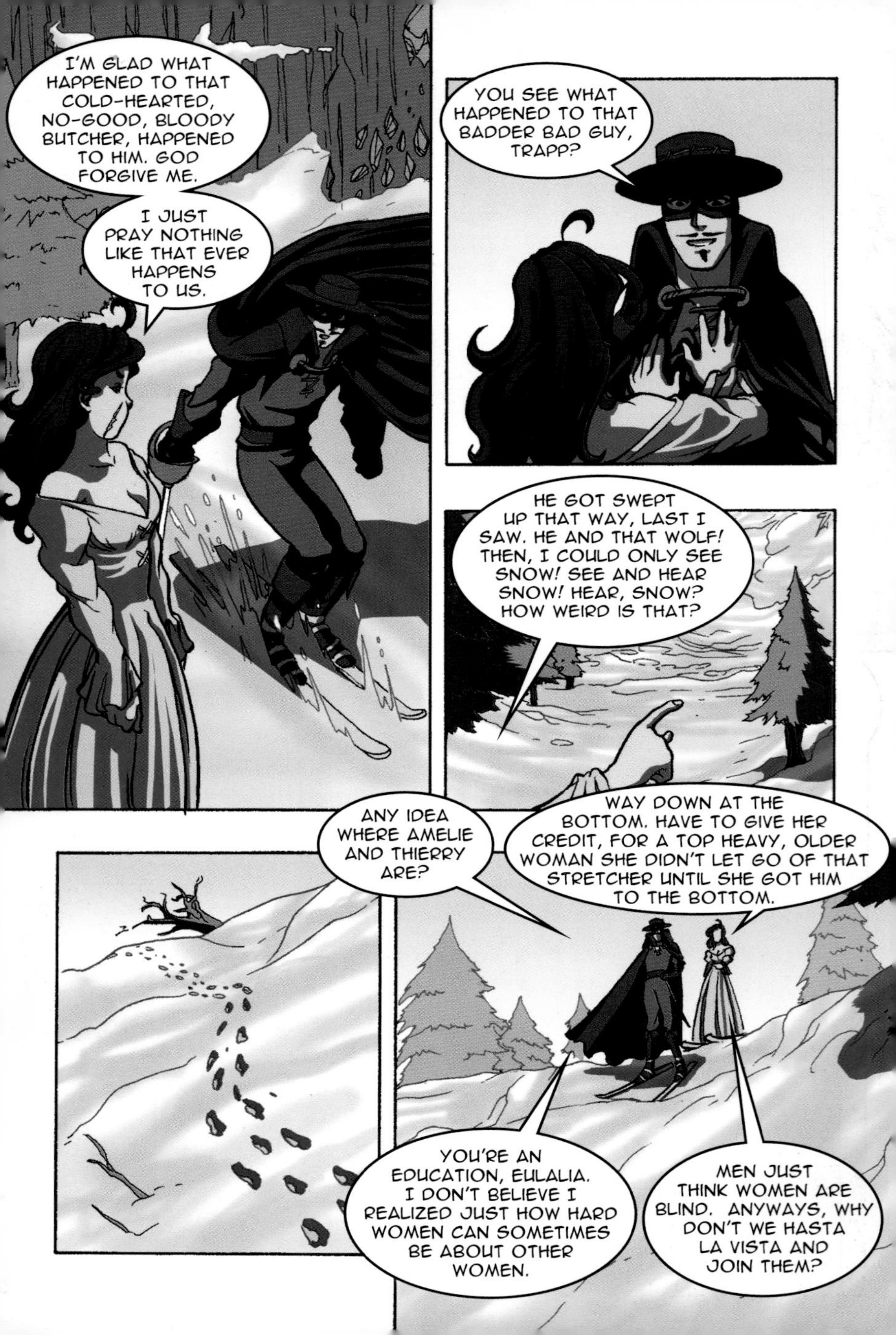
I'M GLAD WHAT HAPPENED TO THAT COLD-HEARTED, NO-GOOD, BLOODY BUTCHER, HAPPENED TO HIM. GOD FORGIVE ME.
I JUST PRAY NOTHING LIKE THAT EVER HAPPENS TO US.
YOU SEE WHAT HAPPENED TO THAT BADDER BAD GUY, TRAPP?
HE GOT SWEPT UP THAT WAY, LAST I SAW. HE AND THAT WOLF! THEN, I COULD ONLY SEE SNOW! SEE AND HEAR SNOW! HEAR, SNOW? HOW WEIRD IS THAT?
ANY IDEA WHERE AMELIE AND THIERRY ARE?
WAY DOWN AT THE BOTTOM. HAVE TO GIVE HER CREDIT, FOR A TOP HEAVY, OLDER WOMAN SHE DIDN'T LET GO OF THAT STRETCHER UNTIL SHE GOT HIM TO THE BOTTOM.
YOU'RE AN EDUCATION, EULALIA. I DON'T BELIEVE I REALIZED JUST HOW HARD WOMEN CAN SOMETIMES BE ABOUT OTHER WOMEN.
MEN JUST THINK WOMEN ARE BLIND. ANYWAYS, WHY DON'T WE HASTA LA VISTA AND JOIN THEM?

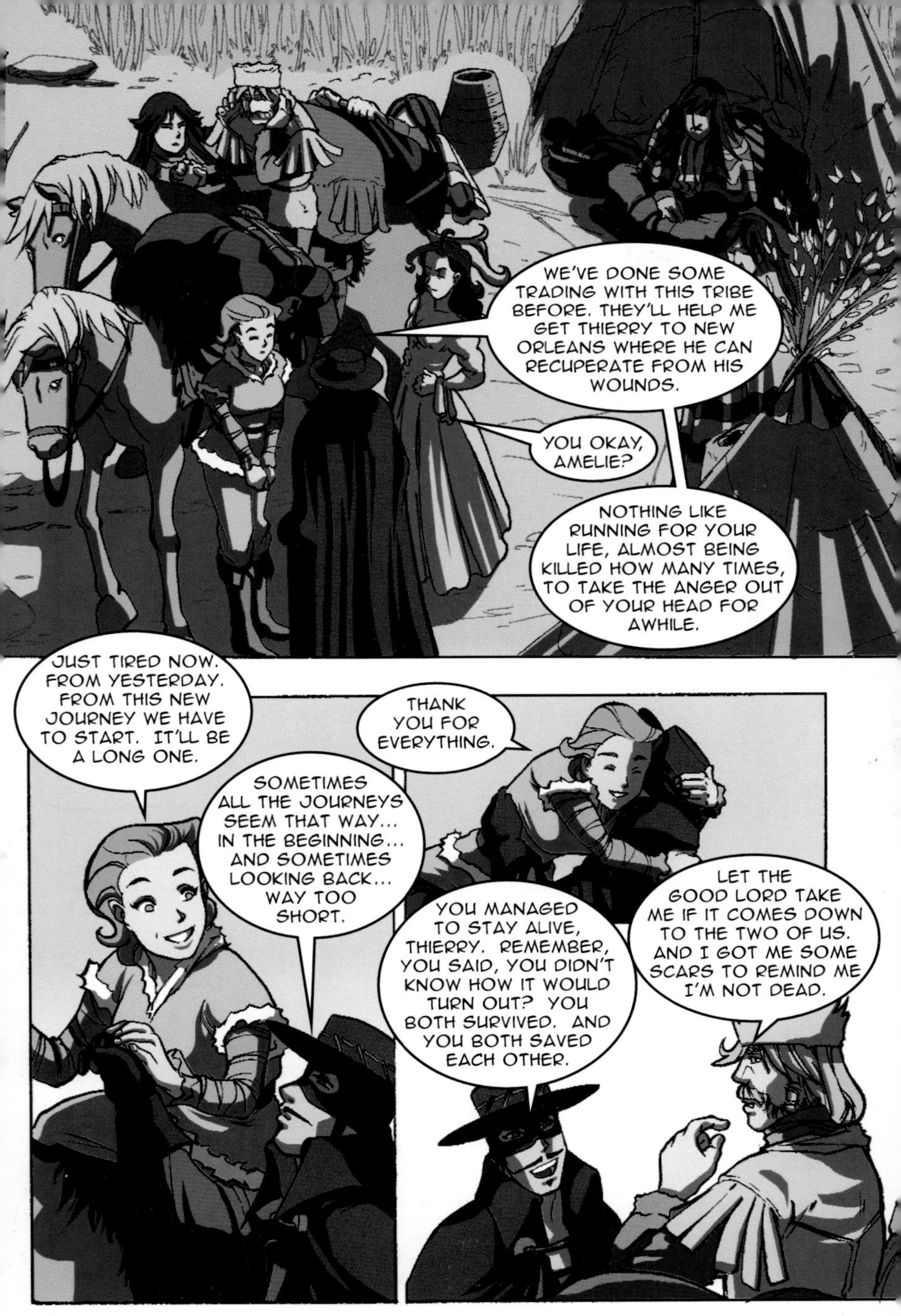
WE'VE DONE SOME TRADING WITH THIS TRIBE BEFORE. THEY'LL HELP ME GET THIERRY TO NEW ORLEANS WHERE HE CAN RECUPERATE FROM HIS WOUNDS.
YOU OKAY, AMELIE?
NOTHING LIKE RUNNING FOR YOUR LIFE, ALMOST BEING KILLED HOW MANY TIMES, TO TAKE THE ANGER OUT OF YOUR HEAD FOR AWHILE.
JUST TIRED NOW. FROM YESTERDAY. FROM THIS NEW JOURNEY WE HAVE TO START. IT'LL BE A LONG ONE.
SOMETIMES ALL THE JOURNEYS SEEM THAT WAY... IN THE BEGINNING... AND SOMETIMES LOOKING BACK... WAY TOO SHORT.
THANK YOU FOR EVERYTHING.
YOU MANAGED TO STAY ALIVE, THIERRY. REMEMBER, YOU SAID, YOU DIDN'T KNOW HOW IT WOULD TURN OUT? YOU BOTH SURVIVED. AND YOU BOTH SAVED EACH OTHER.
LET THE GOOD LORD TAKE ME IF IT COMES DOWN TO THE TWO OF US. AND I GOT ME SOME SCARS TO REMIND ME I'M NOT DEAD.

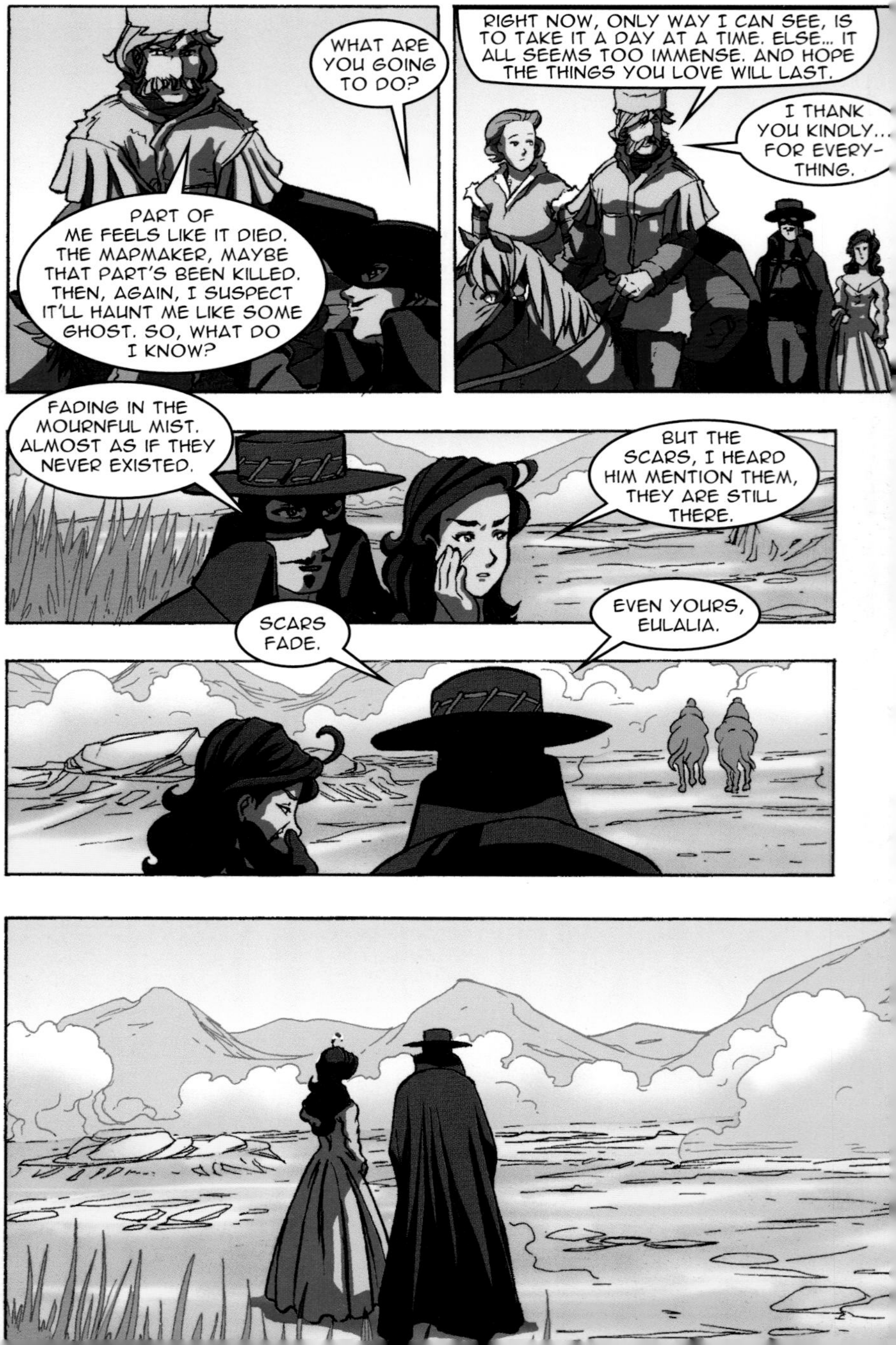
WHAT ARE YOU GOING TO DO?
PART OF ME FEELS LIKE IT DIED. THE MAPMAKER, MAYBE THAT PART'S BEEN KILLED. THEN, AGAIN, I SUSPECT IT'LL HAUNT ME LIKE SOME GHOST. SO, WHAT DO I KNOW?
RIGHT NOW, ONLY WAY I CAN SEE, IS TO TAKE IT A DAY AT A TIME. ELSE... IT ALL SEEMS TOO IMMENSE. AND HOPE THE THINGS YOU LOVE WILL LAST.
I THANK YOU KINDLY... FOR EVERY-THING.
FADING IN THE MOURNFUL MIST. ALMOST AS IF THEY NEVER EXISTED.
BUT THE SCARS, I HEARD HIM MENTION THEM, THEY ARE STILL THERE.
SCARS FADE.
EVEN YOURS, EULALIA.

Special Advance Preview of ZORRO Graphic Novel # 2 – "Drownings!"

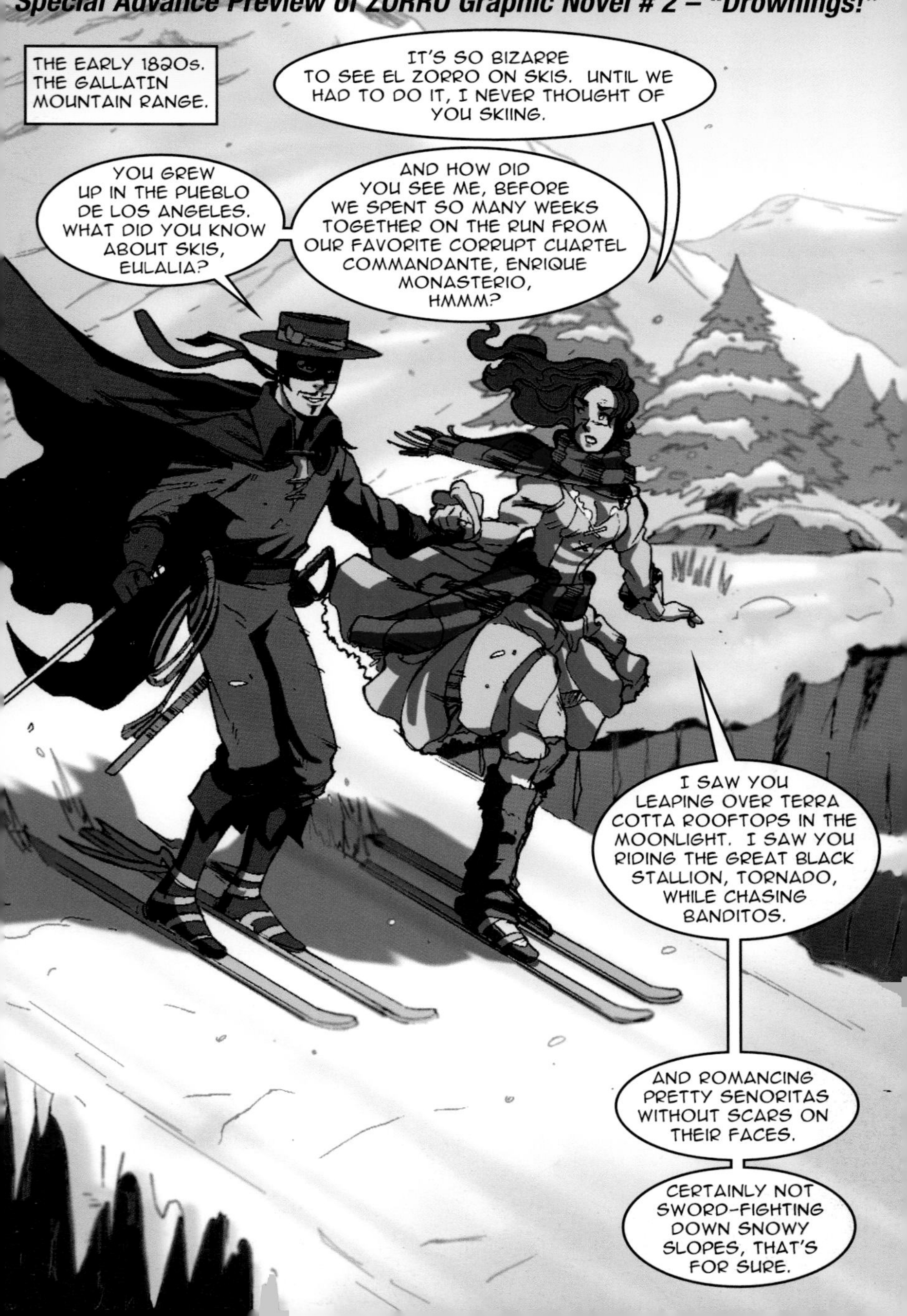

THE EARLY 1820s. THE GALLATIN MOUNTAIN RANGE.
IT'S SO BIZARRE TO SEE EL ZORRO ON SKIS. UNTIL WE HAD TO DO IT, I NEVER THOUGHT OF YOU SKIING.
YOU GREW UP IN THE PUEBLO DE LOS ANGELES. WHAT DID YOU KNOW ABOUT SKIS, EULALIA?
AND HOW DID YOU SEE ME, BEFORE WE SPENT SO MANY WEEKS TOGETHER ON THE RUN FROM OUR FAVORITE CORRUPT CUARTEL COMMANDANTE, ENRIQUE MONASTERIO, HMMM?
I SAW YOU LEAPING OVER TERRA COTTA ROOFTOPS IN THE MOONLIGHT. I SAW YOU RIDING THE GREAT BLACK STALLION, TORNADO, WHILE CHASING BANDITOS.
AND ROMANCING PRETTY SENORITAS WITHOUT SCARS ON THEIR FACES.
CERTAINLY NOT SWORD-FIGHTING DOWN SNOWY SLOPES, THAT'S FOR SURE.

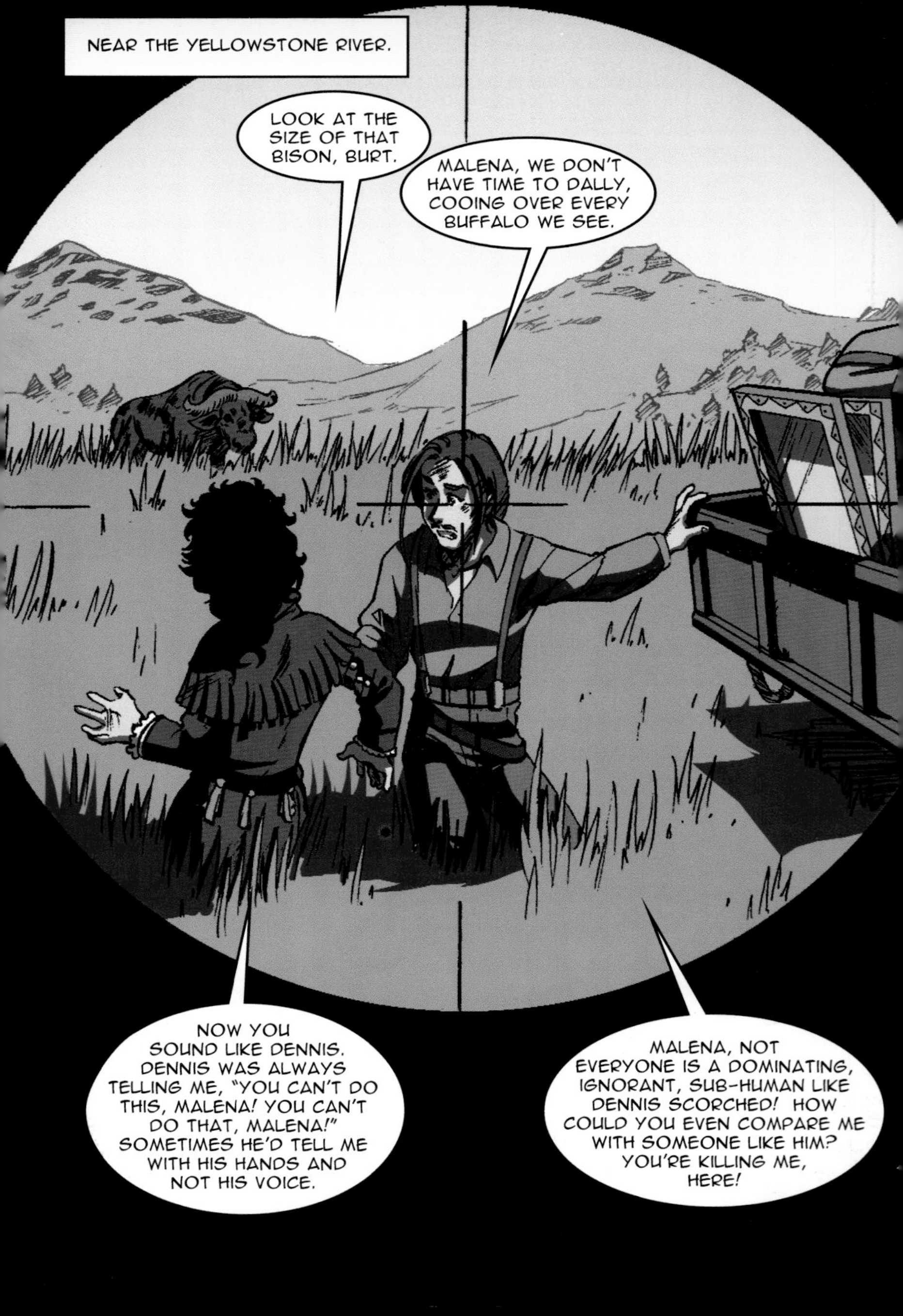
NEAR THE YELLOWSTONE RIVER.
LOOK AT THE SIZE OF THAT BISON, BURT.
MALENA, WE DON'T HAVE TIME TO DALLY, COOING OVER EVERY BUFFALO WE SEE.
NOW YOU SOUND LIKE DENNIS. DENNIS WAS ALWAYS TELLING ME, "YOU CAN'T DO THIS, MALENA! YOU CAN'T DO THAT, MALENA!" SOMETIMES HE'D TELL ME WITH HIS HANDS AND NOT HIS VOICE.
MALENA, NOT EVERYONE IS A DOMINATING, IGNORANT, SUB-HUMAN LIKE DENNIS SCORCHED! HOW COULD YOU EVEN COMPARE ME WITH SOMEONE LIKE HIM? YOU'RE KILLING ME, HERE!

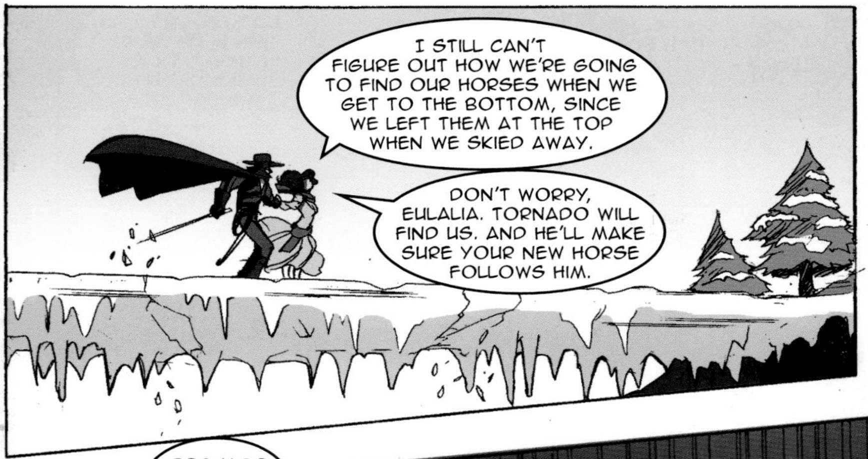
I STILL CAN'T FIGURE OUT HOW WE'RE GOING TO FIND OUR HORSES WHEN WE GET TO THE BOTTOM, SINCE WE LEFT THEM AT THE TOP WHEN WE SKIED AWAY.
DON'T WORRY, EULALIA. TORNADO WILL FIND US. AND HE'LL MAKE SURE YOUR NEW HORSE FOLLOWS HIM.

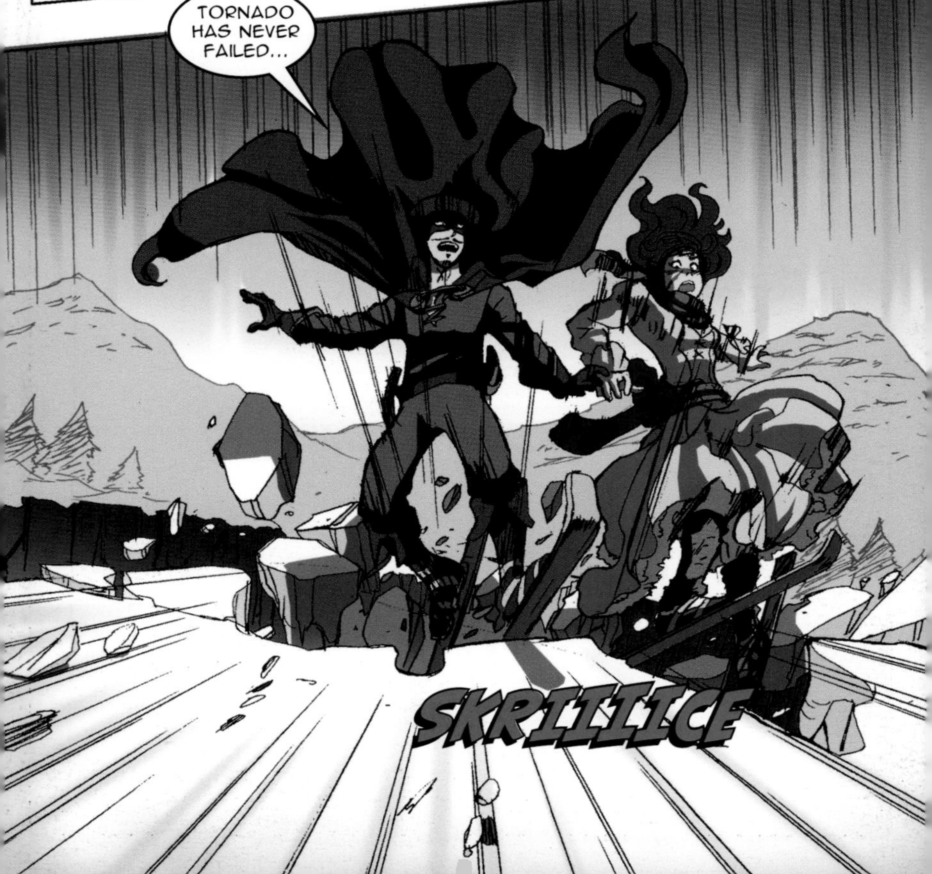
TORNADO HAS NEVER FAILED...
SKRIIIICE

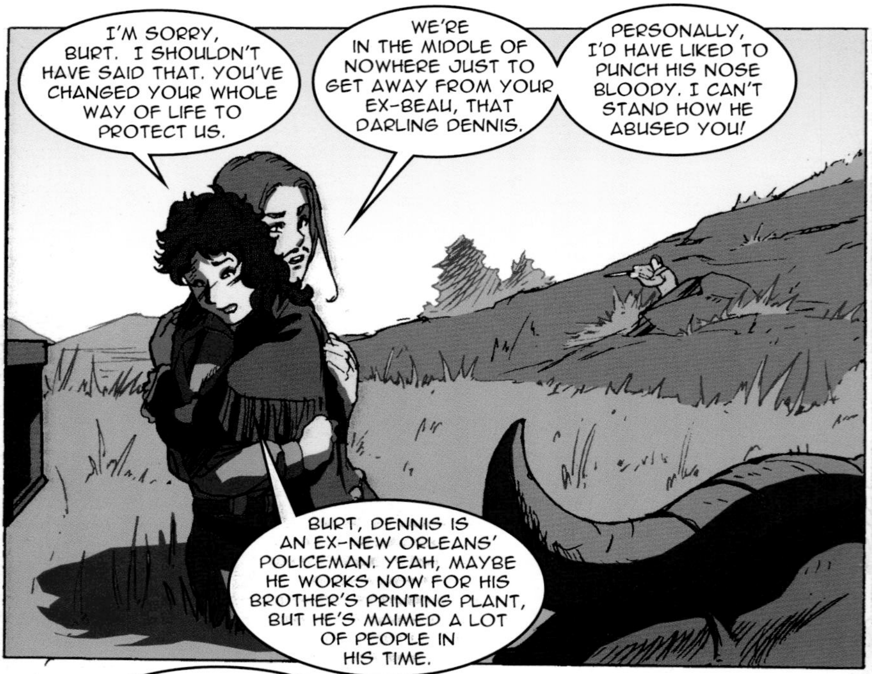
I'M SORRY, BURT. I SHOULDN'T HAVE SAID THAT. YOU'VE CHANGED YOUR WHOLE WAY OF LIFE TO PROTECT US.
WE'RE IN THE MIDDLE OF NOWHERE JUST TO GET AWAY FROM YOUR EX-BEAU, THAT DARLING DENNIS.
PERSONALLY, I'D HAVE LIKED TO PUNCH HIS NOSE BLOODY. I CAN'T STAND HOW HE ABUSED YOU!
BURT, DENNIS IS AN EX-NEW ORLEANS' POLICEMAN. YEAH, MAYBE HE WORKS NOW FOR HIS BROTHER'S PRINTING PLANT, BUT HE'S MAIMED A LOT OF PEOPLE IN HIS TIME.

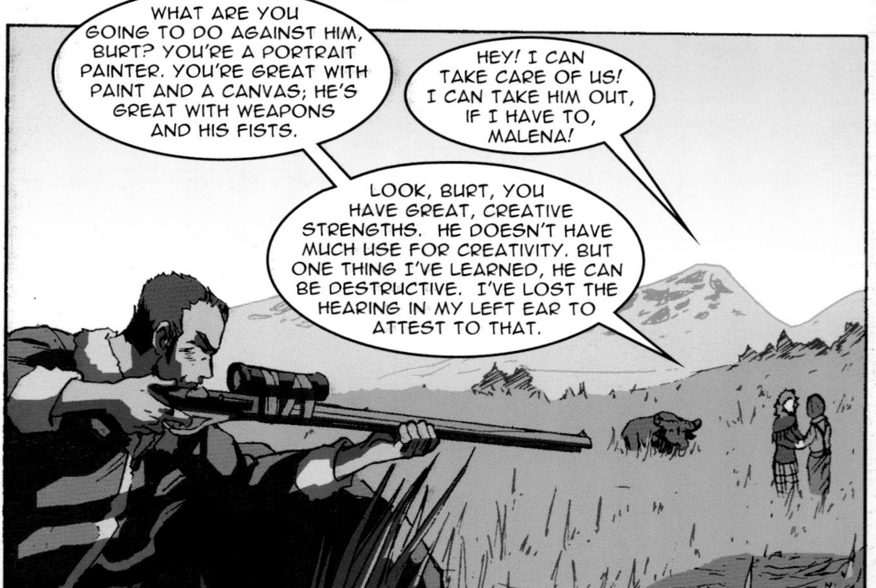
WHAT ARE YOU GOING TO DO AGAINST HIM, BURT? YOU'RE A PORTRAIT PAINTER. YOU'RE GREAT WITH PAINT AND A CANVAS; HE'S GREAT WITH WEAPONS AND HIS FISTS.
HEY! I CAN TAKE CARE OF US! I CAN TAKE HIM OUT, IF I HAVE TO, MALENA!
LOOK, BURT, YOU HAVE GREAT, CREATIVE STRENGTHS. HE DOESN'T HAVE MUCH USE FOR CREATIVITY. BUT ONE THING I'VE LEARNED, HE CAN BE DESTRUCTIVE. I'VE LOST THE HEARING IN MY LEFT EAR TO ATTEST TO THAT.

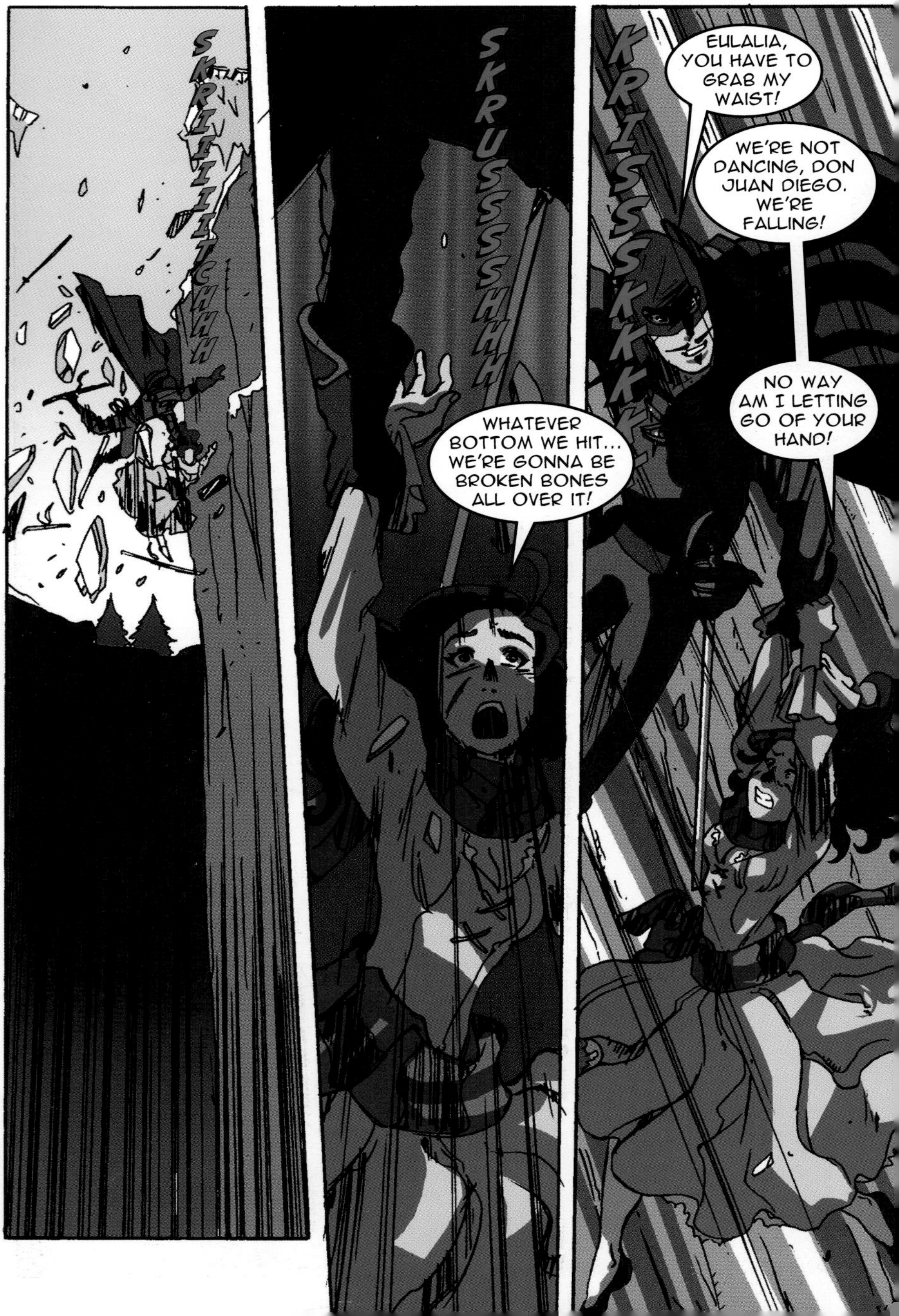
SKRIIIIITCHHH
SKRUSSSSHHH
WHATEVER BOTTOM WE HIT... WE'RE GONNA BE BROKEN BONES ALL OVER IT!
KRISSSSKKK
EULALIA, YOU HAVE TO GRAB MY WAIST!
WE'RE NOT DANCING, DON JUAN DIEGO. WE'RE FALLING!
NO WAY AM I LETTING GO OF YOUR HAND!

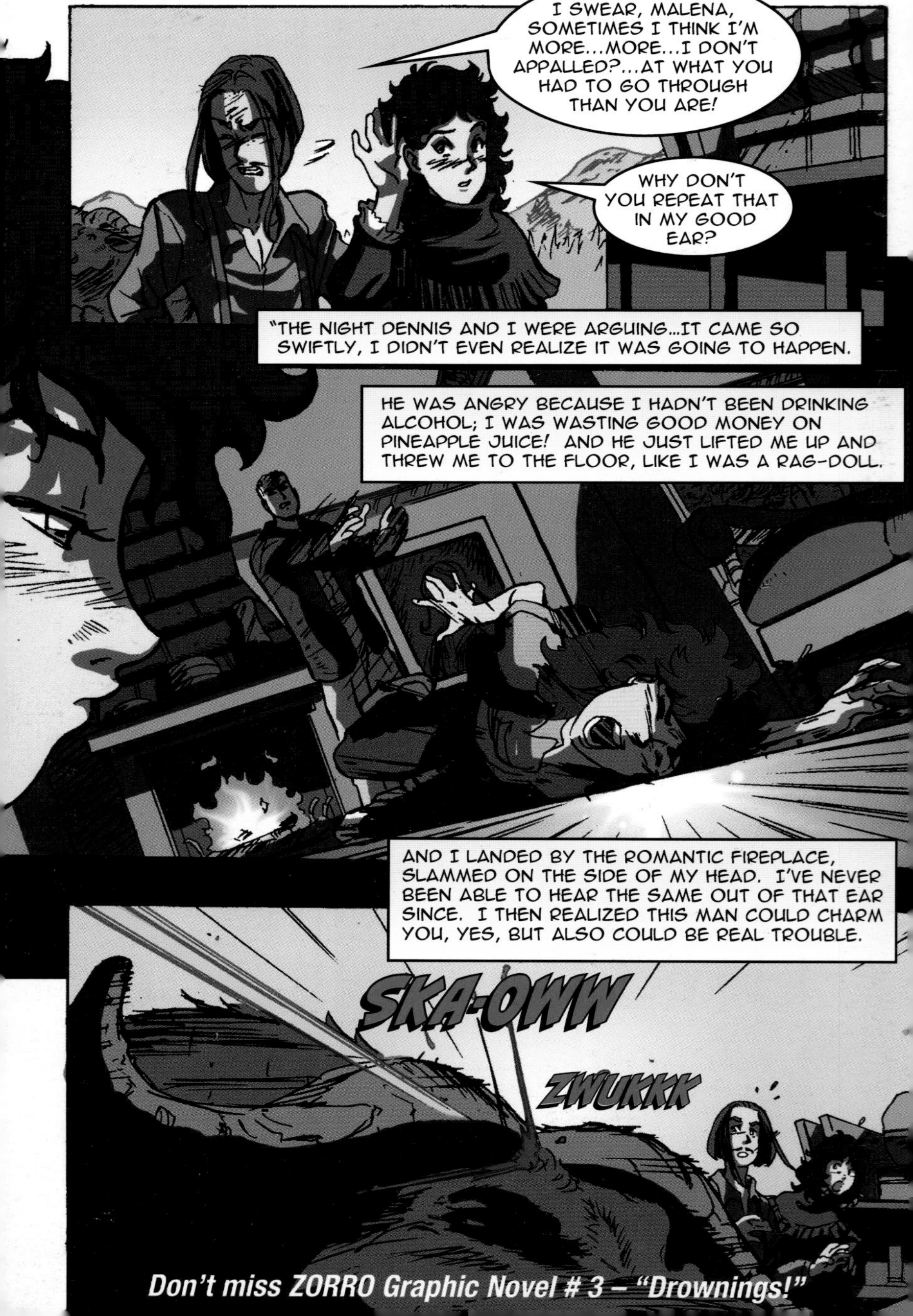
I SWEAR, MALENA, SOMETIMES I THINK I'M MORE...MORE...I DON'T APPALLED?...AT WHAT YOU HAD TO GO THROUGH THAN YOU ARE!
WHY DON'T YOU REPEAT THAT IN MY GOOD EAR?
"THE NIGHT DENNIS AND I WERE ARGUING...IT CAME SO SWIFTLY, I DIDN'T EVEN REALIZE IT WAS GOING TO HAPPEN.
HE WAS ANGRY BECAUSE I HADN'T BEEN DRINKING ALCOHOL; I WAS WASTING GOOD MONEY ON PINEAPPLE JUICE! AND HE JUST LIFTED ME UP AND THREW ME TO THE FLOOR, LIKE I WAS A RAG-DOLL.
AND I LANDED BY THE ROMANTIC FIREPLACE, SLAMMED ON THE SIDE OF MY HEAD. I'VE NEVER BEEN ABLE TO HEAR THE SAME OUT OF THAT EAR SINCE. I THEN REALIZED THIS MAN COULD CHARM YOU, YES, BUT ALSO COULD BE REAL TROUBLE.
SKA-OWW
ZWUKKK
Don't miss ZORRO Graphic Novel # 3 – "Drownings!"

GET A CLUE!

The Hardy Boys and Nancy Drew now in all-new, full-color GRAPHIC NOVELS!

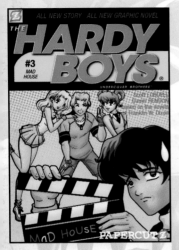

A new one every 3 months.
ON SALE NOW...

THE HARDY BOYS Graphic Novel #3
"Mad House"
Scott Lobdell, writer.
Daniel Rendon, artist.
Frank and Joe Hardy go undercover to find
a murderer on the hit reality TV show.
5 x 7 1/2, 96 pp., full-color paperback:
$7.95, ISBN 1-59707-010-6
hardcover: $12.95, ISBN 1-59707-011-4

NANCY DREW Graphic Novel #3
"The Haunted Dollhouse"
Stefan Petrucha, writer
Sho Murase, artist
Special 75th Anniversary of Nancy Drew
adventure. An antique dollhouse predicts
crimes and the murder of Nancy Drew!
5x7 1/2, 96 pp., full-color paperback:
$7.95, ISBN 1-59707-008-4
hardcover: $12.95, ISBN 1-59707-009-2

AT YOUR STORE NOW!
PAPERCUT Z ™

Order at: 555 8th Ave., Ste. 1202, Dept. P
New York, NY 10018, 1-800-886-1223 (M-F 9-6 EST)
MC, VISA, Amex accepted, add $3 P&H for 1st item, $1 each additional.

Based on the major Motion Picture
from *Columbia Pictures* Starring
Antonio Banderas and Catherine Zeta-Jones

The Legend of Zorro

A Novelization By Scott Ciencin
Based on the Screenplay By Roberto Orci
and Alex Kurtzman-Counter

THE LEGEND LIVES ON!

Zorro behind the mask is a daring defender of freedom and justice, wielding sword and whip with unparalleled skill in defense of the common people. Zorro without the mask is Don Alejandro de la Vega, a wealthy landowner and dedicated family man.

But ruthless men in a deadly conspiracy of power have different ideas. As they threaten the future of a still young state joining the union, they also set Alejandro's two lives in collision, drawing his beloved Elena into a perilous world of shadows and lies. Could the mask ultimately cost the one they call Zorro everything and everyone he holds most dear? Or will the Zorro legacy and de la Vega family prevail?

Available in book stores
October 2005
The Legend of Zorro **0-06-083304-1**